U0131506

Dear English, where did I go wrong?

親愛的英文
我到底哪裡錯了？

史考特・科斯博（Scott Cuthbert）／著

CONTENTS

第 3 關
直擊英文犯罪現場！

第 4 關
這個英文字和你想得不一樣！

第 5 關
親愛的英文，我愈來愈了解你了！

想搞定英文?!其實你只需要這一本！

　　你為什麼需要看這本書呢？

　　因為這本書跟其他學習英文的書不一樣。

　　怎麼不一樣呢？看了書名，你可能會說：「哼！分析英文錯誤的書已經有人寫了。」

　　這點我承認。但是，這本書不一樣的地方是，我列出了許多錯誤，並且為大家分析解釋，這些全部都是真實的錯誤。說清楚一點好了，是真的有人這樣說寫英文，但都是錯的。好吧！好吧！我就有話直說吧！這些都是台灣人用英文表達他們自己的想法時，曾經犯過的錯誤。

課堂上隨時歡迎你來犯錯，下課後保證讓你英語順口溜

　　這為什麼很重要呢？讓我說明一下。我在台灣教英文差不多十年了。上課的時候，學生表達他們的想法，或針對課文相關議題發表心得意見，然後，每當學生說錯的時候，我就會把那個錯誤記在一張紙上，在下課前 10 ~ 20 分鐘，把這堂課學生累積的所有錯誤寫在白板上，全班一起分析、討論、訂正，然後磨成 100%自然的英語。

　　這麼多年的教學經驗顯示，這對學生的幫助很大，學生現學現用，發現錯誤，在課堂裡馬上討論、找出原因，效果最好，再犯的機率小；此外，A 學生犯的錯誤，B 學生雖然沒有犯，但不保證他以後不會犯，同學們的錯誤，在課堂上共同面對，從彼此的錯誤中學習，效果加倍。中文有句成語，「他山之石，可以攻錯」，就是這個意思吧。

十多年的在地英文教學經驗，讓我一手掌握台灣人的聽說讀寫毛病

這本書，就是從我累積十年的龐大錯誤資料庫，擷取精華，所編纂而成的第一本書。手裡有這本書，等於預先知道自己有可能犯這些錯，趕快學習正確的英文應該怎麼說、怎麼寫，你不會覺得很興奮嗎？我再秀一句中文，「千金難買早知道」，買了這本書你就會知道了。

你為什麼要相信我？嗯，好問題。我剛剛說了，每堂課我都把學生的錯誤記錄在一張紙上，這些紙我都保留下來，現在已經厚厚一大疊。我教英文十年，上了將近一萬堂課，學生少說好幾萬，遍佈台灣的北、中、南部，什麼樣的學生都教過，有台大畢業的高材生、上班族、家庭主婦、沒唸完國小的老人、國中生、高中生、大學生和研究生，各行各業都有。後來我連生活中朋友說的、email 裡的、臉書上的英文錯誤都記錄下來了！在這個過程中，我大概記錄過幾十萬筆錯誤，因此，我可以保證，我是華人英文錯誤的專家，也可以保證這本書涵蓋範圍非常廣泛。

為什麼從真實的錯誤來學習很重要，大家應該都知道了，因為這是最有效率的學習方法，我編寫這本書也是希望幫助大家有效的學習好英文。

我怎麼做呢？

這絕對不是一本參考書，它是一套英文學習課程

首先，這本書的編排，是根據大家最常犯的錯誤，按順序排下來的。也就是說，這是一本「英文說寫最常犯的錯誤排行榜」。教書這麼多年，我發現某些特定類型的錯誤發生的頻率比其他類型高，會一而再、再而三地重複出現。大家如果事先知道，導正觀念，正確使用，就可以避免犯下同樣的錯誤，英文說寫一定會有大幅度的進步。

所以，這不是一本參考書，由 A 排到 Z，或從名詞講到動詞，而是一

套英文學習課程。我會帶著你，從最常見的錯誤開始學習，一直到最細微的錯誤，這過程中，你會發現自己犯的錯愈來愈少，說寫出愈來愈完美的英文。

專為母語是中文的讀者量身打造，中英對照，讓你現學現用

再者，這本書是專門針對母語是中文的人會犯的錯誤。許多分析英文錯誤的書是寫給全世界學英文的人，但是這本書是用中文寫的，以說中文的人為目標對象。因為不少英文說寫的錯誤，就是大家嘗試用中文的語法和思維說英文所造成的，經常發生特定類型的錯誤。為了讓大家注意並理解這個問題，我會拿相同意思的中文句子和英文句子做比較，分析為什麼中文語法會造成學習正確英文的障礙，並說明正確的英文應該怎麼表達。

而且，這本書也會增強你的英文表達能力。既然書裡面的句子都是台灣人說的，表示句子的內容都是台灣人需要表達的意思，每一句分析、訂正了之後，就是「現成的英文」，馬上可以運用在日常生活中。坊間眾多英文學習書籍，它們的例句往往不是很實用的，但是這本書裡面的內容都是可以「現學現賣」，它不但會讓你的英文文法有進步，也可以作為日常英文說寫表達的句型用語資料庫。

多功能設計的學習課程，讓你一翻開就想動口又動手

最後，前面說過，這本書是一套英文學習課程，我特別設計了累進學習法，保證你不會再犯這些錯誤。前提是：你不但讀了分析內容，而且還乖乖做練習，包括訂正錯誤、翻譯和造句。我寫這本書的用意，是希望讓大家認識這些一定會犯的錯誤，了解這些錯誤產生的原因，看到錯誤時，迎面痛擊，不會再犯同樣的錯誤。孔子不是說過嗎？「不二過」。

因此，每一章都會有一個「錯誤資料庫」，裡面的句子除了有配合那

一章主題的錯誤，也包括前幾章的主題，請大家做訂正練習。一章一章做下來，你們「除錯」的功力會愈來愈進步。要知道，這個「錯誤資料庫」可是累積過去十年來、數萬名台灣人說英文時實際犯的錯。這本書等於是「踩著別人的錯誤學好英文」，大家可要好好珍惜，努力練習，不要辜負了它。

如果你自認為英文程度很好，那你更需要來比拚一下

最後，真的是最後了，我特別想對英文程度比較好的學生說些話。寫這本書的時候，我曾經拿初稿給一些學生看。有些程度比較好的學生跟我抱怨，「喔，太簡單了！」他們似乎只是看過前面幾章，就作出結論。請這些程度比較好的學生們要注意：這本書的編排是從最簡單和最常見的錯誤，一直到最難與最少見這樣的次序來撰寫，前面的章節若覺得太過簡單，我建議這麼做：馬上跳到「錯誤資料庫」那部分，快速修改錯誤，看看自己是不是真的不會犯相同的錯誤，接著，就可以直接跳到下一章。一直到你認為比較需要學習的章節時，再緩下腳步來詳讀內容。

啊，我答應真的是最後一點了，如果你對這本書有任何的意見、見解、建議、批評、回饋等，請不要害羞喔！你可以跟我聯絡：寫信到dearenglish2014@gmail.com，或加入 Facebook「親愛的英文，我到底哪裡錯了？粉絲團」。

現在，我們馬上開始吧！

第 1 關
搞定這三章
除掉20%的雷

●犯錯排行榜 Top 1：
第三人稱現在式動詞忘記加 s / es（第 1 章）

●犯錯排行榜 Top 2：
複數名詞忘了加 s / es（第 2 章）

●犯錯排行榜 Top 3：
描述過去發生的事，動詞忘記用過去式。（第 3 章）

第 1 章

她不喜歡逛夜市

犯錯排行榜 Top 1：
第三人稱現在式動詞忘記加 **s / es**

有一天，我跟我補習班的學生說我要出書。一個死忠的粉絲立刻站起來，大叫說要志願幫我打廣告：

✘ Everybody need to read Scott's book!

啊，她說錯了。別誤會我，我同意她的看法！但是我不同意她的語法。你知道上面的句子為什麼不是正確的英文嗎？不知道的話，這一章會說清楚、講明白。

這本書裡面所有的句子，就像上面的句子，都是你們親口說出來的。那，為什麼我要用這句英文來開場呢？是因為我要讓你知道已經有人要為我這本書打廣告嗎？呵呵呵，我才不是這種人呢！

只是因為，就像我在序裡說的，這本書的章節順序是從最常見的錯誤類型依序安排的，這樣學習才會有效率，不是嗎？上面的錯誤就是最最最常見的錯誤種類！在台灣，大家說寫英文最常見的錯誤：第三人稱。

「哇！文法專有名詞，我不吃那一套。」我聽到了。我答應你，這本書是提供100%口語、100%用得到的英文。但是為了讓你學習的速度快一點，我們會用一、兩個很簡單的術語。敬請原諒！

那，我們趕快來看大家最常犯的錯誤種類！

我在台灣教英文這麼久了，下面這三種錯誤很少有人不會犯，除非你的母語是英文。它們是：

第一，第三人稱單數的主詞，現在式，動詞沒有加 s。

第二，複數名詞沒有加 s。

第三，描述過去的事情，沒有用動詞的過去式。

你可能會以為我在開玩笑吧。

「這未免太簡單了！我當然知道，第三人稱單數的現在式動詞要加 s，講過去的事要用過去式，複數名詞要加 s。」

是啊，你百分之百「知道」，但只是「偶爾」會忘記。在此，我可要鄭重的告訴大家，這三種問題占所有錯誤的 20%，連英文程度最棒的台灣人也常常無意中犯了錯。

在台灣，很多人學英文，會讀，但是不會說，聽、寫就更不用說了。因此，會考試，但不會聊天，知道了，卻不會應用。這原因主要出在學習語言的認知錯誤！英文不是一種「知識」，而是一種「行為」。像其他行為一樣，愈常練習，就愈能鞏固這個習慣，習慣成自然。

這本書是一套英文學習課程，不是參考書。因此，我會設計很多練習，從我所累積的龐大錯誤資料庫中，選出符合本章的句子，請大家除錯；同時，我也要請大家造句。練習久了，遇到需要用英文的時候，正確的英文就會瞬間脫口而出。

好了，現在我們來分析第一種錯誤，為什麼大家會一犯再犯。我就直接挑明著說，原因就是：中文干涉英文，中文沒有動詞變化，第三人稱現在式動詞沒有加 s / es 這回事。中文可以這麼說：

我喜歡看電影。
她喜歡看電影。

「我」是第一人稱，「她」是第三人稱單數，現在式的動詞一模一樣。但是，英文不是這樣的。英文可以說：

✔ I like to watch movies.

但是，不可以說：

✗　She like to watch movies.

你當然知道，這樣才是對的：

✔　She <u>likes</u> to watch movies.

再說下去，我自己都覺得有一點囉嗦了，那麼，我就直接舉出一些例子：

✗　He go to school every morning at 7:00.
✔　He <u>goes</u> to school every morning at 7:00.

✗　My computer have some problems.
✔　My computer <u>has</u> some problems.

不知道為什麼，do 這個動詞特別有問題。很多人，應該說 does 的時候，反而說 do。比方說：

✗　He do his homework on time every day.
✔　He <u>does</u> his homework on time every day.

否定的時候，也會出錯。例如：

✗　She don't like to go to the night market.（night market = 夜市）
✔　She <u>doesn't</u> like to go to the night market.

「還是太簡單了，不好玩。」好了。我現在要公布連英文高手也會錯的。就是這種：

✗　Everybody have to go to cram schools these days.
　　（cram school = 補習班）

　　這個有點微妙。感覺上，everybody 是指很多人。但是文法上它是單數的。嚴格來講，everybody 是每一個人，文法上，每一個還是一個。正確說法應該是：

✔ Everybody <u>has</u> to go to cram schools these days.

　　就是單數的第三人稱。現在我們來矯正這章開頭的廣告……喔，不，開場那句對大家很有幫助的範例：

✔ Everybody <u>needs</u> to read Scott's book!

　　其實，everybody 還有一些「兄弟」，包括：everyone、somebody、someone、nobody、no one，它們都需要那個第三人稱的 s / es.

✘ Everyone love to take a day off.（take a day off = 請假）
✔ Everyone <u>loves</u> to take a day off.

✘ Somebody have to do it!
✔ Somebody <u>has</u> to do it!

✘ Nobody like to start a diet.
✔ Nobody <u>likes</u> to start a diet.

　　說到 everybody，就是它的形容詞 every，也經常造成問題。看看這個：

✘ Every school have the day off today!
✔ Every school <u>has</u> the day off today!

　　every 就是每一個，一個，但是，很多人不但會用複數的動詞，也會在 every 之後用複數的名詞。如：

✘   Every people in that small town are so friendly.

✔   Every <u>person</u> in that small town <u>is</u> so friendly.

　　自認是英文高手的，請小心不要露出馬腳喔。

　　這類型錯誤的重點就是，用中文的習慣來使用英文，這是以中文為母語的人學英文時特別會犯的錯誤，因此才會榮登英文說寫錯誤排行榜第一名。

　　這本書是針對大家學英文而寫的，除了提醒，分析原因，還要透過反覆的練習來養成使用英文的習慣。現在，為了確定你會正確使用，我要你寫一些用he、she、it 當主詞的現在式句子。

　　等一下，我有一個要求，就是：你造的句子必須是根據真人真事。我的意思是，你要寫出真實的事，或者對某一件事真正的意見。

　　為什麼？因為，學英文畢竟不只是為了「學」而已，而是要在日常生活中用得上。現在，你根據真實的事情寫一句英文，你就有一個現成的句子。以後，生活上有需要時，就馬上可以說出來。但是，如果你光「造句」，隨便編個句子，你可能一輩子也用不到，那不是白白浪費時間了嗎？

　　為了使句子自然一點，你可以把句子的情況或背景放在括號裡（在括號裡寫英文或中文都可以）。

　　現在，我給你們一些用 he、she、it、everybody、every、somebody、nobody 當主詞的現在式句子，都是我自己寫的，我以身作則，這些句子都是描述我生活中的真人真事！

　　再強調一次，這本書是為了在台灣學英文、使用英文的人而寫的，我們就是著重真正可用的句子，真實的情況，真正的用法，為的是讓你學到很多實用、馬上派得上用場的英文。

 史考特的句子

1. （my student）She <u>likes</u> to study English in her free time.

2. （我的機車）It **breaks** down a lot.（break down = 拋錨）

3. It **takes** forty-five minutes for me to get to work.

4. My cell phone **has** a lot of functions.（functions = 功能）

5. （my father）He **calls** me about once a month.

6. China **produces** a lot of goods.

 你的句子

那，我根據真實的情況寫了上面的句子，現在輪到你了：

1. _____

2. _____

等一下，我還有一個要求。

大部分的台灣人對自己的英文會話能力缺乏信心，為了增強這方面的能力，我要你做一個非常簡單的練習。就是，把你剛才在上面寫的句子唸出來。但是，唸的時候，千萬不要看你寫的句子。把它們遮住，或者乾脆闔上書本！因為，當你跟別人說話的時候，手邊不會有書。

記住，英文不是一種「知識」，而是一種「行為」。也就是說，你在外面說英文，就是你對別人的行為。就像其他行為一樣，愈常練習，就愈能鞏固這個習慣。為了養成這個「行為」的習慣，你應該闔上書，把前面的句子多說幾次。以後，遇到一個需要用這句子的情況，因為習慣成自然，正確的英文就會在瞬間脫口而出！

接下來，我要提供我累積了十年的「錯誤資料庫」，簡稱為「錯庫」。

這些錯誤都是台灣人真正犯過的錯。看這些真正發生的錯誤的好處就是，這些句子都是台灣人在描述他們的生活，經過修改，都是馬上可以用的。

為了給你們一些挑戰，我也放進一些正確無誤的句子，希望你們要專心一點。

句子前面的括號表示這句話的情況或背景。

答案就在這一章的最後，為了節省空間，正確的句子不會出現在解答區，這裡只會放修改過的句子。

改句子的時候，我不太要求一定的改法。有些人可能想要重新寫出完整的句子，所以我保留了一些空間。如果你想在句子上做記號修改，這樣也可以，怎麼樣都好，重點是真的去做。

錯庫！蒐集自台灣人真正犯過的英文錯誤，一起來除錯！

1. （派對）If someone invite you, you can go.

2. Taiwan have too many motorcycles.

3. （某個社會問題）The government need to do more.

4. My best friend has a lot of books.

5. Everybody need to follow the law.

6. （My student）She do yoga three times a week.（yoga = 瑜伽）

好，這就是錯誤資料庫。如果你想知道自己改得怎麼樣，解答區就在每一章的最後，以色底呈現，讓你不易看清楚。當然，這只能防君子。若句子本身沒錯，就不會再出現在解答區。

如果你覺得錯誤資料庫的任何句子對你有用，請你用手遮起來，唸出聲音，多唸幾次。

解答

錯庫

1. If someone <u>invites</u> you, you can go.

2. Taiwan <u>has</u> too many motorcycles.

3. The government <u>needs</u> to do more.

4. 正確無誤！

5. Everybody <u>needs</u> to follow the law.

6. She <u>does</u> yoga three times a week.

第2章

我和幾個朋友去KTV

犯錯排行榜 Top 2：複數名詞忘了加 **s / es**

有些學生我教久了，像朋友一樣，除了在教室見面，也會一起出去聚餐聯誼。我發現大家很喜歡去KTV，可以同時吃飯和唱歌。去KTV，多半一群人去，我和幾個朋友去KTV，應該怎麼說呢？

✘　I went to KTV with some of my friend.

幾個朋友啊！這個複數名詞忘了加 s / es。

✔　I went to KTV with some of my <u>friends</u>.

複數名詞忘了加 s / es，是第二個台灣人學英文最常犯的錯誤。

「老師，有沒有搞錯啊？！這太簡單了，我們剛學英文時，就教過這個了。」

我知道啊！你們知道要加 s / es，但實際在使用時就是忘了。這是學習英文非常基本的觀念。學生們都認為自己「會」，可是就是常常忘掉。說真的，這個錯誤每天都會出現在我的課堂上，還有我在課外跟英文很流利的台灣朋友聊天時，千真萬確。

既然是那麼常見的錯誤，我們就得多練習，再舉以下這個例子：

✘　My classmate are all very nice to me.
✔　My <u>classmates</u> are all very nice to me.

作為一個老師，最高興的事，就是學生不犯同樣的錯誤。所以，請記得，複數名詞要加 s / es。

什麼時候加 s，什麼時候加 es？這個問題看似有點微妙，其實很簡單，跟「發音」有關。有些名詞，如果單獨加 s，那個 s 是發不出音的，而發 /ɪz/ 就很順口，這時候就要加 es。以下就是這種情況：

加 es，讀 / ɪz /

wishes （願望）

matches （火柴）

glasses （眼鏡）

加 s，但字尾是有聲子音，加不發音的 e，合在一起也讀 / ɪz /

prizes （獎品）

pages （頁）

bridges （橋）

（注意：以英文為母語的人說得很快或者很輕鬆的時候，那個 / ɪz / 聲音可能會變成 / əz / 的聲音。）

加 s，原本字尾是無聲子音，讀 / s /

cats （貓）

hips （臀）

lakes （湖）

加 s，原本字尾是有聲子音，讀 / z /

heads	（頭）	drums	（鼓）
cars	（汽車）	crabs	（螃蟹）
girls	（女孩）		

不難吧！我現在要寫一些自己的句子。記得，學外語的目的就是要應用，現在練習寫一些和日常生活有關的句子，以後有需要的時候，就有現成的英文可以立即派上用場！

史考特的句子

1. My grandparents' hometown has so many <u>lakes</u>.（lakes 字尾 s 發 / s /）

2. More than half of my students are <u>girls</u>.（girls 後面發音 / z /）

3. I teach several <u>classes</u> every day.（classes 後面發音 / ɪz /）

你的句子

現在請你寫自己的句子,並請註記這個複數名詞尾音是發 / s /、/ z / 或 / ɪz /。

1. _____

2. _____

錯庫!蒐集自台灣人真正犯過的英文錯誤,一起來除錯!

　　這一章的找碴題會比第一章好玩多了,因為我除了會放進這章討論的錯誤,為了複習,也為了鞏固你們在前一章已經養成的正確英文使用習慣,我也會放進第一章的錯誤,就是,he、she、it 開頭的現在式動詞要加 s。當然,對某些企圖心很強的學生,這些可能不夠有挑戰性,所以我還會放進一些百分百正確的句子。

　　不要忘記,下面的錯誤都是台灣人真正說過的。改過之後,它們都是你可以用來描繪日常生活的現成句子!用手遮住這些句子,朗讀出來,多讀幾次之後,你

們就會牢記在心了。

再強調一次，以下的句子有些是正確的，有些句子同時有兩個錯誤。

1.（節日快到了）I have five or six day off.

2. My best friend buys a lot of bags.

3. She always think about the bright side.（bright side = 正面）

4. Our generation exercise less than the older generation.
　（generation = 世代）

5. I have seen a lot of movie about kung fu.（kung fu = 功夫）

6.（好友）He make a lot of joke.

解答

錯庫

1. I have five or six <u>days</u> off.（本章）

2. 正確無誤！

3. She always <u>thinks</u> about the bright side.（第 1 章）

4. Our generation <u>exercises</u> less than the older generation.（第 1 章）

5. I have seen a lot of <u>movies</u> about kung fu.（本章）

6. He <u>makes</u> a lot of <u>jokes</u>.（第 1 章和本章）

第 3 章

我昨晚只睡5個小時

犯錯排行榜 Top 3：
描述過去發生的事，動詞要用過去式。

我的工作是教英文，在課堂上教。教久了，發現許多錯誤不分城市、不分年紀和教育程度，學生不斷在犯。於是，我有了寫這本書的念頭，把所有錯誤，按照犯錯的頻率編排，透過錯誤學習，減少犯錯的機會，希望大家愈來愈喜歡英文。

寫書是額外的工作，為了寫這本書，我常常睡眠不足。有一天下課後，我和學生聊天，學生看我眼皮快要掉下來，問我怎麼了，我跟他說：

「我昨晚只睡5個小時。」

這句話英文應該怎麼說呢？

✘　I only sleep five hours last night.

看出來了嗎？這一章要討論的錯誤就是：說過去的事情，動詞忘了用過去式時態。這個問題名列錯誤排行榜第三名。正確的句子當然是：

✔　I only <u>slept</u> five hours last night.

為什麼這個錯誤這麼容易犯？根源在於，中文根本沒有「過去時態」這個東西。

我們學了sleep 這個單字，直接套用中文句法，不管時態，這是「中式英文」，不是真正的英文啊！

學英文，和交朋友一樣，不會只知道他的名字就好吧？！你還要知道他喜歡什麼？常去什麼地方？藉由他的行為模式來了解他，不是嗎？學英文也一樣，知道這個字，還要知道它屬於什麼類型，在不同的情境該怎麼對待它。只記單字，你跟英文的關係永遠不會熟起來，難怪你不知道錯在哪裡！

英文的動詞，會根據動作發生的時間點而做變化。這一章，我們要學的就是：描述過去發生的事情，動詞要改成過去式的時態。

現在，我們來複習動詞的過去式，從最基本的 am、is、are 開始：

現在式	過去式
I am	I was
I'm not	I wasn't
you（單數）are	you were
you're not	you weren't
he / she / it is	he / she / it was
he / she / it isn't	he / she / it wasn't
we / you（複數）/ they are	we / you（複數）/ they were
we / you（複數）/ they aren't	we / you（複數）/ they weren't

一般而言，動詞加 ed 就是過去式。但是，有一些動詞的過去式是不規則的，以下，是一些常見的動詞，他們的過去式變化：

現在式	過去式		現在式	過去式	
become	became	（變成）	drink	drank	（喝）
begin	began	（開始）	drive	drove	（駕駛）
break	broke	（破）	eat	ate	（吃）
bring	brought	（帶）	fly	flew	（飛）
buy	bought	（買）	forget	forgot	（忘記）
can	could	（可以、能）	get	got	（得到）
come	came	（來）	give	gave	（給）
cost	cost	（值、花費）	hit	hit	（打）
cut	cut	（切）	go	went	（去）
do	did	（做）	grow	grew	（生長）

現在式	過去式		現在式	過去式	
have	had	（有）	see	saw	（看）
hear	heard	（聽）	sell	sold	（賣）
hold	held	（拿）	send	sent	（寄）
hurt	hurt	（痛、傷害）	shut	shut	（關）
keep	kept	（保留）	sing	sang	（唱）
know	knew	（知道）	sit	sat	（坐）
lay	laid	（放）	sleep	slept	（睡）
lead	led	（領導、引導）	speak	spoke	（說）
leave	left	（離開）	spend	spent	（花錢）
lie	lay	（躺）	stand	stood	（站）
lose	lost	（丟掉、失去）	swim	swam	（游泳）
make	made	（做）	take	took	（拿）
meet	met	（見面）	teach	taught	（教書）
pay	paid	（付）	tell	told	（告訴）
put	put	（放）	think	thought	（想）
read	read	（閱讀）	understand	understood	（懂、了解）
ride	rode	（騎）	wake	woke	（醒）
ring	rang	（響）	wear	wore	（穿）
run	ran	（跑）	win	won	（贏）
say	said	（說）	write	wrote	（寫）

現在，我們實際透過句子來看動詞過去式應該怎麼用：

✘ Last weekend I go to Kaohsiung to visit my classmate.
（Kaohsiung = 高雄）

✔ Last weekend I <u>went</u> to Kaohsiung to visit my classmate.

✘ When I was in elementary school, I win a prize in an English contest.

✔ When I was in elementary school, I <u>won</u> a prize in an English contest.

　幾個比較特殊的字要特別提出來說。其中一個就是 can，can 的過去式是 could。can't 的過去式就是 couldn't。例如：

✘ When I was a little kid, I can stay up until 10 pm.
✔ When I was a little kid, I <u>could</u> stay up until 10 pm.

✘ When I was in elementary school, I can't speak English.
✔ When I was in elementary school, I <u>couldn't</u> speak English.

　另一個是 have to，「必須要」的意思，過去式就是 had to。它的用法是：

✘ When I went on vacation last year, I have to get a shot.
（get a shot = 打針）

✔ When I went on vacation last year, I <u>had to</u> get a shot.

　還有，特別要注意的一個字，must，也是「必須要」的意思，它沒有過去式，所以，要說以前 must 做的事情時，就要改成 had to。不只如此，過去 should 做的事也是用 had to，也就是說，have to、must 以及 should 的過去式，實際上都是 had to！

史考特的句子

在這裡，老師我以身作則，提供我真實生活的句子！

1. This morning I <u>had</u> some good Chinese food.

2. （昨晚的課）About 30 students <u>came</u>, but a few were late.

3. My phone <u>rang</u> about 15 minutes ago.

4. I <u>bought</u> some business cards after my class.
   （business cards = 名片）

5. （今早的運動）I <u>drank</u> a lot of water after I finished.

你的句子

現在，我要你根據真實的生活來寫句子。我用心良苦，因為，如果句子是真的，你可以立即派上用場。透過這個練習，你同時也在用英文描述、表達你自己。為了讓句子看起來自然，你可以把情況或背景放在括號裡，就像以上的第二句和第五句一樣，括號裡的東西不太重要，所以英文或中文都行，只看你的程度及志氣。

那麼，開始寫下關於你自己或能描述你的生活、你的看法的句子吧！

1. _____

2. _____

3. _____

超簡單改錯！

　　為了提醒大家注意這樣的錯誤，我們需要多一點練習。以下這些句子都有錯誤，而且與這一章有關，需要你來修改。因為才說明過，所以印象深刻，不費吹灰之力就改好了！

　　一樣再次聲明，這些都是我的學生說寫出來的句子，都和台灣生活有關，你一定很熟悉，可以培養你的語感喔！

1.（以前在金門旅行）When I went to Jinmen, it's sunny.

2.（小時學校的餐廳）We can eat all we wanted.

3.（高中已畢業的人）When I was in high school, our school need seven people for the volleyball team, so I have to play.（volleyball = 排球）

錯庫！蒐集自台灣人真正犯過的英文錯誤，一起來除錯！

　　那麼，我們現在來看看台灣人真正犯過的英文錯誤資料庫，可以提供我們什麼練習。

　　學習很重要，但是複習也一樣重要。因此，這次要請大家挑錯訂正的，除了第一章、第二章，還有本章的錯誤類型。當然，我也會很頑皮地，夾雜一些完美的句子。此外，再提醒你，除了我這個調皮老師所寫的完美句子之外，下面的錯誤都是我的台灣學生親口說出來的。訂正改過之後，我覺

得你可以好好練習、多唸幾次，別人辛辛苦苦表達出來的句子，就變成你的了！

1. （以前的台灣）Most people don't have much money before.

2. （以前的殺人犯）The police can't find him.

3. （學生被問昨天幹嘛）I went to a tea shop with two of my old friends yesterday.

4. My "Mr. Right" have to be kind. （Mr. Right = 理想對象）

5. （以前去旅行）We still need to put up a tent. （tent = 帳篷）

6. （對大學生）How many class do you have per week?

解答

超簡單改錯

1. When I went to Jinmen, it <u>was</u> sunny.

2. We <u>could</u> eat all we wanted.

3. When I was in high school, our school <u>needed</u> seven people for the volleyball team, so I <u>had</u> to play.

錯庫

1. Most people <u>didn't</u> have much money before. （本章）

2. The police <u>couldn't</u> find him. （本章）

3. 正確無誤！

4. My "Mr. Right" <u>has</u> to be kind. （第 1 章：第三人稱現在式動詞忘記加 s / es）

5. We still <u>needed</u> to put up a tent. （本章）

6. How many <u>classes</u> do you have per week? （第 2 章：複數名詞忘了加 s / es）

第 2 關
這個意思
原來英文要這樣說

- 你來自哪裡？
  說 from 和 come from 有什麼不一樣？（第 4 章）

- 這部電影是在說一個英雄拯救全世界。
  電影不會說話！（第 8 章）

- 你到那裡，就右轉！
  到＝ to，那裡＝ here，是這樣嗎？（第 10 章）

我來自威斯康辛州

你來自哪裡？用 from 還是 come from？

第一次上課，總是要自我介紹，從哪裡來的，這是最基本的。我是美國人，我來自威斯康辛州。我有許多學生從台北來的，他們這樣說：

✗　I come from Taipei.

這是錯誤的。這是一個非常基本的錯誤。

說實在的，這個「錯誤」在文法上完全正確。但是，我還是會把它當作一個錯誤，因為母語是英文的人不會這樣說。他們會這樣說：

✔　<u>I'm</u> from Taipei.

這樣的錯誤極可能是來自於中文這個母語的干擾。這句話的中文是這樣說的：
我是從台北來的。

那，你們可能很想把那個「來」翻譯成 come，然後把「從」翻譯成 from。英文，我們的確需要那個 from（從），但是英文在表達家鄉時，其實不需要那個 come（來）。我們就來看一些具體的對錯比較吧：

✗　I come from Taichung.（Taichung = 台中）
✔　<u>I'm</u> from Taichung.

✗　My best friend comes from Hsinchu.（Hsinchu = 新竹）
✔　My best friend <u>is</u> from Hsinchu.

✗　My parents come from a small town near Kaohsiung.
✔　My parents <u>are</u> from a small town near Kaohsiung.

詢問對方從哪裡來時，也容易發生一樣的錯誤。問的時候也不需要用 come。

例如：

✘ Where do you come from?

✔ Where <u>are</u> you from?

　Where do you come from? 這個句子只會在科幻電影中出現，當地球人問外星人是從哪裡來的時候。除非你碰到外星人，不然不准你說這個火星文。那麼，什麼時候才會用到 come from？I'm from 是表達家鄉、出生地或長大的國家城市等。I come from 是用來表達從某一個地方來，為了辦某一件事，from 後面會說你的出發點。比方說，我住台北，但是一個台中的老朋友突然出現，就可以用以下的方式表達：

✔ Me: What are you doing here?

✔ Him: I <u>came from</u> Taichung this morning for a business meeting.

　這並非說他是台中人！他只是在說這件事，台中是他的出發點。

　再舉個例子。前一陣子，我有天臨時起意去淡水玩，晚上有個約，急忙從淡水趕回和朋友約見的地方。我是這麼說：

✔ I'm so tired. I just <u>came</u> here <u>from</u> Tamsui.

　我可不是淡水人，是吧？！

　注意，以上的 came 是過去式。這個 come here 是說從何而來，通常我會用過去式（已經發生了）或者未來式（還沒發生）。

　現在式並不是像很多台灣人想的那麼常用。現在式通常不是說一件事，而是說經常發生的事。所以，真要說現在式的 come from，而不是說你的家鄉，可能是比較特殊的情況。比方說，我有一個朋友住桃園，但每週三來台北拜訪客戶。如果一個住台北的人問為什麼每週三都看到她，她可以這樣回答：

✔ I <u>come from</u> Taoyuan to meet my customers.

但是，這也有一點奇怪，因為很多人，要是他們真的為了工作或上課而經常從某個地方跑到另一個地方，很可能會用另一個字，就是 commute（通勤）。比方說，我現在有個學生，每天從基隆通勤到台北上班。最自然的英文是：

✔ I <u>commute</u> <u>from</u> Keelung <u>to</u> Taipei.

不過，嚴格來講，I come from Keelong to Taipei. 是可以接受的。然後，這個人其實是高雄人！考你：她要說她是哪裡人呢？啊，你猜對了：

✔ I'm <u>from</u> Kaohsiung.

就是這樣！

 史考特的句子

那麼，老師要來示範了，以下是我根據自己的真實生活寫出來的句子：

1. I'<u>m from</u> Wisconsin.（Wisconsin = 威斯康辛州）

2. My co-worker <u>is from</u> Australia.

3. Some of my students <u>are from</u> Jongli.（Jongli = 中壢）

 你的句子

現在，要請你根據真實生活裡發生的事，寫出句子！記住，一定要是真的真的真的真的真的句子……好了，我不鬧你了！

1. _____

2. _____

3. _____

超簡單改錯

　　為了訓練你能迅速辨識出 come from 這個用法是錯的，以下給你一些 come from 的錯。

　　1.（自我介紹）I come from Taoyuan.（Taoyuan = 桃園）

　　2.（自我介紹）I come from Ilan.（Ilan = 宜蘭）

　　3.（對新生）Where are you come from?

錯庫！蒐集自台灣人真正犯過的英文錯誤，一起來除錯！

1.（爸爸）He don't care what I do.

2.（八卦雜誌）They just cover some scandal.
　（cover = 報導，scandal = 醜聞）

3. I have a friend who comes from HK.

4. （921 地震）After the earthquake, the wall have a crack.

5. （可以去旅行的地方）It have a lot of natural beauty.

6. （以前的老師）She had a lot of problems, so she felt unhappy.

7. （下午說的）This morning I have to work.

8. Some of my friends are from Malaysia.

解答

超簡單改錯

1. I'm from Taoyuan.

（Taoyuan = 桃園）

2. I'm from Ilan.

（Ilan = 宜蘭）

3. Where are you come from?

錯庫

1. He doesn't care what I do.

（第 1 章：第三人稱現在式動詞忘記加 s / es）

2. They just cover some scandals.

（第 2 章：複數名詞忘了加 s / es）

3. I have a friend who is from HK.

（本章）

4. After the earthquake, the wall had a crack.

（第 3 章：描述過去發生的事，動詞要用過去式。）

5. It has a lot of natural beauty.

（第 1 章：第三人稱現在式動詞忘記加 s / es）

6. 正確無誤！

7. This morning I had to work.

（第 3 章：描述過去發生的事，動詞要用過去式。）

8. 正確無誤！

我喜歡狗，但我吃狗肉 ?!

表達一般性的看法或意見時，可數的名詞要用複數。

上一章談到自我介紹，最基本的，你來自哪裡？大家已經知道用英文怎麼問、怎麼說了。再多說一點，就會談到喜好和興趣。我有許多學生喜歡動物，特別是狗，我喜歡狗，怎麼說呢？

✘   I love dog.

> 錯！你應該還記得前三章我們討論台灣人學英文最常犯的「三大錯誤」，其中一個是複數名詞忘了加 s。這裡，針對這一點，我們補充說明，在以下情況，名詞要用複數：
>
> 如果你要表達一個看法，或描述一般性的情況，你所用到的名詞，如果是可數的，就要用複數。
>
> 我的說明可能有一點囉嗦，但是我有許多台灣學生都不知道，都犯了這個錯誤，可能也跟中文名詞沒有分單數、複數有關。

前面那個句子，我喜歡狗，就是一個一般性的想法，意思是你喜歡一般的狗，任何的狗，所有的狗，狗這個物種等等。這時候，英文 dog 這個名詞就要用複數。那你就知道，上面的那個錯誤的句子應該這樣講：

✔   I love <u>dogs.</u>

說到 dog 這個字，I like dog 其實是說得通的，但是它的意思是「我喜歡狗肉」。如果你說話的對象是外國人，你肯定會被認為是野蠻人喔！

不多說了，我們來看例子：

✘ I'm interested in flower.

✔ I'm interested in <u>flowers</u>.

✘ I don't like soap opera.（soap opera = 肥皂劇）

✔ I don't like soap <u>operas</u>.

✘ I love reading book about ancient China.（ancient = 古老）

✔ I love reading <u>books</u> about ancient China.

✘ American is friendly.

✔ <u>Americans are</u> friendly.

（注意：因為 Americans 當主詞，是複數的，動詞因此就是 are。）

　　但是，特別提醒你一件事：如果名詞是不可數的，你就不能加 s 喔。不可數名詞是永遠不能加 s 的。譬如：

✔ I like milk.（不可以說 milks）

✔ Beef tastes good.（不可以說 beefs）

✔ I love money.（不可以說 moneys）

　　史考特的句子

老師以身作則，以下真的真的真的是反應我這個人的句子：

　　1. I love <u>dumplings</u>.（dumpling = 餃子）

　　2. <u>Americans</u> eat too much.

　　表達一般性的看法或意見時，可數的名詞要用複數。

3. I'm interested in teaching <u>methods</u>.（method = 方法）

4. I prefer <u>dogs</u> to <u>cats</u>.（記住，dogs 和 cats 都要用複數）

5. I think that new <u>motorcycles</u> are too expensive.
（motorcycle = 摩托車）

 你的句子

現在，輪到你們了，請告訴我你們真實的看法和情況囉：

1. _____

2. _____

3. _____

 超簡單改錯！

以下的句子都是有這個問題的，也是我的台灣學生說出來的，請你訂正！

1. （一般的想法）Firework is beautiful.（firework = 煙火）

2. （對建築一般的想法）I don't like kitchen.

3. I like temple.（temple = 寺廟）

錯庫！蒐集自台灣人真正犯過的英文錯誤，一起來除錯！

1. If your city become famous, it will attract business.

2. （被問為什麼喜歡狗）I just like dog, OK?

3. （自我介紹時）I am come from Taichung.

4. I'm interested in bear.（bear = 熊）

5. （姊妹以前的事）They have a good relationship, before the older sister got a job.

6. （一般的想法）I like teachers who are from America.

解答

超簡單改錯

1. Fireworks are beautiful.

2. I don't like kitchens.

3. I like temples.

錯庫

1. If your city becomes famous, it will attract business.

（第 1 章：第三人稱現在式動詞忘記加 s / es）

2. I just like dogs, OK?（本章.）

3. I am come from Taichung.

（第 4 章：你來自哪裡？用 from 還是 come from？）

4. I'm interested in bears.（本章）

5. They had a good relationship, before the older sister got a job.

（第 3 章：描述過去發生的事，動詞要用過去式。）

6. 正確無誤！

表達一般性的看法或意見時，可數的名詞要用複數。

第 6 章

我有一個朋友讀成功大學

one of 後面的名詞要用複數

關於名詞的複數，還有一個非常普遍的錯誤，就是 one of。是什麼樣的問題呢？

從以下的對錯比較你就知道了：

✗　One of my friend goes to NCKU.（NCKU = 成功大學）

這是非常普遍的錯誤。為什麼會這樣呢？

我認為這個問題主要出在 one 這個字。很多人看到 one，腦子裡就有「單數的思路」，自然而然、毫無意識地說出單數的 friend。

事實上，這個句子裡 one 是主詞，of my friends 是一個介係詞片語，修飾 one，意思是，我所有的朋友中，其中一個讀成功大學，所以 of my friends 是複數的，從那個複數的團體中選出那個 one。所以：

✔　One of my <u>friends</u> goes to NCKU.

好，我們再多看幾個對錯的比較：

✗　One of my teacher is from Japan.
✔　One of my <u>teachers</u> is from Japan.

注意，因為 of my teachers 是個介係詞片語，句子的核心其實是 One is from Japan，動詞要配合單數的主詞 one，而不是介係詞片語裡的 teachers。

以下這一句：

✗　I forgot one of my book.
✔　I forgot one of my <u>books</u>.

史考特的句子

那，現在，老師寫幾句運用 one of 的句子，透過這些句子你們會知道我多一點：

1. <u>One of</u> my student<u>s</u> works for a big engineering company.
   （engineering = 工程）

2. I left <u>one of</u> my umbrella<u>s</u> at work, but I have another one.

3. I got an email last week from <u>one of</u> my former student<u>s</u>.
   （former = 以前的）

你的句子

你現在會用 one of 了吧。我也不用再提醒你要寫出反應你自己的真實例句了，你們應該都懂我的用意了。

1. _____

2. _____

3. _____

超簡單改錯

　　這些句子都反應了本章討論的問題，而且都是我的台灣學生與朋友真正說寫出來的。

　　1. One of the most famous hotel in the world is in Dubai.
　　（Dubai = 杜拜）

　　2. One of my best friend gets giddy when she's drunk.
　　（giddy = 暈暈忽忽而傻笑）

錯庫！蒐集自台灣人真正犯過的英文錯誤，一起來除錯！

　　以下的句子，大部分都是現實生活中我的學生說寫出來的，幾乎都有錯。不過，還是小心一點，裡頭藏有我編出來的正確句子喔。

1. One of my friends went to Hong Kong for Chinese New Year.

2. If one of your friend gets into a car accident, she might need special treatment.

3. I think vampire movie is so terrible.（vampire = 吸血鬼）

4. （最喜歡的球隊最近輸了）I felt sad the Kings lose the game.

5. My best friend is one of my former English teacher.

6. She want you to answer the question.

解答

超簡單改錯

1. One of the most famous hotels in the world is in Dubai.

2. One of my best friends gets giddy when she's drunk.

錯庫

1. 正確無誤！

2. If one of your friends gets into a car accident, she might need special treatment.（本章）

3. I think vampire movies are so terrible.

（第 5 章：表達一般性的看法或意見時，可數的名詞要用複數。）

4. I felt sad the Kings lost the game.

（第 3 章：描述過去發生的事，動詞要用過去式。）

5. My best friend is one of my former English teachers.（本章）

6. She wants you to answer the question.

（第 1 章：第三人稱現在式動詞忘記加 s / es）

第 7 章

我很喜歡奶茶

動詞前面不可加 very

這一章要討論的，就是一個非常典型的中式英文例子。我們來看看以下這句中文，大家就可以看出問題了：

我很喜歡逛街。

所以，我有很多學生會這樣說：

✘ I very like to go shopping.

他們就是把中文的「很」，自動翻譯成 very，然後放在 like（喜歡）前面。
但是，這不是英文！英文並不會把 very 放在動詞前面！
以下才是正確的句子：

✔ I <u>like</u> to go shopping <u>very much</u>.
✔ I <u>really</u> <u>like</u> to go shopping.

> 這兩個句子，又以第二個比較口語，是美國人在日常生活中比較常用的。
> 請記住，在動詞前面，我們不會用 very。但是，我們倒是經常加 really 這個字，在這裡，really 不是「真的」的意思，反而是「很」的意思。
> 因此，之後的錯誤資料庫出現這個問題時，我自己的解答都會用 really 來訂正。

好，再來看例句：
✘ I very love watching movies.
✔ I <u>really</u> <u>love</u> watching movies.

✗ I very hate getting up early.

✔ I <u>really</u> <u>hate</u> getting up early.

✗ I very enjoy going to tea shops with my classmates.

✔ I <u>really</u> <u>enjoy</u> going to tea shops with my classmates.

 史考特的句子

雖然你們的中文嚴重干擾了我教的英文，但是台灣有些干擾我倒是很歡迎的，比如說：奶茶。

為了帶頭示範，我野人獻曝，寫了以下這些句子（都是真的！ＸＤ）：

1. I <u>really</u> <u>like</u> milk tea.

2. I <u>really</u> <u>don't like</u> teaching early in the morning.

3. I <u>really</u> <u>hate</u> loud noises outside my apartment.

4. I <u>really</u> <u>care</u> about my best friend.

 你的句子

那，你現在應該知道怎麼辦。請寫出真實可用的句子！

1. _____

2. _____

超簡單改錯

都是本章的錯誤。改改看！

1. I very like computers and English.

2. I very care about that!

錯庫！蒐集自台灣人真正犯過的英文錯誤，一起來除錯！

1. I got an email from one of my friend.

2. （比較一般的書與漫畫書）I think picture is more interesting.

3. （某個政治活動家）She very cares about Taiwan's environment.

4. Chung Shan Park have some scary people.
（Chung Shan =「中山」的拼音）

5. I very like chicken stuffed with garlic.
（stuffed with garlic = 有蒜頭餡）

6. I really like one of my old English teachers.

解答

超簡單改錯

1. I really like computers and English.

2. I really care about that!

錯庫

1. I got an email from one of my friends.

（第6章：one of 後面的名詞要用複數）

2. I think pictures are more interesting.

（第 5 章：表達一般性的看法或意見時，可數的名詞要用複數。）

3. She really cares about Taiwan's environment.（本章）

4. Chung Shan Park has some scary people.

（第1章：第三人稱現在式動詞忘記加 s / es）

5. I really like chicken stuffed with garlic.（本章）

6. 正確無誤！

第 8 章

電影不會說話！

虛構的事物不能用 talk about

　　最近有一部電影很賣座，大家都在談。有一個人問： 那部電影在演什麼？另一個人回答：這部電影是在說一個救世的英雄。

✘　This movie is talking about a hero who saves the world.

　　電影不能說話！
　　這是很典型的把中文直接翻譯成英文所造成的錯誤。
　　但是，我們美國人不會這樣說。人可以 talking about，但是電影不會。
　　正確的說法是這樣：

✔　This movie <u>is about</u> a hero who saves the world.

　　那麼，我們多看一些對與錯的比較：

✘　This movie is talking about two young people who fall in love.
✔　This movie <u>is about</u> two young people who fall in love.

　　電視節目一樣！

✘　My favorite TV series is talking about a group of friends in New York.
✔　My favorite TV series <u>is about</u> a group of friends in New York.

✘　I recently read a book talking about the Egyptian pyramids
　　（Egyptian pyramids = 埃及的金字塔）
✔　I recently read a book <u>about</u> the Egyptian pyramids.

　　小說（novels）也是！

✘ Pride and Prejudice talks about a girl named Elizabeth.（Pride and Prejudice = 傲慢與偏見）

✔ Pride and Prejudice <u>is about</u> a girl named Elizabeth.

你覺得你逃得了例外嗎？哈，聽到我的苦笑！上面的例子都是描述虛構的事物：電影、電視節目、小說。

不過，還是有例外。有時，非虛構的讀物，尤其是短篇的，特別是討論社會問題，如報紙的文章、專欄等等，可能會說 talk about。為什麼呢？因為，作者像是在扮演教授、政治家、父母等角色，要直接跟你討論並說服你，好像在跟你 talk，所以我們可以接受 His article is talking about... 這樣的說法。但是，虛構的事物不會直接跟你對話，只會呈現某個事件、某個世界。

另外要注意。這類非虛構的事物，除了 talk about 之外，也可以用一些比較「高級」、有深度的同義詞，例如 discuss，句型如下：

His article discusses...

 史考特的句子

為了讓大家精通這個句型，現在我要來寫一些百分之百真實的句子。

1. My favorite book <u>is about</u> a father and his son in Chicago.
   （Chicago=芝加哥）

2. （最近看的電影）It <u>was about</u> life in China in the 1930's.

3. （你們正在看的書！）It<u>'s about</u> English mistakes.

你的句子

那，現在換你上場了。來！說些真實生活中發生的事。

1. _____

2. _____

3. _____

 超簡單改錯

1. （電視節目）It is talk about how a policeman finds criminals.

2. （好萊塢電影）These movies always talk about Western heroes.

錯庫！蒐集自台灣人真正犯過的英文錯誤，一起來除錯！

1.（以前的大事）It's not working out.（work out = 過得好，執行得好）

2. I hate cockroach!（cockroach = 蟑螂）

3.（某個導演）His movies are talking about aliens and robots.
（aliens = 外星人，robots = 機器人）

4.（某一個人）One of his son was drunk!

5.（某一個作家）Her novels are talking about young women in England.

解答

超簡單改錯

1. It <u>is about</u> how a policeman finds criminals.

2. These movies <u>are</u> always <u>about</u> Western heroes.

錯庫

1. It <u>wasn't</u> working out.
（第 3 章：描述過去發生的事，動詞要用過去式。）

2. I hate cockroach<u>es</u>!
（第 5 章：表達一般性的看法或意見時，可數名詞要用複數。）

3. His movies <u>are about</u> aliens and robots.（本章）

4. One of his son<u>s</u> was drunk!
（第 6 章：one of 後面的名詞要用複數）

5. Her novels <u>are about</u> young women in England.（本章）

那裡有一座公園

here 與 there 並不會「有」東西！

不管哪種語言，「這裡」和「那裡」這兩個字應該會扮演很重要的角色，這是日常生活中經常使用的表達，英文也不例外。

但是，英文的「這裡」——here，和「那裡」——there，是很特別的兩個字，如果用中文的思維理解，肯定是錯的，會產生很多「中式英文」的問題。

我們先來看這個中文句子吧：

<u>那裡有</u>一個公園。

這個中文句子完全正確。但是，我的學生，要用英文說或寫這個句子的時候，會自動把這個句子翻譯成英文：

✘　<u>There have</u> a park.

在英文裡面，here 和 there 並不會「有」東西，這兩個字是副詞，表明地方、場所。若想表示「有」這個意思，英文會用 there is / there are 的句型。

上面的句子錯了，以下的句子才是正確：

✔　<u>There is</u> a park <u>there</u>.

注意到了嗎？這個句子裡有兩個 there。不過，它們的意思完全不一樣。句頭的 there is 是一個片語，就是「有」的意思，並非「那裡」的意思。句尾的 there 才是「那裡」的意思。

後面的 there，其實不一定要放進去。

我們應該再多看一些「中式英文」的問題。比方說，某人問你的學校怎麼樣，你要回答：

有幾個老師還不錯。

如果你用中文的方式說英文，會說成以下這種錯誤的句子：

✘   Have several good teachers.

那個「有」不能直接譯成 have。以下這樣才是對的：

✔   <u>There are</u> several good teachers.

「這裡」也是一樣。比方說，描述我自己的學校，我用中文可以說：

這裡有些國中生。

英文的危險你已經感受到了吧：

✘   Here have some junior high school students.
✔   <u>There are</u> some junior high school students <u>here</u>.

再強調一次，前面的 there are 與「那裡」完全沒關係。這個兩個字組合而成的片語，意思就是「存在」或「有」的意思。

是是是！你可以說，there are 和 there 看起來很像，但是，事實上，這真的是兩碼子的事，兩個意思完全不一樣。

如果句子前面有個 there is 或 there are，而你還是想表達「那裡」或「這裡」的話，你就要把 there 或 here 放在句子後面。

另外，可不要忽略否定的句子喔！

我最近碰到一個問題。補習班派我到新的分校教課，但附近都沒有 7-11，真可以說是緊急情況！我可能會用中文這樣表達我的痛苦：

我不敢相信！這裡沒有7-11！

那，用英文怎麼說呢？以下是常見的呆板「中翻英」：

✘　I can't believe it! Here doesn't have any 7-11s!

根據以上的說明，你一定知道如何講出自然正確的英文吧：

✔　I can't believe it! <u>There aren't</u> any 7-11s around <u>here</u>!

簡單的說，肯定的說 there is / there are，否定的說 there isn't / there aren't。

 史考特的句子

以下，是我寫的，中文會說「這裡有……」、「那裡有……」或「有……」的句子，再強調一次，句句屬實。

　　1.（我的城市）<u>There are</u> a lot of dangerous drivers <u>here</u>.

　　2.（我的家鄉）<u>There is</u> a really great Italian restaurant <u>there</u>.

　　3.（我的補習班）<u>There are</u> a few retired people.（retired = 退休的）

 你的句子

那，現在請你用 There is / are...there 或者 There is / are...here 寫幾個句子吧，希望都是描述你真實生活的情況。

　　1. _____

　　2. _____

3. _____

超簡單改錯

1.（餐廳）If there has many people, it might be too crowded.
（crowded = 擁擠的）

2. If there has a hotel, we'll stay in it.

錯庫！蒐集自台灣人真正犯過的英文錯誤，一起來除錯！

1. I like mouse and rabbit.

2. I called one of my neighbor.

3. One of my friends really likes to read.

4. I very admire this ability.

5. There have a vegetarian restaurant.（vegetarian = 素食的）

here 與 there 並不會「有」東西！

解答

超簡單改錯

1. If <u>there are</u> many people <u>there</u>, it might be too crowded.

2. If <u>there is</u> a hotel <u>there</u>, we'll stay in it.

錯庫

1. I like <u>mice</u> and <u>rabbits</u>.

（第 5 章：表達一般性的看法或意見時，可數名詞要用複數。）

2. I called one of my <u>neighbors</u>.

（第 6 章：one of 後面的名詞要用複數）

3. 正確無誤！

4. I <u>really</u> admire this ability.

（第 7 章：動詞前面不可加 very）

5. <u>There is</u> a vegetarian restaurant <u>there</u>.（本章）

你到那裡，就右轉！

here 和 there 前面通常不會放介係詞

你到那裡，就右轉。

「這個句型再簡單不過。沒問題！」其實大有問題：

✘　When you get to there, turn right.

這裡和那裡，here 和 there，簡簡單單兩個字，卻引起不少誤會，產生許多超級常見的錯誤。其中一個就是，在這兩個字前面放介係詞。除了後面會討論的少數例外情況，一般而言，here 和 there 前面不能放介係詞。

用中文的邏輯說英文，就會說成奇怪的英文。這樣才是對的：

✔　When you get <u>there</u>, turn right.

陷阱可能是把「到那裡」的「到」字說成英文的 to。不行！

不只是「到」這個字，「在」也有同樣的問題。比方說，中文可以說：

我住在這裡！

但是，英文是不需要把那個「在」翻譯出來的：

✘　I live at here!

✔　I live <u>here</u>!

　　這個錯誤，我再囉嗦一下，是來自於學習英文的觀念不對，以為學了單字，就把中文的句子用英文的單字替換就好了。這真是大錯特錯！學習英文，就像交新朋友，你要觀察這個朋友的行為模式，才能真正了解他，不能一直用自己的想法去想對方，一直犯錯！

好了，就說到這兒。我們再來多看一些對和錯的比較：

✘ （補習班）I come to here five days a week.

✔ I come <u>here</u> five days a week.

✘ （父母家）I'm going to go to there this weekend.

✔ I'm going to go <u>there</u> this weekend.

✘ （講電話）I'm already at here!

✔ I'm already <u>here</u>!

不過，凡事都有例外。來看一下這幾個句子：

✔ Let's go in there.

✔ Can we go in there?

✔ You can't come in here!

✔ It's pretty cold in here.

我要特別說明，上面這四個句子的 in 都是可以省略的，放那個 in 是要特別提醒對方：那個地方有一個空間，我指的是裡面的空間。

還有一個例外。

我們偶爾會說 over there 與 over here。例如：

✔ （被問洗手間在哪兒）Over there.

✔ （朋友在叫：Where are you?）I'm over here!

這個 over 是什麼意思呢？

首先，over 表示比較遠的地方，有時是距離遠到說話者和傾聽者都看不清楚或根本看不到。

再者，表示你在指出大概的方向，不是很精準的方向。比方說，上面的第一個

句子，問洗手間，你說 over there 的時候，你大概是伸出手臂，指出大約的方向。

　　如果洗手間很近，就在你們都看得很清楚的地方，你可以很準確地指出來，這時候你就乾脆說 right there。

　　至於上面第二句例句，為什麼要說 over here 呢？大概是因為朋友看不到你，你的聲音本身就給了他大概的方向。

 史考特的句子

那麼，我來野人獻曝了：

　　1.（我的學校）I go <u>there</u> six times a week.

　　2.（我現在的城市）I arrived <u>here</u> two months ago.

　　3. My friend comes <u>here</u> to see me on the weekends.

　　4. Living <u>here</u> is a great experience.

　　5.（Australia）I've never been <u>there</u>.

 你的句子

輪到你了：

　　1. _____

　　2. _____

3. _____

超簡單改錯

1. （演唱會）Some people went to there.

2. （提問住什麼城市）I live at here!

錯庫！蒐集自台灣人真正犯過的英文錯誤，一起來除錯！

1. （最近看了一些科幻片）The second movie I saw is talking about a group of scientists.

2. My daughter very loves this dog.

3. （說者的公司會派人到美國去）We send people to there.

4. I don't like bug.

5. In my city have a big temple.

解答

超簡單改錯

1. Some people went ~~to~~ there.

2. I live ~~at~~ here!

錯庫

1. The second movie I saw <u>is about</u> a group of scientists.
（第 8 章：電影不會說話！）

2. My daughter <u>really</u> loves this dog.
（第 7 章：動詞前面不可加 very）

3. We send people ~~to~~ there.（本章）

4. I don't like bug<u>s</u>.
（第 5 章：表達一般性的看法或意見時，可數名詞要用複數。）

5. In my city <u>there is</u> a big temple.
（本章）

我不喜歡這裡

here 與 there 不可以當成受詞和主詞

關於 here 與 there 的問題，其實還沒學完！

我不喜歡這裡。

英文不能直接這樣翻譯：

✗   I don't like here.

這也是中式英文的問題。這樣才對：

✔   I don't like <u>it here</u>.

咦？那個 it 是從哪裡來的呢？

讓我來為你們說明。第一，英文裡，here 與 there 不能當受詞。

然後，第二，說實在的，那個 it 沒有特別的意思，可以說是「這兒的情況」、「這兒的氣氛」、「這兒的樣子」等等，也可以說它根本沒有意思，完全是為了符合我們美國人的文法要求。不管怎麼樣，因為 here 及 there 不能當受詞，所以非要把 it 放進去不可。

再舉些例子來說：

✗   （泰國）I like there.
✔   I like <u>it there</u>.

✗   （這個城市）I love here.
✔   I love <u>it here</u>.

✗   （去過澳大利亞）I didn't enjoy there.
✔   I didn't enjoy <u>it there</u>.

史考特的句子

1.（以前住過的城市）I didn't really <u>like it there</u>.

2.（現在的學校）I <u>love it here</u>.

3.（以前讀過書的一個美國城市）I <u>hated it there</u>.

你的句子

1. _____

2. _____

3. _____

剛剛我們說了 here 與 there 不能當受詞。

同樣的，here 與 there 也不能當主詞。這也是中式英文的問題。中文可以說：

那裡很漂亮。

但是，英文不可以說：

✘ There is beautiful.

這裡，應該用英文的一個句型，就是在前面說 It's，然後把 here 或 there 移到後面。就像這樣：

✔ It's beautiful <u>there</u>.

再多看一些例句：

✘ Here is really noisy.
✔ It's really noisy <u>here</u>.

✘ There is so hot.
✔ It's so hot <u>there</u>.

✘ There is terrible.
✔ It's terrible <u>there</u>.

 史考特的句子

1.（本市）It's really cold <u>here</u>.

2.（紐約）It's so expensive <u>there</u>.

3.（台北）It's a lot more crowded <u>there</u>.

 你的句子

1. _____

2. _____

3. _____

 超簡單改錯

1. I really hate there.

2. There is pretty noisy.

3. I really enjoy here.

4. Here is so ugly!

5. I can't stand here.（can't stand = 受不了）

6. There is pretty wonderful.（這裡的 pretty = 一點）

錯庫！蒐集自台灣人真正犯過的英文錯誤，一起來除錯！

 1.（史考特的補習班！）I come to here to improve my English.

2. Yesterday, I must go out to buy a phone.

3. I really like here.

here 與 there 不可以當成受詞和主詞

4. He need to learn how to get along with other people.

5. My parents think there is dangerous.

解答

超簡單改錯

1. I really hate it there.

2. It's pretty noisy there.

3. I really enjoy it here.

4. It's so ugly here!

5. I can't stand it here.

6. It's pretty wonderful there.

錯庫

1. I come to here to improve my English.

（第 10 章：here 和 there 前面通常不會放介係詞）

2. Yesterday, I had to go out to buy a phone.

（第 3 章：描述過去發生的事，動詞要用過去式。）

3. I really like it here.（本章）

4. He needs to learn how to get along with other people.

（第 1 章：第三人稱現在式動詞忘記加 s / es）

5. My parents think it's dangerous there.（本章）

我喜歡看漫畫書

like、don't like、love、hate 後面
要小心放什麼字！

上一章，我們談到「喜歡那裡」用英文怎麼說，需要小心什麼。

而「喜歡」這個字，也蠻危險的，可能又會讓你犯錯。

先看下面的例句：

✘　I like read comic books.

其實，正確的說法有兩個選擇。你記得嗎？當然記得！就是：

✔　I like <u>to read</u> comic books.
✔　I like <u>reading</u> comic books.

就是，如果 like 後面要接動詞時，不可以直接加動詞，只能加帶有 to 的不定詞或有 ing 的動名詞。

> 從中文的句型，我們很容易看出錯誤的原因：
>
> 我喜歡看漫畫書。
>
> 中文句子的排列組合裡，第一個動詞「喜歡」與第二個動詞「看」，中間沒有任何字詞，很多人就把中文句型直接翻譯成英文，因而犯了這個錯誤！
>
> 請記得：like、don't like、love、hate 這幾個動詞，後面直接加動詞，是錯誤的！
>
> 有人問我，既然不定詞及動名詞都能用，那兩者之間有何差別呢？說實在的，它們並沒什麼差別。對我來說，不定詞感覺上可能會生動一點點，但是對很多以英文為母語的人來說，差別其實是感覺不出來的。

很多人，好像隱約記得這些動詞有 to+verb 及 verb+ing 的用法，可能是過度地追求安全感，結果就同時使用！我聽過很多這樣的句子：

✘ I like to playing computer games.

喔！你以為兩個錯誤會負負得正變成對的嗎？你只能選一個！

✔ I like <u>to play</u> computer games.

或，

✔ I like <u>playing</u> computer games.

愛情和英文，都不可以腳踏兩條船！你要選一個句型，然後死心塌地跟著它。

 史考特的句子

1. I <u>like to watch</u> Chinese movies.

   I <u>like watching</u> Chinese movies.

2. I <u>don't like to ride</u> my scooter in the rain.
   （scooter = 小型的摩托車）

   I <u>don't like riding</u> my scooter in the rain.

3. I <u>love to eat</u> at the night market.

   I <u>love eating</u> at the night market.

4. I <u>hate to wake</u> up early.

   I <u>hate waking</u> up early.

你的句子

不定詞或動名詞，請任選一個，兩個都寫就嫌囉嗦啦！

1. _____

2. _____

超簡單改錯

1. I like use the internet at night.

2. I hate to wasting time at work.

錯庫！蒐集自台灣人真正犯過的英文錯誤，一起來除錯！

1. （報告同學的意見）She says cockroach is terrible.

2. One day my husband drive the car to work.

3. One of my classmates likes to go to the movies every week.

4.（爸爸）He likes drink alcohol.（alcohol = 酒）

5.（某一個城市，有金礦）I only know there have gold.

解答

超簡單改錯

1. I like to use the internet at night.
   （或）I like using the internet at night.

2. I hate to waste time at work.（或）I hate wasting time at work.

錯庫

1. She says cockroaches are terrible.
   （第 5 章：表達一般性的看法或意見時，可數的名詞要用複數。）

2. One day my husband drove the car to work.
   （第 3 章：描述過去發生的事，動詞要用過去式。）

3. 正確無誤！

4. He likes to drink alcohol.（或）He likes drinking alcohol.（本章）

5. I only know there is gold there.
   （第 9 章：here 與 there 並不會「有」東西！）

第 13 章

你喜歡漢堡嗎？喜歡！

有些動詞後面需要接受詞

來看看以下的對話。我不會告訴你 John 是哪一個英文補習班老師的代號。

> Kate: 你喜歡漢堡嗎？
>
> John: 喜歡！

但是，以英文的觀點，John 不可以這樣回答：

✔ Kate: Do you like hamburgers?

✘ John: Yes, I like.

你知道為什麼嗎？

這也是來自於中文語法的影響。

前一章，我們談動詞，討論了如果動詞後面要加動詞，要小心，要加有 to 的不定詞，或是加 ing 的動名詞。這一章，我們還是要繼續探究動詞後面所加的東西。不過，這次我們要談的東西是名詞。

簡單地說，有些動詞後面一定要有受詞，而如果你用中文的思維，可能會說錯，因為中文不需要受詞。

John 其實有兩種正確回答的選擇。首先，他可以簡短回答：

✔ John: Yes, I <u>do</u>.

或者，他在 like 後面加受詞：

✔ John: Yes, I like <u>them</u>.

總而言之，句子不可以停在 like 這個字。說 like 這個字，如果不是接動詞（請

參考上一章），就要接受詞。

英文有很多動詞是不能當作句子的最後一個詞。以下是幾個常常用錯的動詞：

buy	（買）	ignore	（忽視）
do	（做）	like	（喜歡）
enjoy	（享受）	love	（愛）
give	（給、送）	say	（說）
have	（有）	use	（使用）
hate	（恨、討厭）	want	（想要）
hold	（拿、有）		

現在，我們就用上面列出來的幾個動詞做練習，比較對錯：

✘　（提問，要不要一件衣服）No, I don't really like.

✔　No, I don't really like <u>it</u>.

✘　（提問，"Do you love your wife?"）Of course I love!

✔　Of course I love <u>her</u>!

✔　Of course I <u>do</u>!

✘　（以前看過的產品）I really wanted to buy for my friend.

✔　I really wanted to buy <u>it</u> for my friend.

注意：for my friend 不是受詞，而是介係詞片語，buy 後面還需要加受詞。

✘　（新的電腦）I can't use very well.

✔　I can't use <u>it</u> very well.

✘　（跟父母說話時）I should never ignore.

✔　I should never ignore <u>them</u>.

✘ （提問，Do you want to play baseball?）No, I hate!

✔ No, I hate <u>baseball</u>!

✔ No, I <u>don't</u>.

敬請注意，代名詞與一般名詞都可以當受詞使用。

 史考特的句子

1. （cats）I don't like <u>them</u>.

2. （我的新教室）I hate <u>it</u>! It's too small!

3. （movies）I usually enjoy <u>them</u>.

4. （新的軟體）I don't know how to use <u>it</u>.

 你的句子

1. _____

2. _____

超簡單改錯

1.（需要朋友幫忙拿一下你的書包）Can you hold for me?

2.（別人要你煮一種菜）I don't know how to do.

錯庫！蒐集自台灣人真正犯過的英文錯誤，一起來除錯！

1. Yesterday she treat everybody to lunch.（treat = 請客）

2.（某一棟建築）There have air conditioning.

3.（剛才被問及喜不喜歡某種食物）Yeah, I like.

4. One of my friends really likes to go shopping.

5. I like travel.

解答

超簡單改錯

1. Can you hold <u>it</u> for me?

2. I don't know how to do <u>it</u>.

錯庫

1. Yesterday she <u>treated</u> everybody to lunch.

（第 3 章：描述過去發生的事，動詞要用過去式。）

2. There <u>is</u> air conditioning <u>there</u>.

（第 9 章：here 與 there 並不會「有」東西！）

3. Yeah, I like <u>it</u>.（或）Yeah, I <u>do</u>.（本章）

4. 正確無誤！

5. I like <u>to</u> travel.（或）I like <u>traveling</u>.

（第 12 章：like、don't like、love、hate 後面要小心放什麼字！）

第 3 關

直擊英文犯罪現場

- 我缺錢。
  史上最難纏的英文單字：lack（第 15 章）

- 無聊嗎？
  你 boring 還是 bored？這你可要說清楚！（第 17 章）

- 我很容易發胖。
  小心！easy 沒你想得那麼 easy。（第 22 章）

我會考慮

這個動詞後面不需要加介係詞！

第14章

來看一個「英文犯罪現場」。你的朋友請你考慮一件重要的事。你當然會答應他。

✘ I will consider about it.

你們的確是好朋友，不過，你跟英文的友誼卻有待加強！

在上一章，我們認識了一種動詞，後面需要接受詞。如果你能夠忍受一點術語的話，這樣的動詞叫作「及物動詞」。我們已經知道它後面會接受詞，像這樣：

✔ I like it.

沒問題，正確無誤。

但是，卻有另一個問題。就是，這些「及物動詞」是直接接受詞的，但是很多人卻偏偏要放一個介係詞進去，這是錯的。上面「犯罪現場」裡的 consider 是很常見的例子。要這樣說才不會犯罪：

✔ I will consider it.

> 注意，要避開兩種危險！
> 一，這個及物動詞一定要加受詞，不加就錯了。（這就是上一章的主題！）
> 二，動詞與受詞之間不能加介係詞，這也是錯的。

整理一下 consider 的用法，如下：

✘ I will consider.（沒有受詞）
✘ I will consider about it.（加了不需要的介係詞）
✔ I will consider it.

一般來講，很多英文動詞後面不用接介係詞，就是我們剛才介紹的「及物動詞」。根據我的經驗，最常搞錯的是以下這些：

accompany	（陪）	introduce	（介紹）
blame	（怪罪）	lack	（缺）
chase	（追）	mention	（提）
contact	（聯絡）	respect	（尊敬）
consider	（考慮）	study	（學）
date	（約會）	tell	（告訴）
discuss	（討論）	visit	（拜訪、看）
fear	（怕）	waste	（浪費）

　　我把一些特別容易搞錯的字做個對錯比較。不知道為什麼，最常弄錯的是 mention 這個字：

✘　He mentioned.
✘　He mentioned about his job.
✔　He <u>mentioned</u> his job.

　　accompany 也常常搞錯：

✘　I accompanied to the store.
✘　I accompanied with my mother to the store.
✔　I <u>accompanied</u> my mother to the store.

　　contact 一樣：

✘　I contacted.

✘　I contacted with my boss.

✔　I <u>contacted</u> my boss.

consider 也不例外：

✘　We should consider about that choice.

✔　We should <u>consider</u> that choice.

discuss 的錯誤也折磨了我好幾年了：

✘　We are discussing about politics.

✔　We are <u>discussing</u> politics.

　　有些錯誤，我可以理解，是因為這個動詞有相關的名詞，而這個名詞的片語有介係詞。

　　比方說，discuss 的名詞是 discussion，而它的名詞片語的確有介係詞：

✔　We <u>discuss</u> money in class.

✔　We <u>have discussions about</u> money in class.

　　blame、contact、date、discuss、fear、lack、respect、visit、waste 這幾個動詞都一樣，動詞後面沒有介係詞，可是它們的名詞後面其實都有介係詞形成片語，因此在使用上造成了混淆。

　　下面這些句子都是正確的：

✔　I <u>blamed</u> him.（在這裡，blame 動詞）

✔　I <u>put the blame on</u> him.（這 blame 是名詞）

✔　I <u>contacted</u> him.（動詞）

✔　I <u>made contact with</u> him.（名詞）

✔ I <u>dated</u> her.（動詞）
✔ I <u>went on a date with</u> her.（名詞）

✔ We <u>discussed</u> politics.（動詞）
✔ We <u>had a discussion about</u> politics.（名詞）

✔ I <u>fear</u> dogs.（動詞）
✔ I <u>have a fear of</u> dogs.（名詞）

✔ I <u>respect</u> my teacher.（動詞）
✔ I <u>have respect for</u> my teacher.（名詞）

✔ I <u>visited</u> my grandma.（動詞）
✔ I <u>made a visit to</u> my grandma.（名詞）

✔ That <u>wastes</u> money.（動詞）
✔ That <u>is a waste of</u> money.（名詞）

　　總之，你必須記得，很多名詞後面需要加介係詞，然而與它們相關的動詞卻不需要。

　　我們現在來寫些句子吧。就用上面列出的這些單字吧。

 史考特的句子

1. Sometimes I <u>accompany</u> my dad to the store.

2. The book I've been reading <u>mentions</u> college life.

3. I really need to <u>consider</u> my future.

4. Some English schools around here <u>lack</u> resources.
（resource = 資源）

5. A lot of people **blame** their parents for all of their problems.

你的句子

現在，也請你從上面的單字裡選一些來造句。

1. _____

2. _____

3. _____

4. _____

5. _____

超簡單改錯

1.（某些人）They mentioned about family relationships.

2.（對同學建議）Don't waste of money!

錯庫！蒐集自台灣人真正犯過的英文錯誤，一起來除錯！

1.（士林夜市）I like there!

2. They lack of motivation.

3.（對新生）Where are you come from?

4. Their father often contacts with them.

5.（去日本）I went to there to see snow.

6.（某一種機器）I know how to use, but I still don't like it.

解答

超簡單改錯

1. They mentioned ~~about~~ family relationships.

2. Don't waste ~~of~~ money!

錯庫

1. I like ~~it~~ there!

（第 11 章：here 與 there 不可以當成受詞和主詞。）

2. They lack ~~of~~ motivation.（本章）

3. Where are you ~~come~~ from?

（第 4 章：你來自哪裡？用 from 還是 come from？）

4. Their father often contacts ~~with~~ them.（本章）

5. I went ~~to~~ there to see snow.

（第 10 章：here 和 there前面通常不會放介係詞）

6. I know how to use ~~it~~, but I still don't like it.

（第 13 章：有些動詞後面需要接受詞）

第
15 章

我缺錢

細說一個字：lack

✘　I lack of money.

　　我們在上一章談到及物動詞，它們後面不需要接介係詞。其中，在錯庫中，我們看到一個字，lack，它就是一個及物動詞。

　　但是，我覺得 lack（缺少）是個很特殊的案例。我教了差不多十年的英文，前五年，我連一次都沒有聽過有人用對 lack 這個字；接下來的五年，正確使用的次數沒有超過五次。十、年、用、對、了、五、次。雖然每次用錯我都會提醒！嗚！好、痛、苦！

　　以單字來說，lack 榮登大家最容易用錯的單字第一名，超級巨星！

　　可能是因為 lack 有動詞、形容詞與名詞的詞性，然後詞性的用法都不一樣，因此大家把它們全部混在一起了。今天，我們在這裡好好的來看待這個字。

lack 的正確用法如下：

動詞（lack）：所謂的及物動詞，一個字，單獨用，後面不需要加介係詞。

✔　I <u>lack</u> money.

形容詞（lacking）：三個字，be lacking in，後面的介係詞一定是 in，不可以用別的介係詞：

✔　I <u>am lacking in</u> money.

名詞（lack）：四個字，have a lack of，後面的介係詞一定是 of，不可以用別的介係詞：

✔ I <u>have a lack of</u> money.

我們再看一個例子，都是對的，第一是動詞，第二是形容詞，第三是名詞：

✔ That library <u>lacks</u> English books.
✔ That library <u>is lacking in</u> English books.
✔ That library <u>has a lack of</u> English books.

用法就是這樣。動詞單獨使用；形容詞則用三個字表示，介係詞一定是 in；名詞就用四個字表示，介係詞一定是 of。

這個字 lack 真的是英文老師的敵人。如果你們真的學會這一章的內容，然後開始正確應用 lack，我真的會感激終身！

 史考特的句子

讓我來說說誰缺什麼。動詞、形容詞、名詞全部都會用到！

1. Right now, I <u>lack</u> time for studying Chinese.（動詞）

2. Taiwan <u>lacks</u> natural resources.
   （動詞，natural resources = 自然資源）

3. My friend <u>is lacking in</u> confidence, so he doesn't talk to many girls.（形容詞）

4. My area <u>is lacking in</u> good American restaurants.（形容詞）

5. Some students <u>have a lack of</u> opportunities to practice English.（名詞）

6. This afternoon I <u>had a lack of</u> energy, so I took a nap.（名詞）

你的句子

換你！每一種詞性都用一用啊。

1. _____

2. _____

3. _____

超簡單改錯

注意，改成動詞、形容詞或名詞都可以。

1. （要買某一個東西）He couldn't buy it because he was lack of money.

2. In the future, we will lack of oil.

錯庫！蒐集自台灣人真正犯過的英文錯誤，一起來除錯！

1. I can go to a lot of place to have special experiences.

2. （某一個地方）There is convenient.

3. Only people who lack of self-confidence do that.
    （self-confidence = 自信心）

4. In the future, I will very like children.

5. I like action movies.（action movies = 動作片）

6. One of my colleague, she live near my house.

7. When you get old, your children can accompany with you.

超簡單改錯

1. He couldn't buy it because he lacked money.

（或）He couldn't buy it because he was lacking in money.

（或）He couldn't buy it because he had a lack of money.

2. In the future, we will lack oil.

（或）In the future, we will be lacking in oil.

（或）In the future, we will have a lack of oil.

錯庫

1. I can go to a lot of places to have special experiences.

（第 2 章：複數名詞忘了加 s / es）

2. It's convenient there.

（第 11 章：here 與 there 不可以當成受詞和主詞）

3. Only people who lack of self-confidence do that.（本章）

（或）Only people who are lacking in self-confidence do that

（或）Only people who have a lack of self-confidence do that

4. In the future, I will very really like children.

（第 7 章：動詞前面不可加 very）

5. 正確無誤！

6. One of my colleagues she lives near my house.

（第 6 章：one of 後面的名詞要用複數；第 1 章：第三人稱現在式動詞忘記加 s / es）

7. When you get old, your children can accompany with you.

（第 14 章：這個動詞後面不需要加介係詞！）

第 16 章

我正在聽韓國流行音樂

進行式如果搞錯,一切都進行不了!

我打電話給朋友,問她,So what are you doing?,她回答:

✘　I listening to Korean pop music.（Korean = 韓國的）

看到錯在哪裡了嗎?這句話沒有動詞啊!

嚴格來講,listening 是個形容詞。

　　這一章的錯誤雖然很簡單,但卻很常見。很多人要表達現在正在做的事情時,他們忘了加 be 動詞,這是錯的。

　　如果你願意讓我稍微囉嗦一下,很煩人,我知道,但我必須介紹一點文法的專用術語。這樣的形容詞叫作「現在分詞」,他就是一種形容詞,上面的 listening 就是現在分詞。那個「現在」,理應會讓你意識到,要用現在時態。

以下的句子才是正確的:

✔　I'm listening to Korean pop music.

很簡單,對不對?可是我要提醒你,如果用一般動詞,就不用那個 be。例如:

✔　I listen to music every day.

這個 listen 是個動詞,上面的 listening 卻是個形容詞。我知道它們長得很像,所以要更小心使用喔!

再來一些對錯的比較:

✘ My best friend talking to her boyfriend.

✔ My best friend <u>is talking</u> to her boyfriend.

在否定的句子中，可能會有一樣的問題：

✘ I not doing anything right now.

✔ I'<u>m</u> not <u>doing</u> anything right now.

還有一個相關的問題。就像以上的說明，現在時態是這樣形成的：be ＋ 動詞 ing。剛才說，大家可能會忘記寫 be 動詞，不過，有些人忘的是動詞後面的 ing。比方說：

✘ I'm read an English book right now.

正確的應該是：

✔ I'm rea<u>ding</u> an English book right now.

過去進行式也一樣，會有人忘了說 ing。比方說，你的朋友問你昨天下午一點在幹嘛，你可能會這樣回答：

✘ I was eat lunch.

✔ I was eat<u>ing</u> lunch.

 史考特的句子

那，我隨便說一說我的事！

1. My parents <u>are sleeping</u> right now.

2. One of my students <u>is eating</u> a huge meal.

你的句子

1. _____

2. _____

 超簡單改錯

1. A: What's up?　B: I preparing for my big test.
（What's up = 近來如何？）

2. My sister is not do her homework!

錯庫！蒐集自台灣人真正犯過的英文錯誤，一起來除錯！

1. （家鄉）I love there, because it's a small village.

2. （史考特剛才問學生他們在做什麼？）We talking about the first question in the book.

3. （某個公園）Have some cool models of tanks.
（model = 模型，tank = 坦克）

4. （剛被問 What's up?）I'm talking to one of my friends about cars.

5. （跟朋友說在做什麼）I am study hard for my test tomorrow.

解答

超簡單改錯

1. A: What's up? B: <u>I'm preparing</u> for my big test.
2. My sister <u>isn't</u> <u>doing</u> her homework!

錯庫

1. I love <u>it</u> there, because it's a small village.（第 11 章：here 與 there 不可以當成受詞和主詞）

2. We <u>are talking</u> about the first question in the book.（本章）
3. <u>There are</u> some cool models of tanks.（第 9 章：here 與 there 並不會「有」東西！）
4. 正確無誤！
5. I am study<u>ing</u> hard for my test tomorrow.（本章）

第 17 章

我們那堂課很無聊

無聊有兩種：你很 boring 還是很 bored，
你真的不能不管！

你去上課。台上的人巴拉巴拉巴拉講了老半天（你一定知道這位老師不叫史考特），無聊死了。終於結束了，你應該怎麼跟朋友描述這堂課呢？恐怕很多人會這樣說喔：

✘　Our class was so bored!

這裡請特別小心，注意以下我的說明。

bored 這個字的意思是無聊，是一種感受，引發那個感受的東西要用 ing，接收到那個感受的人要用 ed。所以，上面那個錯誤的句子，那個 class 讓你覺得很無聊，是它引發那個無聊的感覺。正確的句子已經浮現在你的腦海裡了吧：

✔　Our <u>class</u> was so bor<u>ing</u>!

我們再說一部恐怖片：

✘　The movie was really bad. I was so boring.

主詞是 I，是你接收到那個感覺，這樣的情況，你就要說：

✔　The movie was really bad. <u>I</u> was so bor<u>ed</u>.

看一下這個小圖表：

引發　　　→　　　感受
ing　　　→　　　ed

你已經看出來了，這可以歸納出一個原則，在一般的情況下，都會有這樣一對互補的句子，一個可以形容引發那種感覺的東西，另一個則是接收到那種感覺的人。

這樣由 ed / ing 形成的一組字，我們來整理出一張漂亮的清單吧！

引發的東西是……	感受的人是……	
amazing	amazed	（驚奇）
boring	bored	
confusing	confused	（困惑）
embarrassing	embarrassed	
exciting	excited	
exhausting	exhausted	（疲倦）
fascinating	fascinated	（非常感興趣）
frustrating	frustrated	（挫折／沮喪）
humiliating	humiliated	（丟臉）
interesting	interested	
relaxing	relaxed	
shocking	shocked	（驚人）
tiring	tired	

我們來考慮一些情境。比如，你看了一本很有趣的書。以下兩種說法都正確：

✔ The book was really interesting. （書是引發者）
✔ I was really interested in that book. （我是接受者）

注意：這兩個句子的意思一樣！

下面是形容無聊的旅行，兩句都可以通用：

✔ The trip was so boring.
✔ I was bored by the trip.

以下兩句的意思都一樣：

✔ <u>The test</u> was frustrat<u>ing</u>.
✔ <u>I</u> was frustrat<u>ed</u> by the test.

很多表達情緒的字往往跟在 feel（覺得……）的後面。那，你覺得 feel 後面應該用 ed 還是 ing 的形容詞呢？

因為 feel 是用來說你感受到什麼情緒，一定是用 ed 的。但是，你們還是常常表錯情啊！例如：

✘ When NBA stars come to Taiwan, I feel so exciting!
✔ When NBA stars come to Taiwan, I <u>feel</u> so <u>excited</u>!

我們可以看出，一般來說，「東西」或「活動」大部分都用 ing，「人」多半都用 ed。比方說，我們可以正確地說：

NBA（東西）很 excit<u>ing</u>.
我看 NBA的時候，我（人）很 excit<u>ed</u>.

但是，還是有些特殊情況。例如，引發者跟接收者都是人。

我們又要來舉那個很無聊、不叫史考特的老師為例。這一堂課，老師說的話很無趣，讓你覺得很無聊。因為老師是無聊這種感覺產生的原因，形容這個老師就要說：

✔ Oh my god, <u>the teacher</u> was so bor<u>ing</u>.

說到你自己的反應，你要說：

✔ Oh my god, <u>I</u> was so bor<u>ed</u> by the teacher.

看了這些例子之後，我們就可以了解為什麼很多人會搞錯。因為中文一個詞「無聊」，可以說老師，也可以說學生。英文卻有兩個字，要區分情況來用。

很多人內心是這麼想的：「哦，『無聊』就是 boring 的意思。當遇到任何中文會說『無聊』的情況，那就可以用這個英文字 boring。」

我告訴你，可沒有那麼簡單！英文的「無聊」有兩種，你要選對！

那，我為什麼一直強調 bored/boring 這兩個字呢？因為這是最容易讓大家出糗的一個英文字。根據上面的討論，你猜得出原因吧。就是，其實你是要講一件很無聊的事情，卻說出這樣的話……

✘　Ah! I'm so boring!

這句話還說得通，它的意思是：我讓別人覺得很無聊，我就是產生無聊感覺的東西，我說的話很無趣，我的笑話冷，我的動作不生動，我的衣服不吸睛，我的 email 不值得看，我臉書上的照片拍得不好，等等。

I am boring，說出這句話，是相當激烈地在批評自己！根據我學生交上來的幾萬篇報告，他們是全世界最 boring 的人。我深刻地希望他們真正的意思是 bored，這只是英文的錯誤而已。但再想想，他們搞不好真的是全世界最……不不，不可能吧。

所以，上面真的只是個英文錯誤，正確的說法應該是：

✔　Ah! I'm so <u>bored</u>!

英文不是很煩嗎？哦，對不起，我打錯字了，我要打的是：「英文不是很 fun 嗎？」（哈哈，請容忍我的冷笑話！）

那，恐怕我們要再來 fun 一下。

以上有很多對形容詞，一個是 ed，一個是 ing。不過，其實還有一些單字的變化不是那麼規律。為了避免害你腦袋爆炸，我只列出日常生活裡大家比較容易誤用的。

引發者	意思	威受者	意思
addictive	會害人上癮的	addicted	上了癮的
impressive	令人留下深刻印象的	impressed	留下深刻印象的
offensive	會冒犯他人的	offended	被別人冒犯了的
scary	可怕/嚇到人的	scared	怕/被嚇到了的
stressful	給人壓力的	stressed out	受到了很多壓力的

注意：不知道為什麼，現在說 stressed 的時候，我們都還會說第二個字 out，那個 out 沒什麼意思，只是口語的習慣。

這批單字裡頭，最容易讓人丟臉的一定是 scary 與 scared 這一組。遇到可怕的事情，很多人會說：

✘　I was so scary!

這句的意思是：「我嚇到了人！」

你不是這個意思啦，對吧對吧？！這跟你的本意剛好是相反的。你其實是要這麼說：

✔　I was so scared!

要是你說 I am so scary，而對方搞不懂你是說錯英文，以他來說，你的話可能會帶有一點威脅的味道。I am so scary 可能會暗示人家：「我是會嚇到人的人，害人也無所謂。人們應該不想看到我的厲害吧，你們走著瞧。」

> 我還記得我第一次來台灣教英文，是教一些高中女生。瘦瘦的、矮矮的、很多人帶 Hello Kitty 的書包。開學的日子，她們一個一個走進教室跟我說：
> 「Teacher, I'm so scary!」
> 哇，好可怕，小女生還會威脅老師，這是什麼樣的鬼國家呢？後來才發現台灣人會搞錯 scary 跟 scared 的語法，她們原來是要說，第一次上有外籍老

師的英文課讓她們很 scared，但是每一個都對著老師説「她們很 scary」。
當時，真正很 scared 其實是我！

 史考特的句子

1. The <u>book</u> I'm reading is pretty interest<u>ing</u>.（這裡，pretty = 相當）

2. <u>I</u> was so bor<u>ed</u> at my company's meeting.（meeting = 會議）

以下這一組也是有關係而且互補的句子，說的都是同樣一件事：

3a. The <u>kids</u> were excit<u>ed</u> by the lantern festival.
（lantern festival = 元宵節）

3b. The lantern <u>festival</u> was excit<u>ing</u> for the kids.

 你的句子

1. _____

2. _____

（以下兩句請仿造第 3a 句和第 3b 句，寫出有關係而且互補的句子。）

3a. _____

3b. _____

超簡單改錯

1. The first time I went abroad, I was so exciting!

2. This year, Chinese New Year was pretty bored.

錯庫！蒐集自台灣人真正犯過的英文錯誤，一起來除錯！

1.（某一個風俗習慣）In Taiwan we always do this way.

2.（家的狗）It was exciting about mice.（mice = 老鼠，複數的拼法）

3.（老人說的）When I'm in junior high school, I went to cram school every day.（cram school = 補習班）

4.（學生在討論食物）I really like one of the restaurants near my house.

5.（學生不要做可能會出糗的事）That will be embarrassed.

超簡單改錯

1. The first time I went abroad, I was so excit<u>ed</u>!
2. This year, Chinese New Year was pretty bor<u>ing</u>.

錯庫

1. In Taiwan we always do <u>it</u> this way.
（第 13 章：有些動詞後面需要接受詞）
2. It was excit<u>ed</u> about mice.（本章）
3. When I <u>was</u> in junior high school, I went to cram school every day.
（第 3 章：描述過去發生的事，動詞要用過去式。）
4. 正確無誤！
5. That will be embarras<u>ing</u>.（本章）
（或）I will be embarrass<u>ed</u>.

第18章 慢跑是一種好運動

動詞開頭的句子，要用加 ing 的動名詞。

有時候，我們要把一個動作放在句子前面，也就是說，這個動作是句子的主詞。用中文很簡單，例如：

看書很好玩。

有些人這麼認為，「看書」這個動作，英文是 read，所以他們就這樣說：

✘ Read is fun.

說中文的時候，不管「看書」當動詞或名詞，它還是「看書」，完全不會改變。

但是，英文可不一樣了！動詞的「看書」，當然是 read。文法上，一個句子的主詞必須是名詞，動詞後面加 ing 就會變成所謂的「動名詞」，動名詞才可以當主詞：

✔ Read*ing* is fun.

很多人問我，To read is fun 可以嗎？可以，但是 to + 動詞是很正式、很具詩意的用法，一般日常的說、寫不會像莎士比亞那樣！動詞 + ing，99% 的時候就可以了。

再看兩個：

✘ Jog is good exercise.（jog = 慢跑；exercise = 運動）
✔ Jogg*ing* is good exercise.

✘ Listen to my noisy neighbors makes me crazy.（neighbor = 鄰居）
✔ Listen*ing* to my noisy neighbors makes me crazy.

還有一個問題要小心。就是，有些動詞後面我們會放完整的句子，像 say,

think 什麼的。比方，中文說，「我認為存錢非常重要。」這可要小心：

✘　I think save money is really important.

think 後面有句子，所以還是要遵守這章介紹的規定：

✔　I think <u>saving</u> money is really important.

注意：這樣的句子裡，think 後面可以加 that：

✔　I think that <u>saving</u> money is really important.

口語英文中，這樣的 that 常常會省略，不過這樣是100% 正確的，that 可放可不放。

我們不妨再來練習一個：

✘　He said deal with his boss makes him unhappy.
✔　He said <u>dealing</u> with his boss makes him unhappy.

再提醒一下：said 後面也可以說 that。

那，你知道英文有一句話：Use it or lose it. 意思是「不用就作廢」。為了不 lose 我們的英文，我們就去 use 它來造句。當然是真實生活中用得上的句子。Me first!

 史考特的句子

1. Study<u>ing</u> Chinese is one of my hobbies.

2. My dad said that <u>riding</u> a motorcycle in Taiwan is really scary.

3. Eat<u>ing</u> sticky rice dumplings makes me happy.

（sticky rice dumplings = 粽子）

 你的句子

1. _____

2. _____

 超簡單改錯

1. I think eat at restaurants is a little too expensive for me.

2. Meet girls for the first time makes him nervous.（nervous = 緊張）

錯庫！蒐集自台灣人真正犯過的英文錯誤，一起來除錯！

 1. I love movies about robots.（robot = 機器人）

2. （某一種活動）That will be tired.

3. One of my friend is not from a big city.

4.（一般的想法）We rely on computer too much.（rely on = 依賴）

5. Go hiking is part of my weekly routine.

（routine = 慣常做的事情）

解答

超簡單改錯

1. I think eat<u>ing</u> at restaurants is a little
   too expensive for me.
2. Meet<u>ing</u> girls for the first time makes
   him nervous.

錯庫

1. 正確無誤！
2. That will be tir<u>ing</u>.
   （第 17 章：無聊有兩種：你很
   boring 還是很 bored，你真的不能不
   管！）

3. One of my friend<u>s</u> is not from a big
   city.
   （第 6 章：one of 後面的名詞要用複
   數）
4. We rely on computer<u>s</u> too much.
   （第 5 章：表達一般性的看法或意見
   時，可數名詞要用複數。）
5. <u>Going</u> hiking is part of my weekly
   routine.（本章）

他有很多錢

名詞是可數的還是不可數的？

「他有很多錢。」在台灣，這是很常聽到的，也是相當簡單的句型。但在台灣教了十年的英文，我聽了一大堆這個：

✘ He has a lot of moneys.

靠你現在的英文語感及習慣，你應該知道這樣才是對的：

✔ He has a lot of <u>money</u>.

> 不過，為什麼這樣才是對的呢？啊，親愛的讀者，敬請原諒，我需要說些文法術語。但是我向你保證，你「學」了一定馬上就會「說」。
>
> 我們要學的是這個：英文有一個中文所沒有的現象，就是我們的名詞分成「可數的」和「不可數的」。這是什麼意思呢？
>
> 基本上，可數的名詞可以用數字來計算：1、2、3……等，可以用1、2、3這樣數出來，就是可數的，就這麼簡單。

✔ one dog, two dogs, three dogs...

one dog 也可以說：

✔ a dog

有很多的話，就可以說：

✔ many dogs
✔ a lot of dogs

記住，這些 dogs 都加 s。

但是，有些東西不容易計算。

例如，我們說水，water。可以說 one waters, two waters, three waters 嗎？
不可以。那怎麼計算呢？

不可數的名詞，通常不會加複數的 s。我們只能說：

✔ some water（一些水）
✔ much water（很多水）
✔ a lot of water（很多水）

記住，這些 water 都不加 s。

這裡，我還要說一下 much 與 a lot of 的差別。

簡單地說，它們的意思一樣。我知道很多台灣的英文學習書都是這麼說，要說
「很多」的時候，就說 much。的確，這是沒錯的。

但是，這本書要教你怎麼說最口語、美國人真的會說的英文。我們美國人說話
時，要說「很多」不可數的東西，我們真正會說 的是 a lot of。例如：

✔ much money
✔ a lot of money（這是我們真正會說的）
✔ much sugar
✔ a lot of sugar（這是我們真正會說的）

因此，這樣的錯誤出現在我們的錯庫裡，我都會改成 a lot of。更重要的
是，說話的時候，你應該馬上養成美國人說 a lot of 的習慣，戒掉 much 這
個字，因為我們真的不會這麼說。

接著，我們來看一下一些對錯的比較。最常見的錯誤就是把不可數的名詞當作
可數的名詞，加上不該有的 s。

✘　I have a lot of moneys.

✔　I have a lot of <u>money</u>.

✘　After school, I have some free times.

✔　After school, I have some free <u>time</u>.

以下我列出最常誤用的名詞。都是不可數的哦！

常用錯的不可數名詞

Chinese	（中文）	news	（新聞）
English	（英文）	pollution	（污染）
equipment	（設備）	research	（研究、研究出來的資訊）
feedback	（回饋）	sand	（沙）
food	（食物）	scenery	（風景）
homework	（功課）	software	（軟體）
ice	（冰）	stuff	（東西）
information	（資訊、資料）	time	（時間）
Japanese	（日文）	water	（水）
money	（錢）		

　　我們現在扭轉一下焦點。上面都是說人們把不可數的名詞當作可數的。也會出現相反的情況：把可數的名詞當成不可數，忘了加該有的 s。舉一個例子來說：

✘　You eat too much calories.（calorie = 大卡、卡路里，是可數的詞）

✔　You eat too <u>many</u> calories.

　　這個例子同時也呈現一個重要的對比。要說「太多」的時候，可數名詞我們說 too many，不可數名詞則說 too much。例如：

✔ He has <u>too many</u> girlfriends.（girlfriend 是可數的）

✔ He has <u>too much</u> money.（money 是不可數的）

　　另一個問題是，可數名詞前面可以加 a / an，不可數名詞不可以說 a / an，只能說 some。舉個例子：

✔ I have a motorcycle.（motorcyle = 機車，是可數的）

✔ I have some rice.（rice = 米飯，是不可數的）

　　再來一個對錯相比：

✘ I have <u>a</u> food in my refrigerator.（refrigerator = 冰箱）

✔ I have <u>some</u> food in my refrigerator.

　　food 通常是不可數的，所以我們不可以說 a food。

　　還有一件事我要提醒你。文法上，不可數名詞是單數的。因此，要用單數的動詞：

✘ The waters, when they are cold, freeze quickly.（freeze = 冷凍起來）

✔ The <u>water</u>, when <u>it</u> is cold, <u>freezes</u> quickly.

　　不但要用單數的動詞，還要用單數的代名詞，it。如果你把不可數的名詞當作可數的，就會出現一連串的錯誤喔！

 細說一個字：news

　　我們在第15章認識了最讓英文老師抓狂的一個字，lack。你想知道第二名是哪一個字嗎？我不好讓你久等，它就是 news。

　　敬請注意，news 是不可數的！後面這個 s，並不表示這是複數的字，很單純的就是這個字的字尾。它仍然是不可數的名詞！這是一個大家常常搞錯的字。而

且有很多種錯誤！比方說，用中文，我們可能會說：

我聽到了一個消息。

唉，很多人經不起說這「一個」的誘惑：

✘　I heard a news.

哇，不可數的東西前面都不可以說 a！你應該記得吧，a 就是「一個」的意思，不可數的東西根本不能加 a！正確的應該是：

✔　I heard <u>some</u> news.

很多學生帶著懷疑問我，「嘿，人們不會真的這樣說吧。」讓我告訴你：美國總統派我來台灣的主要任務就是要跟你們說這兩句話：

1　英文根本沒有 a news 這個說法
2　some news 真的真的真的是再自然不過的說法了

而且，任何配合可數名詞的形容詞都行，像 a little、some、enough、a lot of 等等，就像上面曾經討論過的情況，不太會說 much，但 too much 與 so much 則是很常用的。以下這些都是百分之一百正確的英文：

✔　I've got <u>a little</u> bad <u>news</u>. I have to cancel the party.
✔　I've got <u>some</u> good <u>news</u> for you: you passed the test!
✔　This is the only TV news show that has <u>enough news</u> about Europe.
✔　There has been <u>a lot of news</u> about Jeremy Lin.
　　（美國人真的不會說 much！）
✔　In America there is <u>so much news</u> about the president.
✔　I think there is <u>too much news</u> about TV stars.

109

如果真的要用英文說一個消息,兩個新聞的時候,怎麼辦呢?我們有別的說法,比方說,report/reports(報告)、story/stories(故事)、article/articles(文章/篇)都是可數的,前面可以說 a、one、two、three 什麼的,它們都可以代替 news。比方說,這些都是沒問題的:

✔ I saw <u>a report</u> on TV last night about the economy.
✔ There were <u>two stories</u> in yesterday's newspaper that were so sad.
✔ I have to read <u>ten articles</u> from the English newspaper for my class!

如果,你真的很想強調這是新聞,但還是要用數字,news 就可以當形容詞,然後放在 report/reports、story/stories、article/articles 的前面。像以下這些這樣:

✔ Last night I heard <u>a news story</u> that really surprised me.
✔ <u>Three news articles</u> really got my attention recently.
✔ Wow, there are about <u>twenty news reports</u> on Yahoo that I want to read!

嚴格來講,因為 a、three、twenty 是形容名詞 story、news、reports,並不是形容這裡做形容詞的 news,這是沒問題的。上面的例句也都是美國人真的會用的說法。

很多台灣人知道這個問題的存在,明明知道不能說 a news,但是,他們就是有「辦法」,他們的「辦法」就是說成 a piece of news:

✘ Yesterday I heard a piece of news.

然後,很多學生很激烈地跟我爭辯這是正確的說法。朋友,告訴你,我這輩

子從來沒聽過任何一個以英文為母語的人說 a piece of news。根本沒有人這樣說，這是錯的。以下這樣才是正確的：

✔ Yesterday I heard <u>some news</u>.

✔ Yesterday I heard <u>a news report</u>.

✔ Yesterday I heard <u>a news story</u>.

還有一個問題！因為 news 的字尾是 s，它當主詞的時候，很多人會機械性的把它當作複數的字，然後使用複數的動詞。不行！

✘ The news are pretty interesting today.（這裡，pretty = 相當）

這種不可數的名詞需要配合單數的動詞：

✔ The news <u>is</u> pretty interesting today.

因此，搭配 news 的一般動詞就會有第三人稱的 s：

✘ The news make me so angry.

✔ The news <u>makes</u> me so angry.

好了，我說出了讓我抓狂的 news，紓解了很多心裡累積多年的痛苦。謝謝你們的聆聽。

Aah，發洩了不滿，我就可以輕輕鬆鬆的、豪豪爽爽的造些句子。為了練習大家真的常誤用的字，我會從上面的清單裡選一些「慣犯」。

 史考特的句子

1. I only have **<u>a little</u>** free **<u>time</u>** on Friday.

2. I admit I've eaten **<u>thousands of</u> <u>calories</u>** in recent meals.

3. I don't have <u>a lot of</u> money.

挑戰自己，你也從常誤用的名詞清單來造句吧。

1. _____

2. _____

超簡單改錯

1. It's raining, and there are a lot of waters on the ground.

2. That ice cream has a lot of calorie.

錯庫！蒐集自台灣人真正犯過的英文錯誤，一起來除錯！

1.（某工業）It will make a lot of pollutions.

2. Going to work is very tiring for my mother.

3. The ice, when they accumulate, are blue.
（accumulate = 累積）

4. When we raised our children, it was so tired.（raise = 養大）

5. Taiwanese people very like to take medicine.

解答

超簡單改錯

1. It's raining, and there <u>is</u> a lot of <u>water</u> on the ground.

2. That ice cream has a lot of <u>calories</u>.

錯庫

1. It will make a lot of <u>pollution</u>.（本章）

2. 正確無誤！

3. The ice, when <u>it accumulates</u>, <u>is</u> blue.（本章）

4. When we raised our children, it was so <u>tiring</u>.

（第 17 章：無聊有兩種：你很 boring 還是很 bored，你真的不能不管！）

5. Taiwanese people <u>really</u> like to take medicine.

（第 7 章：動詞前面不可加 very）

電影看了沒？

搞不清楚 a / an 和 the

我們來看一齣小話劇：

Scott:　　Hey, George! I haven't seen you for so many years! Any big news?

George:　Yeah, last year I bought the house!

Scott:　　Wow, congratulations!（congratulations = 恭喜）

啊，這齣戲其實是悲劇，因為裡面有一句英文錯了。你找得到嗎？暗示：當然不是 Scott 說的！

那，我就好心地洩漏結局喔！George 的問題就是他搞不清楚 a 和 the。正確的是：

✔　Yeah, last year I bought <u>a</u> house!

但是，George 並不孤單。《A/THE搞錯俱樂部》有很多成員，而且台灣的每一個城市都有分部！

現在《A/THE搞錯俱樂部》就要舉辦 party，我就是主持人！

the，一般來講，是用來形容已知的東西。也就是說，說者與聽者都知道他們說的特定的東西是什麼。舉幾個具體的例子你們就會明白我在說什麼了。

比方說，你最近跟朋友一直在聊快要上映的電影《超人》。然後，週一，你要問他有沒有去看那部電影。你可以這樣問：

✔　Did you see the movie?

這裡，在 movie 之前的 the 是對的，因為你們最近聊過這部電影，提到電影的時候，他跟你都會知道你是提到那一部特定的電影。

但是，假如你週一跟朋友碰面，完全不知道對方在上週末做了些什麼，而你很好奇她有沒有去餐廳吃飯，這下子，你應該這樣問：

✔ Did you go to <u>a</u> restaurant?

這個餐廳，不是特定的、你們都知道的或聊過的餐廳，是任何一間餐廳。

再假如，你的朋友是這樣回答上面的問題：

✔ Yes, I went to <u>a</u> dumpling shop near my apartment.

（**翻譯**：有，我去了我住的公寓附近一間水餃店。）

因為她回答的時候，你也不知道她說的是哪一個地方，她就只能說 a dumpling shop。

不過，因為她現在已經回答了，這間水餃店就不是任何一家餐廳，是特定的、你們雙方都知道的一間餐廳了。那麼，如果你要問 「餐廳怎麼樣」，你現在就要說：

✔ So how was <u>the</u> restaurant?

> 我試圖整理出超精簡的日常應用原則：
> →如果要講最新的情況/東西，你應該用 a / an（複數的話，就要用
>   some）。
> →情況/東西是已經熟悉的，說 the。

比方說，一上班，同事就問你，「昨晚怎麼樣？」，你說你開始看一本小說。你應該這樣回答：

✔ I started to read <u>a</u> novel.

你提到的是同事不知道的東西，就要用 a。

可是，假如第二天，你跟同事說你很喜歡那本書，現在情況不一樣了，你們兩個大概都知道是在說哪一本書，因此，你就要說 the。比方說，你的同事如果要

問你，他應該這麼說：

✔ So how's <u>the</u> novel?（小說怎麼樣？）

這個 the 就是對的。

複數名詞，原則也是一樣，但是不會說 a，而會說 some。

比方說，現在你外國朋友打電話給你，問你在幹嘛，你要報告你剛才烤了些熱狗。你應該這麼說：

✔ I just cooked <u>some</u> hot dogs.

Some 是對的。這些熱狗，你的朋友已經知道嗎？沒有。

你已經說了這些熱狗，現在它們是**特定、兩方都知道的東西了**。如果，你們要繼續談這些熱狗的話，就要用the。例如，你要跟朋友說，你可以給他兩個，你應該這麼說：

✔ Well, I can give you two of <u>the</u> hot dogs.

狡猾的一招：用 that 來當你的尺

既然 the 是指特定的東西，它的用法跟 that 就很像。當你不知道該用什麼冠詞時，就實驗性地放進 that，如果感覺是對的，就用 the，如果不對，就用 a。

這個原則的絕妙之處就是，你也可以用中文實驗。在那樣的情境裡，可不可以說「那個」。

比方說，一個男孩碰到一個女性朋友，很久沒見，完全不知道她最近在做什麼。假設，這個女生剛好買了新包包（但男生不知道）。他可以問：

妳最近怎麼樣？

如果女生這樣回答：

我最近買了那個包包。

不會很奇怪嗎？這就是我說的「那個／that 考驗」。這裡，很清楚，「那個／

that」是不合適的,所以,我們就要用 a:

✔ Recently I bought <u>a</u> backpack.

不能用 that,所以 the 也是不對勁的:

✘ Recently I bought the backpack.

但是,如果要繼續談下去的話,用中文講「那個」就是很自然的:

欸,妳有帶那個包包嗎?

這裡,中文和英文都通用的「那個/that」測試是行得通的,我們就可以放心地說 the:

✔ Hey, did you bring <u>the</u> backpack with you?

再說下去,兩方都應該說 the backpack 了。

我們的原則,用最最最濃縮的方式整理,如下:

→第一次提到,説 a / an

→繼續講,説 the

注意:到底是用 a / an /some 或 the,完全依情況、語境、上下文來判斷。你要想,「對方知道我在說特定的哪一個東西嗎?」若沒有的話,請説 a / an。若有的話,就說 the。

但是,這裡有一個小小的問題。就是,在這本書裡,我和你分享的問題都是單一句子,沒有上下文可以判斷。因此,很難判斷應該用 a 或 the。所以,這樣的錯誤在我的錯庫裡會比較少。而且,我只會給你「語境足以判斷對錯,再來訂正」的練習。

但是,這個 a / an /the 真的很重要,我建議你要常常複習這一章。

開始造句和訂正錯誤之前，還有一件事要講。就是，上面的原則有一些例外！英文什麼都有例外！「什麼都有例外」是唯一沒有例外的原則！

就是，一些生活中經常出現的地方都要用 the。不管你有沒有跟說話的對象提過，你還是應該說 the。我們列出最常見的例子如下：

She'll go to the store.（商店）
Can you buy me something at the supermarket?（超級市場）
I went to the bank.（銀行）
I'll take you to the hospital.（醫院）
My dad went to the pharmacy.（藥局）
He has to go to the post office tomorrow.（郵局）

以上這些例子，如果你真的要堅持，是可以使用不定冠詞 a。但是，我告訴你，the 的說法比較常用，請相信史考特叔叔！

然後，有些地方、有些情況，我們一律、百分之百用 the，而這個 the 也絕對不能省略。最常見的是：

the internet（網路）

還有

the government（政府）

而且，不管是哪裡的政府，都要說 the：

the Taiwanese government
the American government
the Japanese government
the Taipei City government
the Taoyuan County government（Taoyuan County = 桃園縣）

史考特的句子

OK，說心裡想說的事喔。因為 a / an /the 的用法完全看情況，我會特別小心說明這句是在什麼情況下說的。

1. （週一看到學生，他完全不知道我上週末做了什麼？）I saw <u>a</u> movie over the weekend.（因為這不是特定的、我們已經說過的電影。）

2. （朋友以前說過要參加派對，現在派對已經結束了。）So how was <u>the</u> party?（因為這是他以前說過的，就算是特定的一個派對。）

3. （突然發現沒筆）Hey, do you have <u>a</u> pen?（因為我根本不知道他會給我哪一支筆，這就不算是我們都知道的一個物件。）

4. （跟同班同學說，我們才剛考完試。）<u>The</u> Chinese test was so hard! （因為我們是同班，我提到考試，同學就知道我是說哪一場考試。）

5. I need to go to <u>the</u> bank soon.（因為不管怎麼樣，bank 通常有 the。）

 你的句子

就像我上面做的，這一章的練習得看語境，你得先寫一下這是在什麼情況下說的。為了練習，請交替使用a / an 和 the 來造句。

1. _____

2. _____

3. _____

4. _____

 超簡單改錯

說真的，簡單到我都不好意思要你改了！

1. （下課回家了。你媽不知道你下課之後做什麼。）Mom, I bought the book after class.

2. （你的朋友以前建議了一家餐廳，你現在要報告你終於去了那家餐廳。）
I finally went to a restaurant.

錯庫！蒐集自台灣人真正犯過的英文錯誤，一起來除錯！

1. We are discussing about Harry Potter.

2. It's hot there.

3. The change give students more pressures.

4.（第一次認識新同事）I worked at the foreign company before I came here.

5. I very hate the cold day.

6. For work, Microsoft software are more useful.

解答

超簡單改錯

1. Mom, I bought ~~the~~ a book after class.
2. I finally went to ~~a~~ the restaurant.

錯庫

1. We are discussing ~~about~~ Harry Potter.
　（第14章：這個動詞後面不需要加介係詞！）
2. 正確無誤！

3. The change gives students more pressures.
　（第 1 章：第三人稱現在式動詞忘記加 s / es；第 19 章：名詞是可數的還是不可數的？）
4. I worked at ~~the~~ a foreign company before I came here.（本章）
5. I ~~very~~ really hate the cold days.
　（第 7 章：動詞前面不可加 very；第 5 章：表達一般性的看法或意見時，可數名詞要用複數。）
6. For work, Microsoft software ~~are~~ is more useful.（第 19 章：名詞是可數的還是不可數的？）

第21章 你上週末做什麼？ 看電影啊。

一樣東西（是可數的話）前面需要冠詞！

這章一開始還是來看齣「悲劇」，你找得出我們台灣版羅密歐與茱麗葉「致命」的那一句嗎？

✘ Owen: What did you do last weekend？
　Katy: I saw movie.

> 我保證救回這個茱麗葉。
>
> 上一章我們討論如何分辨及正確使用 a/ an 和 the。其實，這兩個冠詞，還有另一種很常見的情況，容易讓你犯錯，就是——根本忘了說 a / an 或 the！

就像這本書裡很多問題一樣，可能是中文的習慣把你們帶壞了。中文沒有冠詞這種用法，所以，上面的「悲劇」用中文演，則是：

A：你上週末做什麼？

B：看電影啊。

啊，中文是輕輕鬆鬆、快快樂樂的「無冠詞世界」。問題是，英文不是啊！movie 是可數的名詞，這樣的名詞前面需要加冠詞。所以：

✔ John: What did you do last weekend？
　Katy: I saw <u>a</u> movie.

或者：

✔ John: What did you do last weekend？
　Katy: I saw <u>the</u> movie.

那，怎麼判斷要用 a / an 還是 the 呢？

喂！上一章我們不是才說過了嗎！已經忘了？很丟臉欸！如果 Katy 去看電影之前沒有跟 John 提過那部電影，她就應該用 a；如果 Katy 去看電影之前他們已經談過那部電影了，就應該用 the。

好了，好了！再舉一個例子。
你正在吃一顆蘋果，然後朋友打電話來，問你在幹嘛：

✘　I'm eating apple.

你應該說：

✔　I'm eating _an_ apple.

如果一個朋友問你，「昨晚做什麼」，然後你要說「買了一本書」：

✘　I was buying book.

這樣說才是對的：

✔　I was buying _a_ book.

根據上一章所討論的，一件東西前面，如果說者和聽者都知道是什麼，就要用 the。比方說，剛才提到的那本 book，以後如果朋友再提起，就要用 the。總之，就是不能省略冠詞：

✘　Did you finish book?
✔　Did you finish _the_ book?

也請注意，所有格代名詞可以代替冠詞：

✗   I can lend you bicycle.

✔   I can lend you <u>my</u> bicycle.

就這樣。

還有一點要提醒你，這一章討論的原則是，一件東西，可數的，要加冠詞。

但是，如果是複數的話，就不一定要冠詞了。你還記得我們在第5章談過的原則吧？！「表達一般的想法，可數名詞要用複數的。」這樣的情況通常不需要加冠詞：

✔   I like <u>movies</u>.

如果要強調「一<u>些</u>」東西，你可以說 some。例如：

✔   I went to the supermarket yesterday. I bought <u>some eggs</u>.

不過，複數比單數彈性。單數，冠詞不能不說。一個東西的 a / an / the 是必須要的，一些東西的 some 並不是必須要的：

✔   I went to the supermarket yesterday. I bought <u>eggs</u>.

複數名詞前面也可以用 the，規則和 a / an / the 一模一樣。已經提過了，some 會換成 the。我們以剛剛上面的 eggs為例，現在你跟聽者都知道你是說哪些雞蛋，所以這時候你應該這樣講：

✔   I want to cook some of <u>the eggs</u> right now.

我知道，這一點都不難，只是提醒你一些在國中已經學過的用法，而且不一樣的是，不只是學，學了是為了要用！

史考特的句子

1. I have **a** printer on my desk.

2. **The** last chapter of this book is worth studying!（chapter = 章）

3. I finished **a** really good book last week.

4. I have to go to <u>the</u> supermarket for some vegetables.

 你的句子

希望你拿自己比較容易說錯的字彙來練習：

1.

2. _____

 超簡單改錯

1. I don't have job.

2. （上課時對我史考特說的）I have question!

錯庫！蒐集自台灣人真正犯過的英文錯誤，一起來除錯！

1. One of my friends really likes milk tea.

2. I very like to see that.

3. （異鄉的好友）We don't have many time to see each other.

4. （做個自我介紹）I come from Taichung.

5. （進入美國的大學）You have to have interview.

6. （公園）There have a skating rink.（skating rink = 溜冰場）

解答

超簡單改錯

1. I don't have a job.

2. I have a question!

錯庫

1. 正確無誤！

2. I ~~very~~ really like to see that.
   （第 7 章：動詞前面不可加 very）

3. We don't have ~~many~~ much time to
   see each other.
   （第 19 章：名詞是可數的還是不可數
   的？）

4. ~~I come from~~ I'm from Taichung.
   （第 4 章：你來自哪裡？用 from 還是
   come from ？）

5. You have to have an interview.
   （本章）

6. There ~~have~~ is a skating rink（there）.
   （第 9 章：here 與 there 並不會
   「有」東西！）

大部分台灣人都很「打拚」

most 的用法：可以用一個字，也可以用三個字，就是不能用兩個字！

我們來看看下面這句話：

✗　Most of Taiwanese are hard-working.

你們是不是這樣想：「欸，沒錯喔！我們台灣人很打拚，學生用功，上班族勤勞！」

內容的確是沒錯啦！你們真的很拚，不過文法還是要再拚一點。

為了向我們老外展示你們台灣人的工作態度，我們來打拚學習一個字，就是 most。

most，這個字很簡單，意思是「大部分」或「大多數」。沒問題吧！

但是，說實在的，這個字在犯錯榜上赫赫有名，老是被用錯，挺糗的。我們來看看：

✗　Most of fast food restaurants are unhealthy.（fast food = 速食）
✔　(1) <u>Most</u> fast food restaurants are unhealthy.
✔　(2) <u>Most of the</u> fast food restaurants are unhealthy.

> 　你可以看到，fast food restaurants 前面可以用一個字，most，也可以用三個字，most of the，就是不可以用兩個字，most of。
>
> 　這是為什麼呢？說真的，沒有為什麼。用法是一種習慣，道地的美國人就是這麼說的。
>
> 　那麼，我們怎麼判斷應該說一個字 most，或三個字 most of the 呢？
>
> 　答案是，根據第 20 章的原則來決定。你受得了再複習一次嗎？如果 most 後面的東西是，(1)特定的一個或特定的一群，還有(2)聽者已經聽過的，這時候就必須要用 the，就會成為 most of the 三個字。沒有符合以上這兩個條件的，用 most 一個字就可以了。

那，我們現在再回去拜訪上面你介紹過、格外打拚的台灣人。如果你真的有打拚研讀這一章的內容，你會知道正確的句子應該是：

（A）Most Taiwanese are hard-working.

或是

（B）Most of the Taiwanese are hard-working.

我認為這是說所有的人，不是特定的一群人，所以要選 （A）。

再舉個例子：

你跟一個朋友一起去看過很多部電影，然後你想向朋友說你覺得大部分的電影都還不錯，你應該說下面哪一句呢？

（A）Most movies are good.

還是

（B）Most of the movies are good.

這次，你是說特定的一些電影，然後你朋友已經知道你在說哪些電影（因為他跟你去看的！）因此，要選（B）。

不過，你非要牢記不可，在這兩個例子裡，要表達「大部分」，可以用一個字（「Most」 Taiwanese...），也可以用三個字（「Most of the」 movies...），但是我們從來沒有用過兩個字 Most of...，因為，我們根本沒有那樣的用法。

另外，還有一點也要注意。有時候，所有格形容詞會代替 the 那個字，但是整個組成還是三個字。例如：

✔ Most of my friends are good students.
✔ Most of her books are really boring.
✔ Most of our teachers are ugly.
✔ Most of their problems are not too bad.

還有一點要補充。

some 這個字的用法其實和 most 是一樣的。可以說一個字 some，或三個字 some of the，但是沒有人說兩個字 some of。你看：

✘ Some of bookstores don't have many English books.
✔ Some bookstores don't have many English books.

✘ Some of restaurants in my neighborhood are closed in the afternoon.
✔ Some of the restaurants in my neighborhood are closed in the afternoon.

我們也不該忽略 one 與 all. 它們有一模一樣的問題。就是：一個字（one dog、all dogs）行，三個字（one of the dogs、all of the dogs）行，但是兩個字（one of dogs、all of dogs）永遠不行！

不過，不知道為什麼，對於這樣的錯誤，most 發生的次數遠比 one、some，以及 all 更多，這也就是為什麼這一章會特別強調 most 的用法。

還有一種特殊情況。如果你要用英文說「大部分的時候」，通常我們會用三個字的 most of the，就是 most of the time。大家也經常在這個時候誤用：

✘ Most of time I don't like to drink beer.
✔ Most of the time I don't like to drink beer.

這裡，我們也不會只說 most 一個字：

✘ Most time I get to class early.
✔ Most of the time I get to class early.

簡單地說，你乾脆把 most of the time 這四個字當做片語背起來就好了。

現在，你應該想看到一些對錯比較的句子吧。好，不讓你失望：

✗　Most of English books are challenging.（challenging = 有挑戰性）

✔　<u>Most</u> English books are challenging.

✗　Most of people at my company like me.

✔　<u>Most of the</u> people at my company like me.

✗　Most of make-up looks ugly on me.（make-up = 化妝品）

✔　(1) <u>Most</u> make-up looks ugly on me.

✔　(2) <u>Most of my</u> make up looks ugly on me.

 史考特的句子

1. <u>Most</u> Americans should go on a diet.（go on a diet = 減肥）

2. <u>Most of the</u> students at my school think I'm awesome.
（awesome = 讚）

 你的句子

1. _____

2. _____

超簡單改錯

1. Most of Taiwanese want to get good grades in school.

2. Most of chapters in Scott's book are very interesting.

錯庫！蒐集自台灣人真正犯過的英文錯誤，一起來除錯！

這些都是從台灣人打拚學英文產生的錯誤句子中精挑出來的，幫幫他們吧！

1. I very hate smoking.

2.（高中已畢業的人）When I was in high school, I don't like PE class, so I try to make excuses not to go.（PE class = 體育課）

3.（台灣的工廠）Most of companies are moving to China.

4. He saw a lot of shiny sands on his foot.（sand = 沙子）

5. Most of time I am a chicken.（在這裡，chicken = 膽小鬼）

解答

超簡單改錯

1. <u>Most</u> Taiwanese want to get good grades in school.

2. <u>Most of the</u> chapters in Scott's book are very interesting.

錯庫

1. I <u>really</u> hate smoking.

（第 7 章：動詞前面不可加 very）

2. When I was in high school, I <u>didn't</u> like PE class, so I <u>tried</u> to make excuses not to go.

（第 3 章：描述過去發生的事，動詞要用過去式。）

3. <u>Most</u> companies are moving to China.（或）<u>Most of the</u> companies are moving to China.（本章）

4. He saw a lot of shiny <u>sand</u> on his foot.

（第 19 章：名詞是可數的還是不可數的？）

5. <u>Most of the time</u> I am a chicken.

（本章）

第 23 章

我很容易發胖

說「容易」不一定很容易！

我很容易發胖。

怎麼用英語表達呢？

小心！因為習慣上面這樣的中文句子，我們很容易被誘惑，把「容易」翻譯成 easy to，就會說出以下這樣的英文：

✘ I am easy to get fat.

這又是一個「中式英文」的問題。

這其實是錯的。使用英文的 easy to 要非常謹慎。

如果主詞是人，我們不能說 easy to，只能說 easily。要這樣說才對：

✔ I get fat <u>easily</u>.

Easily 可以移動，也可以放在前面：

✔ I <u>easily</u> get fat.

不過，easily 放在句末比較常見。

請注意，easily 這個副詞通常會放在句子後面。總之，中文說「人很容易……（動詞）……」的時候，英文要這樣講：

人……（動詞）……easily

但是，你印象裡一定看過 easy to 這個片語，那，什麼時候可以說 easy to 呢？

當主詞不是人的時候，才可以說 easy to。事實上，easy to 的主詞通常是 it。例如：

✔ <u>It's easy to</u> watch movies on the internet.

✔ <u>It's easy to</u> get lost in a big city.

✔ <u>It's easy to</u> forget your umbrella somewhere on a rainy day.

注意，有時候我們是有選擇的。

在某些情況下，你可以選「人……（動詞）……easily」的句型，也可以選「It's easy to...」的句型，意思一模一樣。

譬如，你要說，「我很容易背生字。」以下這兩個句子都是正確的：

✔ <u>I</u> learn new words <u>easily</u>.
✔ <u>It's easy</u> for me <u>to</u> learn new words.

注意，在第二個例子，easy to 的主詞是 it，但是我們套進了一個 for me，這樣是可以的。

再多看些例子吧：

✘ I am easy to learn musical instruments.（musical instruments = 樂器）
✔ <u>I</u> learn musical instruments <u>easily</u>.
✔ <u>I</u> <u>easily</u> learn musical instruments.
✔ <u>It's easy</u> for me <u>to</u> learn musical instruments.

✘ She is easy to cry.
✔ <u>She</u> cries <u>easily</u>.
✔ <u>She easily</u> cries.

注意！最後一個例子，容易哭的女生，我不會用 it's easy to... 這個句型。形容人們容易有什麼情緒，我們習慣用 easily。硬要說 it's easy... 很勉強，反而會讓英文是母語的人覺得怪怪的。She cries easily 感覺是，她很多情緒，動不動就哭。It's easy for her to cry 感覺是，她是個演員，任何時候都可以產生眼淚，是她演技的特色。表達情緒的都是類似這樣：easily 暗示這個情緒是自然流露出來的，it's easy to 暗示情緒是演出來的或刻意努力出來的。

啊！不過，英文像是連體嬰，一個頭叫「原則」，另外一個頭叫「例外」，他們一向都在一起。這用法果然有個例外。有時，如果有比較被動的意思，我們可能會說「（人）⋯easy to⋯」。譬如說，一個人很容易被騙，我們可能會說：

✔ He is <u>easy to</u> trick.

注意那個被騙的因素。上面的「（人）⋯easily」句型，都是說那個人自己很會或主動地去做的事。像你這位學習高手：

✔ I <u>learn</u> new things <u>easily</u>.

learn 是你自己去做的事，而且你做得很順利。這個例外呢，通常是指你很容易受到別人的影響。再加上，這個說法實際上會常常帶有「弱者很好搞，很容易被影響」的意味，不是他主動做什麼，是他被別人害的。像：

He is easy to trick.　他很容易被騙。

He is easy to please.　他很容易滿足（也意味著因為標準低）

He is easy to bully.　他很容易被欺負。

He is easy to control.　他很容易被控制。

He is easy to kill.　他很容易被殺。

He is easy to push around.　他很好搞定。

但是，不要讓這少見的例外使你分心。說某人很容易做什麼，99%的時候，你後面要說 easily。

那，我們來造些句子吧。

 史考特的句子

1. <u>I</u> forget my water bottle at school <u>easily</u>.

（或）It's easy for me to forget my water bottle at school

2. I make friends easily.

（或）It's easy for me to make friends.

 你的句子

1. _____

2. _____

 超簡單改錯

1. I am easy to forget my keys.

2. My best friend is easy to get angry.

錯庫！蒐集自台灣人真正犯過的英文錯誤，一起來除錯！

 1. I don't like.

2. People are easy to remember your name.

3. One of my friends likes to eat hot dogs.

4. I like to eat everything my mom cook.

5.（一間沒有道德的公司）Most of time, they just dump chemicals into the ground.（dump = 倒掉; chemicals = 化學品）

解答

超簡單改錯

1. I forget my keys easily.（或）It's easy for me to forget my keys.

2. My best friend gets angry easily.

錯庫

1. I don't like it.

（第 13 章：有些動詞後面需要接受詞）

2. People remember your name easily.（或）It's easy for people to remember your name.（本章）

3. 正確無誤！

4. I like to eat everything my mom cooks.

（第 1 章：第三人稱現在式動詞忘記加 s / es）

5. Most of the time, they just dump chemicals into the ground.

（第 22 章：most 的用法：可以用一個字，也可以用三個字，就是不能用兩個字！）

她很愛抱怨她的老師

這個動詞後面要放介係詞！

第 24 章

你的朋友注意到你在看這本書。她說：「嗚……英文，一定很難。」那你當然要抗議。不過，如果你是這樣跟她說：

✘　No way! I don't agree that!

那……，這一章你就要吃下去喔！

你應該還記得，在第13章，我們提過有些動詞的後面需要接受詞。

這裡，請再原諒我，我可能要再複習一下一、兩個文法術語。這樣的動詞叫「及物動詞」，那個「物」就是「受詞」的意思。

一般來說，那樣的動詞，不但「可以」接受詞，也「必須要」接受詞。例如，buy 是個及物動詞，以下的句子就是錯的：

✘　（某一個產品）I bought.

下面這句才是對的：

✔　I bought <u>it</u>.

這一點應該沒問題吧，這只不過是複習而已。

但是，有很多動詞，它們後面不用接受詞，它們可以當句子的最後一個字。這種動詞就叫作「不及物動詞」。

不及物動詞中，talk 是很常見的字。它可以是句子的最後一個字：

✔　（A）What did you do with your friend?（B）We talked.

talked 後面沒有受詞。

當然，如果有需要，你可以加副詞或介係詞片語：

✔ We talked loudly.

✔ We talked for two hours.

這裡提醒一下，loudly 與 for two hours 都不是受詞。名詞才可以當受詞。

這些都很簡單。

但是，現在你的腦海裡可能出現一個問題，就是：欸，在中文裡，「說」這個字是可以接受詞的。例如：

我們在談我們的學校。

用英文的話，不及物動詞後面不必接受詞，如果 talk 不能接受詞，那我們怎麼表達我們在說什麼呢？

答案就是，你要加一個介係詞。以 talk 為例，介係詞就用 about。「我們在談我們的學校」就要這樣說：

✔ We're <u>talking about</u> our school.

沒有介係詞就是錯的！

✘ We're <u>talking</u> our school.

你看，中文，「談」與「我們的學校」之間不用放任何字眼，但是，英文要放一個介係詞。英文有很多動詞是這樣的，因此，如果你用中文來想英文，「中式英文」所造成的錯誤將是一直存在的陷阱。

我們多看一些例子。

不及物動詞		agree
可以單獨使用？可以。		I agree.
陷阱	（中文）後面繼續說不需加介係詞	我同意你的看法。
	（英文）後面繼續說需要加介係詞	I agree <mark>with</mark> your opinion.
搭配使用的介係詞		with

不及物動詞	depend
可以單獨使用？可以。	That depends.
陷阱 （中文）後面繼續說不需加介係詞	那得看你幾點要去。
陷阱 （英文）後面繼續說需要加介係詞	That depends on what time you want to go.
搭配使用的介係詞	on

不及物動詞	invest
可以單獨使用？可以。	You should invest.
陷阱 （中文）後面繼續說不需加介係詞	你應該投資股票。
陷阱 （英文）後面繼續說需要加介係詞	You should invest in stocks.
搭配使用的介係詞	in

你可以看出，動詞後面都有不一樣的介係詞。

現在，我會列出經常誤用的不及物動詞，以及它們後面應該放哪一個介係詞，如下：

disagree（不同意）	
單獨使用	I disagree!
有話要說，後面接字	I disagree with him.

care（在乎）	
單獨使用	I really care.
有話要說	I really care about my dog.

apply（申請）	
單獨使用	I forgot to apply.
有話要說	I forgot to apply to that school. I forgot to apply for that job.

注意，不及物動詞後面的介係詞多半會改變，得看你要說什麼。

以 apply 為例，向說向哪個機構申請，就說 apply to；要說申請哪一個你想要得到的東西，就要說 apply for。

以下我來告訴你哪些動詞可以接不一樣的介係詞。來，繼續吧：

complain（抱怨）	
單獨使用	She loves to complain.
有話要說	She loves to complain about her teacher.
跟誰說	She loves to complain to her friends.

以上的句子可以合併，同時說（1）抱怨什麼及（2）跟誰說話。這兩種都行：

She loves to complain about her teacher to her friends.

She loves to complain to her friends about her teacher.

現在，為了節省空間，我們比較緊湊地列出所有常出錯的不及物動詞：

動詞	有話要說，用什麼介係詞	意思
agree	with	同意
apply	to（機構）/ for（你要的東西）	申請
care	about	介意
complain	about	抱怨
concentrate	on	專心，專注

cut	down（樹，森林等）		砍
depend	on		得看，靠
disagree	with		不同意
discriminate	against		歧視
fill	in（表格的一項）/ out（表格的全部）		填
focus	on		專心
graduate	from（學校）		畢業
invest	in		投資
listen	to		聽
look	for		找
live	in		住
participate	in		參加
pay	for（產品）		付
prepare	for		準備
register	for（課程）/ at（機構）		報名，註冊
respond	to		回答，反應
search	for		找
study	at（哪個學校）/in（哪個科系）		唸
	for（哪個學位）		
talk	to（人）/ about（話題）		說、聊
think	about		考慮、想
wait	for		等

如果還要再深入一點，我們可以說，介係詞加上後面所接的字，就形成所謂的

介係詞片語。比方我說：

✔　I want to invest in stocks.

這個 in stocks 就是一個介係詞片語。

說實在的，動詞後面可以放很多介係詞片語。例如，我也可以說：

✔　I want to invest in stocks at the bank on July 15th for my mom.

這裡，in stocks、at the bank、on July 15th、還有 for my mom，可以說都是介係詞片語，而 in、at、on、還有 for 都是介係詞。

既然如此，為什麼在上面常見的不及物動詞列表裡，只列出一個介係詞呢？

我在此說明，這只是那個動詞後面最常見、最典型的介係詞。你要記得，視情況而定，加什麼介係詞是有彈性的。

這份列表如果列出兩個介係詞，當然可以同時使用。比方說，在 apply 的後面有 to 與 for，可以同時使用：

✔　I applied <u>to</u> the company <u>for</u> a job.

就像我說的，你可以加很多一般的介係詞片語:

✔　I applied <u>to</u> the company <u>for</u> a job <u>on</u> Saturday <u>in</u> their office <u>next to</u> the big street.

哇！我好像太囉嗦了。你現在對不及物動詞和介係詞片語應該一清二楚了吧。

可是，我還是要冒著你可能會生氣的風險，再提出最後一個問題。

就是，有時候知道動詞需要一個介係詞，但是用錯了介係詞！

不知道為什麼，有些字特別容易出錯。其中兩個是 concentrate 與 focus：

✘　I concentrated about my job.
✔　I <u>concentrated</u> on my job.

✗   I want to focus at my book.

✔   I want to <u>focus</u> **on** my book.

所以，現在有朋友說英文很難，只有一種回答：

✔   No way! I don't agree <u>with</u> that.

好了，不要再囉嗦下去了。因為這一章的問題根源是「中式英文」，我們就來做點中英翻譯吧。

 翻譯成英文

1. 我不想投資股票。

_____

2. 我喜歡聽音樂。

_____

3. 我的朋友喜歡抱怨她的壞男朋友。

_____

4.（網路上）我會找些有用的資訊。

_____

5. 不要歧視外國人！

_____

6. 我討厭等公車。

_____

7. 我同意你。

_____

8. 哇，我要找我的鑰匙！

_____

現在，我們從上面的清單選幾個常錯的字來造些句子吧。

 史考特的句子

1. I <u>invest</u> in mutual funds every month.（mutual funds = 共同基金）

2. I don't <u>listen</u> to music very often.

3. I'll <u>search</u> for a beautiful girl to marry.

4. I need to <u>prepare</u> for my vacation.

5. I want my students to <u>concentrate</u> on their English homework.

你的句子

1. _____

2. _____

超簡單改錯

這一章介紹的字彙比較多，練習就會多一點。

1. When it's noisy, I can't concentrate my homework.

2. Don't complain your job. Everybody has a tough job.
（tough = 辛苦）

3. A：Do you want to go to the movies?
   B：It depends the time.

4. I live a big apartment building.

5. I like to listen pop music.

6. In my city, some people discriminate foreign workers.

7. I'll apply a new job soon.

8. I don't agree about you.

9. I should focus about my English.

10. I need to prepare about my vacation.

錯庫！蒐集自台灣人真正犯過的英文錯誤，一起來除錯！

1. I talked about one of my teachers with my mom.

2. （以前同學不理我）They ignored.

3. （某些研究）We cannot trust those research too much.

4. I'll study to prepare the test.

5. You are easy to find a job.

6. At the test, there were a lot of people who were from my school.

7. People don't care this too much.

8. （介紹台灣）There have different religious groups.

翻譯

1. I don't want to <u>invest in</u> stocks.

2. I like to <u>listen</u> to music.

3. My friend likes to <u>complain about</u> her bad boyfriend.

4. I'll <u>look for</u> some useful information.

5. Don't <u>discriminate against</u> foreigners!

6. I hate <u>waiting for</u> the bus.

7. I <u>agree with</u> you.

8. Woah, I have to <u>look for</u> my keys!

超簡單改錯

1. When it's noisy, I can't <u>concentrate on</u> my homework.

2. Don't <u>complain about</u> your job. Everybody has a tough job.

3. A：Do you want to go to the movies?

   B：It <u>depends on</u> the time.

4. I <u>live in</u> a big apartment building.

5. I like to <u>listen to</u> pop music.

6. In my city, some people <u>discriminate against</u> foreign workers.

7. I'll <u>apply for</u> a new job soon.

8. I don't <u>agree with</u> you.

9. I should <u>focus on</u> my English.

10. I need to <u>prepare for</u> my vacation.

錯庫

1. 正確無誤！

2. They ignored <u>me</u>.

   （第 13 章：有些動詞後面需要接受詞）

3. We cannot trust <u>that</u> research too much.

   （第 19 章：名詞是可數的還是不可數的？）

4. I'll study to <u>prepare for</u> the test.（本章）

5. You can find a job <u>easily</u>.

   （第 23 章：說「容易」不一定很容易！）

6. 正確無誤！

7. People don't <u>care about</u> this too much.（本章）

8. <u>There are</u> different religious groups <u>here</u>.

   （第 9 章：here 與 there 並不會「有」東西！）

即使你不想，你還是必須要！

even if 和 even though，不能沒有 if 和 though。

第 25 章

就算現在天氣很糟糕，我還是得上班。錢少事多離家遠，還下雨了耶。很可惜，這就是我正在面對的事實。怎麼用英文說呢？

✘　Even the weather is terrible, I still have to go to work.

即使你不想，你還是必須要努力地學習。這句呢？

✘　Even you don't want to, you need to study hard.

嗯，我對於這兩句的內容都很認同，沒有什麼好討論的。不過，我們的痛苦還沒結束，還有英文錯誤要解決。因為，上面這兩個句子，我們漏掉了 even 後面的 though 或 if。

這個句型很簡單，就是：

（公式1）

Even if + 句子 A, 句子 B

Even though + 句子 A, 句子 B

這是英文很常用的兩個句型，中文的意思就是「就算 A⋯，也 B」或「即使 A⋯，還是 B」。

現在，我們可以幫助上面可憐的老師，教可憐的學生說正確的英文：

✔　<u>Even though</u> the weather is terrible, I still have to go to work.

✔　<u>Even if</u> you don't want to, you need to study hard.

請看清楚，前面都是兩個字。第一個有 even if，第二個有 even though。但是，很多時候，在使用這個句型時，卻常常錯誤地只用一個字。 例如：

✘ Even he is ugly, I still love him.
✔ <u>Even though</u> he is ugly, I still love him.

✘ Even the test is hard, you shouldn't give up.
✔ <u>Even if</u> the test is hard, you shouldn't give up.

even though，even（一！）though（二！），兩個字！
even if，even（一！）if（二！），兩個字！

你可能想問：
「哇，等一下！even though 和 even if，它們有什麼差別呢?」

這是個好問題。一般來說，even though 用於實際發生的狀況，even if 用於假設和建議。比方說，你今天真的很累，可是還是要拜訪親戚：

✔ Even though I'm tired, I still have to visit my grandma today.

這是真正的情況，所以你就要用 even though。
我們再思考一種情況。你的一個女性朋友要去一間酒吧，你得提醒她：
就算一個男生很帥，妳還是不應該把電話號碼給他。
這是還沒發生的事，算是假設/建議的情況，我們就要用 even if：

✔ Even if a guy is handsome, you still shouldn't give him your phone number.

一般性的建議，因為不是真實發生過、特定的例子，也是用 even if。例如：

✔ Even if you make a lot of money, you should try to be frugal.
（frugal = 節儉）

這樣的句型相當彈性，就是裡面的兩個句子，前後可以隨便交換。公式 1 可以換成：

even if 和 even though，不能沒有 if 和 though。

（公式2）

句子 B， even if + 句子 A.

句子 B， even though + 句子 A.

比方說，這兩個句子都可以：

✔ Even if you've graduated from school, you should still practice your English.

✔ You should still practice your English, even if you've graduated from school.

 細說一個字：even

唉，我又知道你在想什麼了。

你要說：「等一下！我真的有印象看過一些句子，第一個字是 even，但是後面並沒有 though 或 if。」

你想的並沒有錯，不過那是不一樣的句型。那是「連……都／也……」的句型。

譬如說，你要說一本書超簡單，連笨笨的史考特也會懂。中文是這麼說：

連史考特也看得懂。

英文則是：

✔ Even Scott understands.

這個句型只有一個 even，沒有 though 或 if。

這兩種句型不難分辨。even though / if 通常有兩個動詞，是被逗點分開：

✔ Even though he bought new shoes, he still wears the old ones.

bought 與 wears 都是動詞。

至於 even 一個字開頭的句型，後面只會有一個動詞。比方說，台灣的便利商店到處都是，連小鎮也會有。英文可以這樣表達：

✔ <u>Even</u> small towns <u>have</u> a lot of convenience stores.

總而言之，even though / if 兩個字是「即使……還是」的意思，even 一個字是「連……都……」的意思。

為了克服「中式英文」造成的混淆，我們先來做些中英翻譯。

 翻譯

1. 就算他不是很有錢，他的女朋友還是很多!

_____

2. 連最糟糕的學生都可以看得懂最基本的英文文法。

_____

3. 即使一個人對你很好，也不要過度信任他。

_____

4. 連最餓的人都吃不下那個意大利麵。

_____

5. 雖然這兩個人常常講話，但他們不是好朋友。

_____

6. 連那個可愛的女生也會孤單。

_____

史考特的句子

好，我們現在造些句子。我會用幾個 even if / though 的，還有幾個 even 的。

1. <u>Even though</u> I'm really tired today, I'm still writing my book.

2. <u>Even if</u> I do my job well, my boss still doesn't give me more money.

3. <u>Even though</u> America is powerful, it still has a lot of problems.

4. <u>Even</u> strong guys cry sometimes.

5. <u>Even</u> my best students make mistakes once in a while.

6. <u>Even</u> the simplest books have some interesting parts.

 你的句子

1. _____

2. _____

3. _____

4. _____

5. _____

6. _____

 超簡單改錯

1. Even the weather was terrible, I went to Scott's class.

2. Even you win the lottery, you might not be happy.

3. Even I don't have a car, I can still go anywhere I want.

錯庫！蒐集自台灣人真正犯過的英文錯誤，一起來除錯！

1. Most of Taiwanese want to have a white-collar job.
   （white-collar job = 白領階級的工作）

2. （她喜歡我）She like me.

3. Most horror movies make me feel very scared.
   （horror movie = 恐怖片）

4.（學生對另外一個學生說的）I just want to respond your comment.

5. I feel there is good.

6. Even you are walking on the street, drivers don't slow down for you.

7. I hate kitten.（kitten = 小貓）

8. One of the person who helped me was my uncle.

翻譯

1. <u>Even though</u> he doesn't have a lot of money, he still has a lot of girlfriends!

2. <u>Even</u> the worst students can understand the most basic English grammar.

3. <u>Even if</u> someone is very good to you, don't trust him too much.

4. <u>Even</u> the hungriest person couldn't finish this spaghetti.

5. <u>Even though</u> these two people talk a lot, they're still not good friends.

6. <u>Even</u> that cute girl will be lonely.

超簡單改錯

1. <u>Even though</u> the weather was terrible, I went to Scott's class.

2. <u>Even if</u> you win the lottery, you might not be happy.

3. <u>Even though</u> I don't have a car, I can still go anywhere I want.

錯庫

1. <u>Most</u> Taiwanese want to have a white-collar job.

（第 22 章：most 的用法，可以用一個字，也可以用三個字，就是不能用兩個字！）

2. She like<u>s</u> me.

（第 1 章：第三人稱現在式動詞忘記加 s / es）

3. 正確無誤！

4. I just want to <u>respond to</u> your comment.

（第 24 章：這個動詞後面要放介係詞！）

5. I feel <u>it's</u> good <u>there</u>.

（第 11 章：here 與 there 不可以當成受詞和主詞）

6. <u>Even if</u> you are walking on the street, drivers don't slow down for you.

（本章）

7. I hate kitten<u>s</u>.

（第 5 章：表達一般性的看法或意見時，可數名詞要用複數。）

8. One of the <u>people</u> who helped me was my uncle.

（第 6 章：one of 後面的名詞要用複數）

我很滿意我的學校

嘿，你忘了動詞！

英文的句子結構，最基本的一定要有主詞與動詞。

但是，很多人會漏掉動詞！我覺得這也是「中式英文」的問題。在中文裡，很多句子沒有動詞。譬如說：

他很高。

「他」是代名詞，「很」是副詞，然後「高」是形容詞。

但是，用英文表示，一般句子都需要動詞。當然有些例外，不過這裡暫不討論。

我覺得有兩種句子特別會讓中文是母語的人說錯：

（1）把形容詞當作動詞。這包括把現在分詞或過去分詞當作動詞，這兩種詞其實都是形容詞。

（2）光用介係詞片語，而沒有加動詞，事實上，一定要有動詞！

我們先看第一種，把形容詞當作動詞：

✘　My mom swimming right now.

那個 swimming 很像動詞，可是，嚴格來講，他是現在分詞，一種形容詞而已。正確的是：

✔　My mom <u>is</u> swimming right now.

你應該記得，我們在第 14 章討論過這個問題，就是現在進行式的時態，要加 be 動詞才完整。

其實，過去分詞也常搞錯。

✘　I satisfied with my school.（satisfy = 滿意）

satisfied 是過去分詞。像我在上面寫的，過去分詞畢竟是形容詞，這個句子沒

有動詞，所以是錯的。正確的句子應該是：

✔ I <u>am</u> satisfied with my school.

一般的形容詞也會有類似的問題：

✘ He a little angry.
✔ He<u>'s</u> a little angry.

✘ I always busy with homework.
✔ I<u>'m</u> always busy with homework.

第二種常導致錯誤的類型是介係詞片語，「中式英文」是主因，因為中文可以說：

他在教室裡。

這會誘惑大家用英文翻譯成：

✘ He in the classroom.

「在」固然可以翻譯成 in，可是英文的 in 是介係詞，這個句子仍然需要一個動詞！

✔ He<u>'s</u> in the classroom.

另外，還有一些很容易說錯的情況。一個是把副詞或介係詞當作動詞。譬如：

✘ I back home.

這可能是「我回家」的翻譯。但是，在英文裡，back 不是個動詞，而是副詞。要再加一個真的動詞啊：

✔ I <u>went</u> back home.

再來，拿英文的 against 來說。英文裡，against 是介係詞。但是很多人會講：

✘　I will never against my father.

✔　I will never <u>go</u> against my father.

詞類我們要分清楚，然後確定我們的句子都有動詞！

那，先看一下一些很容易讓你犯錯的中文，再請你翻譯成英文。

 翻譯

1. 他在澳洲。

_____

2. 我的學校在我家附近。

_____

3. 我對那個過敏。

_____

4. 他醉了！

_____

5. 我要回學校。

_____

6. 我在博物館前面。

_____

好，因為「句子要有動詞」是一個那麼廣泛的建議，這一章我就不請大家寫句子了，畢竟那太簡單了。但是我們的「超簡單改錯」會長一點。記得哦！這些錯誤都是來自於現實生活中我的學生或朋友。

 超簡單改錯

1. I so angry at my mom.

2. Her English teacher a little bit strict.（strict = 嚴格）

3. I want to next to the road.

4. I invited to a secret party.

5. Which university you going to?

6. I impressed by his English（impress = 讓人留下好印象）

接下來，我們直接來看錯誤資料庫。

錯庫！蒐集自台灣人真正犯過的英文錯誤，一起來除錯！

 錯一點都不酷啊！

1. I don't know how to say.

2. I like to listen some classical music.

3. （NBA比賽）It's a live game, and everybody excited.

4. Even you have a job, you can still live at home.

5. （昨天看電視）I watching TV and I saw the news about terrorists.（terrorist = 恐怖分子）

6. I very like dumplings.（dumpling = 餃子、水餃）

解答

翻譯

1. He's in Australia.（in 是介係詞）
2. My school is near my home.
   （near 也是介係詞）
3. I'm allergic to that.
   （allergic 是形容詞）
4. He's drunk!
   （drunk 是過去分詞的形容詞）
5. I'll go back to school.（back 是副詞）
6. I'm in front of the museum.
   （in front of 是介係詞）

超簡單改錯

1. I'm so angry at my mom.
2. Her English teacher is a little bit strict.
3. I want to walk/stand/sit next to the road.
4. I am/was invited to a secret party.

5. Which university are you going to?
6. I am/was impressed by his English.

錯庫

1. I don't know how to say it.
   （第13章，有些動詞後面需要接受詞）
2. I like to listen to some classical music.
   （第24章，這個動詞後面要放介係詞！）
3. It's a live game, and everybody is excited.（本章）
4. Even if/though you have a job, you can still live at home.
   （第25章：even if 和 even though，不能沒有 if 和 though。）
5. I was watching TV and I saw the news about terrorists.（本章）
6. I really like dumplings.
   （第 7 章：動詞前面不可加 very）

第27章 如果她和我約會，我會很快樂！

你說了助動詞，卻忘了主要動詞！

我會冷！

「這麼簡單的情境，用英文說哪有可能會錯？」所以，很多人會沒頭沒腦地闖進這個陷阱：

✘　I will cold.

想一下，語感是不是回來了？對，這句話應該要這樣說：

✔　I will <u>be</u> cold.

你看出來了！這一章和上一章有密切關係，就是，動詞又被忘記了！

> 你應該知道英文有「助動詞」和「動詞」這個分別。說寫英文時，你要記得，助動詞後面需要加一個動詞。
>
> 不難看出大家為什麼會說錯。在中文裡，說未來的事，動詞後面可以直接說形容詞。英文可不一樣囉！在現實生活中，超常見的錯誤就是 will 後面直接加形容詞，這超級超級常見的。

例如：

✘　If she goes on a date with me, I will happy.
✔　If she goes on a date with me, I <u>will</u> **be** happy.

✘　They have dogs? I will afraid of them!
✔　They have dogs? I <u>will</u> **be** afraid of them!

will 不是唯一會產生問題的助動詞。can 也會。例如：

✘　I can back home after lunch.

back 不是動詞，是副詞，它的意思是指方向。應該要這樣講才對：

✔　I can **go** back home after lunch.

should 也是！

✘　I should to school at 8 am.
✔　I should go to school at 8 am.

must 也是！

✘　I must more hard-working.
✔　I must **be** more hard-working.

have to 也是！

✘　You're an adult now. You have to responsible!
✔　You're an adult now. You have to **be** responsible!

祈使語氣的句子也是！

✘　Don't crazy!
✔　Don't **be** crazy!

來造句吧！

　史考特的句子

以下這些句子都反映我真實的人生：

1. I will **be** happy if this book makes a lot of money!

2. I <u>should</u> **go** back to America and see my parents this year.

你的句子

和我分享你的生活吧：

1. _____

2. _____

超簡單改錯

1. The boy will scared.

2. Many people will maybe afraid of marriage.

錯庫！蒐集自台灣人真正犯過的英文錯誤，一起來除錯！

1. I have different opinion.

2. On the internet have a special disk I can use.（disk = 硬碟）

3. （一般的想法）I don't like detective novel.
   （detective novel = 偵探小說）

4. （台南）Even there are policemen, they can't control the traffic.

5. （某一件以前可怕的事情）Actually, everybody feared about that.

6. You will happier if you pray to this goddess.
   （goddess = 女神）

7. One of my teachers really hates students talking in class.

解答

超簡單改錯

1. The boy <u>will</u> <u>be</u> scared.

2. Many people <u>will</u> maybe <u>be</u> afraid of marriage.

錯庫

1. I have <u>a</u> different opinion.
   （第 21 章：一樣東西〈是可數的話〉前面需要冠詞）

2. On the internet ~~have~~ <u>there is</u> a special disk I can use.
   （第 9 章：here 與 there 並不會「有」東西！）

3. I don't like detective novels.
   （第 5 章：表達一般性的看法或意見時，可數名詞要用複數。）

4. <u>Even though</u> there are policemen, they can't control the traffic.
   （第 25 章：even if 和 even though，不能沒有 if 和 though。）

5. Actually, everybody feared ~~about~~ that.
   （第 14 章：這個動詞後面不需要加介係詞！）

6. You will <u>be</u> happier if you pray to this goddess.（本章）

7. 正確無誤！

那就是我擔心的！

很多形容詞後面需要介係詞，對的介係詞！

「我對 Scott 的書很滿意。」

我很感謝你願意跟我說真心話。但是，如果你這樣說：

✘　I'm satisfied Scott's book.

那…，Scott 自己可不會滿意！

很多形容詞的後面，如果你有話要繼續講，需要加介係詞。我本來以為這應該不會太難，因為中文有很多類似的說法。比方說，「我對 Scott 的書很滿意」這個句子裡，那個「對」，以英文的詞性來比擬，就是個介係詞。

啊，我知道了，我現在就會了。應該是這樣說：

✘　I'm satisfied to Scott's book.

哇，這也是錯的！很多人會把那個「對」在腦子裡自動轉換成為 to。但是，搭配英文形容詞的介係詞不一定跟中文一樣。以 satisfied 為例，跟它搭配的介係詞是 with。這樣才對：

✔　I'm <u>satisfied</u> **with** Scott's book.

那，怎麼知道哪一個介係詞搭配某個形容詞呢？啊，現在你已經是我的老朋友，所以我覺得可以跟你說實話：壞消息就是，不但搭配的介係詞跟中文不一定會一樣，而且沒什麼原則讓你系統性地猜出正確的介係詞。結論就是，你要一個一個背下來。

也不一定是背！我應該說，要一個一個去習慣。比方說，美國的小孩不會去背單字，但是他們都很有把握，當然是因為他們聽了大人說了幾次，自己說了幾次，自然而然那兩個字在他們的腦子裡就會連接在一起。所以，以下我列出最常搞錯的形容詞／介係詞的搭配。最好的方法是選擇你比較沒把握的字多說幾次或多寫幾次，以後在你的大腦裡它們就是焊接在一起的。

形容詞	接名詞就要放這個介係詞	意思
addicted	to	（對⋯⋯上癮）
bad	at	（不擅長、對⋯⋯沒能力）
crazy	about	（對⋯⋯瘋狂）
compared	to	（跟⋯⋯比起來）
curious	about	（對⋯⋯好奇）
dissatisfied	with	（對⋯⋯不滿）
familiar	with	（對⋯⋯熟悉）
full	of	（充滿⋯⋯）
good	at	（擅長）
high	in（卡洛里、養分等）	（有高程度的⋯⋯）
impressed	with/by	（留下深刻的印象）
interested	in	（對⋯⋯有興趣）
related	to	（跟⋯⋯相關）
satisfied	with	（對⋯⋯滿意）
serious	about	（重視⋯⋯）
suitable	for	（適合⋯⋯）
worried	about	（擔憂⋯⋯）

注意：

（1）形容詞後面的介係詞都不一樣，沒有什麼原則可以讓你知道哪個形容詞需要什麼介係詞，你就是得背下來⋯⋯喔，說錯了，我的意思是就要練習到熟。

（2）上面這些英文詞彙，有時翻譯成中文是形容詞，有時是別的詞性。我要提醒你，死板地從中文翻譯過來是很危險的，英文即使有同樣的意思，很可能是

不一樣的詞性，用法也就不同。

現在，我們來看一下對錯的比較：

✗   I'm very worried that.
✔   I'm very <u>worried</u> <mark>about</mark> that.

✗   My English paper is full mistakes!
✔   My English paper is <u>full</u> <mark>of</mark> mistakes!

✗   I'm interested foreign cultures.
✔   I'm <u>interested</u> <mark>in</mark> foreign cultures.

這裡，我要特別講一個特殊的錯誤。按照我剛才寫的，介係詞是連接形容詞與名詞。有時候，那個名詞會移到前面，但是介係詞還是需要！請看以下的例子：

✗   That's the teacher who I am impressed.
✔   That's the teacher who I am <u>impressed</u> <mark>with</mark>.

who，（在這裡 whom 也是正確的），是個關係代名詞，表示哪一位老師讓你留下好印象（他代替前面的 teacher 這個字）。就算他在前面，impressed 還是需要你用 with 來連接它。我們多舉些例子：

✗   That's the thing that I'm worried.
✔   That's the thing that I'm <u>worried</u> <mark>about</mark>.

在這裡，that 是 about 的受詞。最微妙的是，有時候關係代名詞會省略，但是，後面的介係詞還是不能少！。例如：

✗   Math is the only subject I'm good.
✔   Math is the only subject I'm <u>good</u> <mark>at</mark>.

第二句省略了 that，後面的那個 at 是連接 good 及省略的 that！當然，你也

可以說出那個省略的 that：

✔ Math is the only subject <u>that</u> I'm <u>good</u> **at**.

還有一個相關的問題。有人，尤其是程度比較好的學生，雖然知道這個形容詞後面需要一個介係詞，他們卻用錯了介係詞！例如：

✘ I'm satisfied about my life.
✔ I'm <u>satisfied</u> **with** my life.

✘ I'm curious at her.
✔ I'm <u>curious</u> **about** her.

✘ This food is high with calories.
✔ This food is <u>high</u> **in** calories.

> 這裡，我可能腳步要放慢一點，說一個比較哲學性的話。
>
> 很多學生，發現形容詞後面的介係詞要接什麼，是沒有什麼原則可循的，就會抱怨：
>
> 「哇，英文太難了，背單字已經很辛苦，現在你跟我們說還要背後面的介係詞，實在太辛苦了，人生好不公平！」
>
> 什麼？！什麼？！
>
> 你們的抱怨會觸及一個很重要的問題：
>
> 我們什麼時候才可以說我們「了解」一個字？
>
> 很多學生認為，背了那個單字，然後背了他的中文譯文，就表示你「了解」這個字。
>
> 哦，你這個天真的孩子！希望是這樣，但並不是！
>
> 說實在的，你不但需要知道這個字的定義，不管定義是背英文的還是中文的，你也需要知道這個字的「行為」，才能說你「了解」這個字。

什麼叫作字的「行為」呢？

這就像了解一個人。你知道一個人的名字，就可以說你「了解」這個人嗎？當然不是。至少需要知道他的一些行為：他會做什麼、他會去哪裡、他會跟誰在一起等等。

英文詞彙也是一樣。知道這個英文字的「中文名字」根本不夠。你還需要知道這個字會「去哪裡」，也需要知道它的「朋友」是誰。我的意思是，你需要知道這個字會用在什麼情況，也需要知道一個字會跟什麼詞搭配。

了解一個字的很多「行為」，你才可以說「了解」這個字。包括我們在這一章討論的，知道形容詞會跟什麼介係詞搭配，才能說你開始「了解」它。

好了，哲學課讓我很累，也應該讓你很累。我們回去做正常的事。先來造些句子吧。

 史考特的句子

我是用上面清單的字彙來造句的呦：

1. I'm not <u>satisfied</u> **with** my salary!

2. I'm <u>crazy</u> **about** old Chinese movies.

3. Unfortunately, a lot of my favorite foods are <u>high</u> **in** calories.

4. Shanghai is the city <u>that</u> I'm most <u>curious</u> **about**. （注意，介係詞的受詞在前面）

你的句子

奉勸你也多多練習前面清單的字彙：

1. _____

2. _____

3. _____

 超簡單改錯

1. I'm not satisfied the security in Taiwan.（security = 治安）

2. （某一個思想）I'm not familiar that.

錯庫！蒐集自台灣人真正犯過的英文錯誤，一起來除錯！

1. Some young people are easy to get H1N1.（H1N1是一種病毒）

2. I want a job that is related English.

3. （學日文的人說……）Learn English is easier.

4. Even though he is learning to swim quickly, he doesn't enjoy it.

5. （某個挑戰）It very hard.

6. Why is he so addicted in scary novels?

7. Usually celebrity is a media darling.
（celebrity = 名人; media darling = 被媒體喜愛的人）

8. We are still introduce ourselves.

解答

超簡單改錯

1. I'm not <u>satisfied with</u> the security in Taiwan.

2. I'm not <u>familiar with</u> that.

錯庫

1. Some young people <u>get</u> H1N1 <u>easily</u>.
（第 23 章：說「容易」不一定很容易！）

2. I want a job that is <u>related to</u> English.（本章）

3. <u>Learning</u> English is easier.
（第 18 章：動詞開頭的句子，要用加 ing 的動名詞。）

4. 正確無誤！

5. It<u>'</u>s very hard.
（第 26 章：嘿，你忘了動詞！）

6. Why is he so <u>addicted to</u> scary novels？（本章）

7. Usually celebrit<u>ies are</u> ~~a~~ media darling<u>s</u>.
（第 5 章：表達一般性的看法或意見時，可數名詞要用複數。）

8. We are still introduc<u>ing</u> ourselves.
（第 16 章：進行式如果搞錯，一切都進行不了！）

中場休息　錯庫發瘋

Part 1

> ### 大家出了那麼多錯，快拯救他們吧！

到現在，你們應該學到了不少吧！

為了休息一下，也為了複習一下，我在這一章不會介紹新的內容，反而會有一個超級大的錯庫。我們學過的每一個錯誤在這裡會至少出現一次。不過，我也會調皮地放進一些正確的句子。希望你真的可以發現收穫很多，進步很大。

1. （做自我介紹時說你的家鄉）I come from Taipei.

2. （某個地方）There have poor people.

3. （某個消息）One of my teacher told me.

4. I like!

5. （很久以前請朋友吃飯）We can saw that Mr. Wang enjoyed the meal.

6. We are discuss purchasing items over the internet.

7. Most of people hate America.

8. Even she is fat, she is really good at her job.

9. I very like to do exercise.

10. （以前犯了交通規則）I stopped by a policeman.

11. There is beautiful.

12. （書）It just give me a lot of things to imagine.

13. The job is too tired for me.

14. （老師們）They showed our homeworks to people.

15. I can contact with my friends in the USA.

16. Did you hear the news? Kaohsiung will build the MRT system.

17. A lot of building have to have renovations.
（renovations = 裝修）

18. One of my friends is interested in music.

19. I've never been to there.

20. When you look this word one time, you'll remember it.

21. They can't easy find a job.

22. Learn grammar is hard.（grammar = 文法）

23. In my school, have some snobby girls.
（snobby = 勢利眼的，自以為了不起的）

24.（一般的想法）Panda should live in a certain environment.
（certain environment = 特別的環境）

25.（要得到好工作）You have to be good everything.

26. I like play basketball.

27. Most of the students at my school are making progress.

28. We just angry at him.

29. There was a TV show talking about people on an island.

30. It's easily to make a typo.（typo = 打錯的字）

31.（某些人造的生物）Even we have a good plan to control them, I will still be worried.

32.（某些歌手）Their voices make me very exciting.

33. Most of students in my class speak pretty good English.

34. One of my friend lives in Japan.

35. I took pictures of beautiful sceneries there.

36. Some teacher are too old.

37. （被忽略的一個英雄）People don't concentrate about him.

38. Most of Taiwanese guys want to buy a fancy car.
（fancy = 豪華的，炫耀的）

39. （對自己的城市的想法）We don't need high building.

40. （比較網路上互動與當面溝通）I think talk to people has more feeling.

41. There didn't have a really nice hospital.

42. It makes me very want to sleep.

43. Are you interested for your job?

44. （自我介紹）I like go to movies.

45. （某地方）It's really hot there, so I don't want to go.

46.（比較男性和女性，這句當然是個男生說的!）Man is better!

47. He is dating with a teacher.

48.（某地方）I hate there!

49.（某一種食物）It's high calories!

50. I like go roller skating.（roller skating = 路上的溜冰）

51.（某一個東西）You must see very often.

52. Even China has economic power, in some ways it's still struggling.（struggle = 辛苦）

53.（Scott 的學生說我們補習班的新老師）He's come from England.

54. Taiwan is a bored country!

55. I hate loud motorcyles. They are so annoying.

56. I respect to my parents.

57.（電視節目）It talks about a police officer.

58. Read novels is great, because you can read them again and again.

59. Right now we talk about fried foods.

60. People very care about their salaries.

61. （一般的想法）Education influence people.

62. （某個公園）Young people love to hang out at there.

63. You will want too many times or money.

64. （以前婚禮的歌手們）They can't sing that song.

65. I study Kun Shan University.（Kun Shan = 崑山的拼音）

66. Yes, I like.

67. A: What's your dream?　B: I want to ride the camel across the desert.（camel = 駱駝）

68. Raising dogs is one of her hobbies.（這裡，raise = 養）

69. （某一種運動）You don't easy to get hurt.

70. I good at geography in high school.（geography = 地理）

71. （唸大學時）The courses were in literature, which I was not interested.（literature = 文學）

72.（台灣的小島）I went to one of the island.

73. I can't go there, because there is dangerous.

74.（有趣的地方）You can go to there.

75.（科幻電影）That movie is talking about cloned humans.
（cloned humans = 複製人）

哇，改了那麼多，恭喜你。佩服，佩服。這一章就是這樣哦，但下一章會有新的內容哦！

解答

1. I'm from Taipei.
　（第 4 章：你來自哪裡？用 from 還是 come from？）
2. There are poor people there.
　（第 9 章：here 與 there 並不會「有」東西！）
3. One of my teachers told me.
　（第 6 章：one of 後面的名詞要用複數）
4. I like it/them!
　（第 13 章：有些動詞後面需要接受詞）
5. We could see that Mr. Wang enjoyed the meal.
　（第 3 章：描述過去發生的事，動詞要用過去式。）

6. We are discussing purchasing items over the internet.
　（第 16 章：進行式如果搞錯，一切都進行不了！）
7. Most of people hate America.
　（或）Most of the people hate America.
　（第 22 章：most 的用法：可以用一個字，也可以用三個字，就是不能用兩個字！）
8. Even though she is fat, she is really good at her job.
　（第 25 章：even if 和 even though，不能沒有 if 和 though。）
9. I really like to do exercise.

（第 7 章：動詞前面不可加 very）

10. I <u>was</u> stopped by a policeman.

（第 26 章：嘿，你忘了動詞！）

11. It's beautiful <u>there</u>.

（第 11 章：here 與 there 不可以當成受詞和主詞）

12. It just give<u>s</u> me a lot of things to imagine.

（第 1 章：第三人稱現在式動詞忘記加 s / es）

13. The job is too tir<u>ing</u> for me.

（第 17 章：無聊有兩種：你很 boring 還是很 bored，你真的不能不管！）

14. They showed our homework<u>s</u> to people.

（第 19 章：名詞是可數的還是不可數的？）

15. I can contact <s>with</s> my friends in the USA.

（第 14 章：這個動詞後面不需要加介係詞！）

16. Did you hear the news? Kaohsiung will build <u>an</u> MRT system.

（第 20 章：搞不清楚 a / an 和 the）

17. A lot of building<u>s</u> have to have renovations.

（第 2 章：複數名詞忘了加 s / es）

18. 正確無誤！

19. I've never been <s>to</s> there.

（第 10 章：here 和 there 前面通常不會放介係詞）

20. When you look <u>at</u> this word one time, you'll remember it.

（第 24 章：這個動詞後面要放介係詞！）

21. They can't find a job <u>easily</u>.

（第 23 章：説「容易」不一定很容易！）

22. Learn<u>ing</u> grammar is hard.

（第 18 章：動詞開頭的句子，要用加 ing 的動名詞）

23. In my school, <u>there are</u> some snobby girls.

（第 9 章：here 與 there 並不會「有」東西！）

24. Panda<u>s</u> should live in a certain environment.

（第 5 章：表達一般性的看法或意見時，可數名詞要用複數。）

25. You have to be <u>good</u> at everything.

（第 28 章：很多形容詞後面需要介係詞，對的介係詞！）

26. I like <u>to play</u> basketball.（或）I like <u>playing</u> basketball.

（第 12 章：like、don't like、love、hate 後面要小心放什麼字！）

27. 正確無誤！

28. We <u>are</u> just angry at him.

（第 26 章：嘿，你忘了動詞！）

29. There was a TV show <s>talking</s> about people on an island.

（第 8 章：電影不會説話！）

30. It's <u>easy</u> to make a typo.

（第 23 章：説「容易」不一定很容易！）

31. Even <u>if</u> we have a good plan to control them, I will still be worried.

（第25章：even if 和 even though，不能沒有 if 和 though。）

32. Their voices make me very excit<u>ed</u>.

（第 17 章：無聊有兩種：你很 boring 還是很 bored，你真的不能不管！）

33. Most of the students in my class speak pretty good English.

（第 22 章：most 的用法：可以用一個字，也可以用三個字，就是不能用兩個字！）

34. One of my friends lives in Japan.

（第 6 章：one of 後面的名詞要用複數）

35. I took pictures of beautiful scenery there.

（第 19 章：名詞是可數的還是不可數的？）

36. Some teachers are too old.

（第 2 章：複數名詞忘了加 s / es）

37. People don't concentrate on him.

（第 24 章：這個動詞後面要放介係詞！）

38. Most of Taiwanese guys want to buy a fancy car.

（第 22 章：most 的用法：可以用一個字，也可以用三個字，就是不能用兩個字！）

39. We don't need high buildings.

（第 5 章：表達一般性的看法或意見時，可數名詞要用複數。）

40. I think talking to people has more feeling.

（第 18 章：動詞開頭的句子，要用加 ing 的動名詞）

41. There wasn't a really nice hospital there.

（第 9 章：here 與 there 並不會「有」東西！）

42. It makes me really want to sleep.

（第 7 章：動詞前面不可加 very）

43. Are you interested in your job?

（第 28 章：很多形容詞後面需要介係詞，對的介係詞！）

44. I like to go to movies.（或）I like going to movies.

（第 12 章：like、don't like、love、hate 後面要小心放什麼字！）

45. 正確無誤！

46. Men are better!

（第 5 章：表達一般性的看法或意見時，可數名詞要用複數。）

47. He is dating with a teacher.

（第 14 章：這個動詞後面不需要加介係詞！）

48. I hate it there!

（第 11 章：here 與 there 不可以當成受詞和主詞）

49. It's high in calories.（第 28 章：很多形容詞後面需要介係詞，對的介係詞！）

50. I like to go roller skating.（或）I like going roller skating.

（第 12 章：like、don't like、love、hate 後面要小心放什麼字！）

51. You must see it/them very often.

（第 13 章：有些動詞後面需要接受詞）

52. Even though China has economic power, in some ways it's still struggling.

（第25章：even if 和 even though，不能沒有 if 和 though。）

53. He's come from England.
（第 4 章：你來自哪裡？用 from 還是 come from？）
54. Taiwan is a boring country!
（第 17 章：無聊有兩種：你很 boring 還是很 bored，你真的不能不管！）
55. 正確無誤！
56. I respect to my parents.
（第 14 章：這個動詞後面不需要加介係詞！）
57. It is about a police officer.
（第 8 章：電影不會説話！）
58. Reading novels is great, because you can read them again and again.
（第 18 章：動詞開頭的句子，要用加 ing 的動名詞。）
59. Right now we are talking about fried foods.
（第 16 章：進行式如果搞錯，一切都進行不了！）
60. People really care about their salaries.
（第 7 章：動詞前面不可加 very）
61. Education influences people.
（第 1 章：第三人稱現在式動詞忘記加 s／es）
62. Young people love to hang out at there.
（第 10 章：here 和 there 前面通常不會放介係詞）
63. You will want too much time or money.
（第 19 章：名詞是可數的還是不可數的？）
64. They couldn't sing that song.
（第 3 章：描述過去發生的事，動詞要用過去式。）
65. I study at Kun San University.
（第 24 章：這個動詞後面要放介係詞！）
66. Yes, I like it/them.（或）Yes, I do.
（第 13 章：有些動詞後面需要接受詞）
67. A: What's your dream? B: I want to ride a camel across the desert.
（第 20 章：搞不清楚 a／an 和 the）
68. 正確無誤！
69. You don't get hurt easily.
（第 23 章：説「容易」不一定很容易！）
70. I was good at geography in high school.
（第 26 章：嘿，你忘了動詞！）
71. The courses were in literature, which I was not interested in.
（第 28 章：很多形容詞後面需要介係詞，對的介係詞！）
72. I went to one of the islands.
（第 6 章：one of 後面的名詞要用複數）
73. I can't go there, because it is dangerous there.
（第 11 章：here 與 there 不可以當成受詞和主詞）
74. You can go to there.
（第 10 章：here 和 there 前面通常不會放介係詞）
75. That movie is talking about cloned humans.
（第 8 章：電影不會説話！）

第 **4** 關
這個英文字和
你想得不一樣

●他的生活很奢華，手上戴只名牌表。
　到底是 luxury 還是 luxurious？囧。（第 30 章）

●我曾經去過美國。
　小心！用錯 ever，史考特不讓你再去美國。（第 33 章）

●我對你好，因為你值得！
　worth？worthwhile？worthy？怎麼用？（第 39 章）

關於這個問題，我的看法不同

詞性搞錯了（一）：形容詞 vs. 副詞

啊，想一想，中文這個語言真是太好了！文法上好簡單，不是嗎？！

就拿形容詞和副詞來說。很多形容詞與副詞，不管用在什麼句型，詞本身都不會改變。例如，你可以說：

我很愉快。

我玩得很愉快。

這兩個句子裡，那個詞「愉快」是一模一樣的。

但是，英文並沒有那麼簡單。上面的第一句，用英文可以說：

✔ I'm very happy.

但是，第二句不能說：

✘ I play very happy.

第二句的「愉快」，從英文的詞性而言，應該是副詞，字的結構會改變，你要說：

✔ I play very <u>happily</u>.

在英文裡，形容詞與副詞通常有不同的拼法。

原則上，分辨形容詞與副詞很簡單。形容詞是形容名詞的，它可能在名詞的正前面：

✔ He is a happy boy.（boy 是名詞，happy 是形容詞）

有時候，可能會有 be 動詞分開名詞與形容詞，像這樣：

✔ That dog is cute.（dog 是名詞，cute 是形容詞）

副詞也很簡單。它們經常用來形容動詞是怎麼做的。像：

✔ He ate quickly.（ate 是動詞，quickly 是副詞）

但是，很多人會忘記副詞不但可以形容動詞，而且經常形容形容詞。譬如：

✔ She was extremely angry.（angry 是形容詞, extremely 是副詞）

這一點，副詞形容形容詞，很多人會忘記。

現在，我們進一步分析第一個問題，就是你應該用副詞，卻用了形容詞。

以下，是我根據累積的實際錯誤，整理出最容易搞混的單字：

你誤用了形容詞	其實你應該用副詞	
clear	clearly	（清楚）
effective	effectively	（有效）
different	differently	（不一樣）
general	generally	（一般）
good	well	（好）
independent	independently	（獨立）
perfect	perfectly	（完美）
personal	personally	（個人）
previous	previously	（以前）
strange	strangely	（奇怪）
total	totally	（完全）

還有一個很常見的問題，就是如果要放一個字在句子的開頭，而且是單獨使用，這個字通常是副詞，不是形容詞。例如：

✘ Previous, I had a lot of money.
✔ <u>Previously</u>, I had a lot of money.

偶爾會有類似這樣兩個字的說法：

✘ General speaking, Asian students work hard.
✔ <u>Generally</u> speaking, Asian students work hard.

當然，最常見的是很基本的錯誤，雖然在動詞的後面，但是大家還是會誤用形容詞。再次提醒大家，副詞才是正確的。

✘ I did really good on my test.
✔ I did really <u>well</u> on my test.（did 是動詞，well 是副詞）

✘ That soccer player played perfect.
✔ That soccer player played <u>perfectly</u>.（played 是動詞，perfectly 是副詞）

✘ I look at this issue different.
✔ I look at this issue <u>differently</u>.（look 是動詞，differently 是副詞）

還有，上面曾經提到的，副詞也可以用來形容形容詞。

✘ Everything is total different now!
✔ Everything is <u>totally</u> different now!（different 是形容詞，totally 是副詞）

注意：total 這個字是常常會用錯。

✘ This paper isn't clear written.
✔ This paper isn't <u>clearly</u> written.（written 是形容詞，clearly 是副詞）

應該用形容詞，卻誤用了副詞
現在，我們來看相反的情況，就是你誤用了副詞，但其實應該用形容詞。

我來列出最常被誤用的字：

你誤用了副詞	其實你應該用形容詞	
badly	bad	（不好、差）
carefully	careful	（小心）
extremely	extreme	（極端、非常）
loudly	loud	（大聲）
quickly	quick	（快）
really	real	（真的）
strictly	strict	（嚴格）
well	good	（好）

有時，就算這個單字明明擺在名詞的前面，大家竟然還是會忘了用形容詞：

✘　That was a loudly sound!

✔　That was a <u>loud</u> sound!（sound 是名詞，loud 是形容詞）

✘　He is not a carefully driver.

✔　He is not a <u>careful</u> driver.（driver 是名詞，careful 是形容詞）

 細說一個字：really

我們需要慢下來，然後細說一個字。早先我們已經介紹了最邪惡的兩個「通緝犯」：第一名是 lack，第二名是 news，第三名是誰呢？就是躲在上面清單裡的 really。

不知道為什麼，很多很多（很多）人，在任何中文會使用「真的」的情況時，只會千篇一律地說 really。錯！錯！還有，再來一個錯！根據上面的說明，當形容詞的時候，只能說 real。比方說，中文會說：「嘿，她告訴了我她的真實年齡

喔！」的時候，很多很多（很多）人會說：

✘ Hey, she told me her really age!
✔ Hey, she told me her <u>real</u> age!

你不知道真實的情況怎麼樣嗎？你想知道嗎？如果你用以下的英文問美國人，他們可能會氣到不想回答你：

✘ Can you tell me what the really situation is?
✔ Can you tell me what the <u>real</u> situation is?

還有一個問題。用中文表達時，懷疑對方說話的真實性，這樣回答很自然：
真的嗎？
用英文表達時要特別小心。用一個英文字回答，你的確可以說：

✔ Really?

不過，關鍵的、要死記的一點，就是：超過一個字，我們就不說 really 了。比方說，中文的「真的」可以加些字：

是真的嗎？
真的假的？

英文不一樣！超過一個字，就不能說：

✘ Is it really?

我知道你心裡在打什麼主意了：「啊，那改成 real 就可以了！」

啊，朋友，你又掉進了一個陷阱。在這種需要判斷資訊、資料、人是否屬實的情況，我們並不會用 real，反而會用 true。所以「是真的嗎？」而最自然的英文是：

✔ Is it true?

把 real 與 true 分清楚是很重要的事。簡單的說，real 是形容情況，true 是形容資訊。資訊包括別人說的話。所以懷疑別人說話不是真的，會說 true。所以上述的例子，really 與 real 都是錯的！

再舉個例子。中文可以很自然地說，「他說的話不是真的。」要小心「真的」所埋下的陷阱：

✘ What he said isn't really.

✘ What he said isn't real.

✔ What he said isn't <u>true</u>.

總而言之，在中文會說「真的」的情況中，英文有三個選擇：

（1）really　副詞。可以單獨使用，自己就是完整的句子。

（2）real　　形容詞。用來說情況是否存在。

（3）true　　形容詞。用來說資訊是否正確。

在堅持你的說法是對的、台灣人會說「真的！」的情況之下，美國人會乾脆說：

✔ It's true!

相信我，這本書裡寫的東西都是 true。

重要：這些動詞後面要用形容詞

好，我們換一個主題，來說另一種副詞／形容詞的問題。有時，形容詞和名詞被 be 或 become 分開，也可能會造成錯誤：

✘ That teacher is very strictly.

✔ That teacher is very <u>strict</u>.（teacher 是名詞，strict 是形容詞）

✘ He is becoming very rudely.

✔ He is becoming very <u>rude</u>. （he 是名詞，rude，不禮貌，是形容詞）

　　還有一種特殊類型。有些表達知覺、感官的動詞，像 seem、look、feel、taste、smell 等等，後面也要放形容詞，不是副詞。比方說：

✘ Wow, this fruit tastes sourly!

✔ Wow, this fruit <u>tastes</u> <u>sour</u>! （sour = 酸）

✘ He seems sadly.

✔ He <u>seems</u> <u>sad</u>.

✘ She looks beautifully.

✔ She <u>looks</u> <u>beautiful</u>.

　　不難懂！但是外語的終點線不是懂，而是用！那麼我們就來用英文表達自己的想法吧。

 史考特的句子

　　那，現在，我從以上的清單選一些容易犯錯的單字來造句，寫兩個有形容詞的句子，兩個有副詞的句子。

1. When my students write English, they are usually very <u>careful</u>.

2. I feel embarrassed when I speak <u>bad</u> Chinese.

3. I <u>totally</u> agree with people who say we should spend more time learning foreign languages.

4. **Generally** speaking, Asian people save more money than Westerners.

 你的句子

我建議你也從清單裡挑一些對你而言比較有挑戰性的單字來造句。

1. _____

2. _____

 超簡單改錯

1.（美國）The culture is total different.

2.（歐洲人）Their English is very well.

3.（打球的人）He plays very good.

4. It is quickly.

1. I'm never satisfied my life.

2. Hey, I like chain store!（chain store = 連鎖店）

3. It's kind of embarrassed.

4. Previous, Hong Kong is not a rich country.

5. Generally speaking, there are a lot of friendly people in the world.

6. In my neighborhood have a park, but some people don't like to go to there.

7. You need a strictly law.

8. You can visit to them.

解答

超簡單改錯

1. The culture is <u>totally</u> different.

2. Their English is very <u>good</u>.

3. He plays very <u>well</u>.

4. It is <u>quick</u>.

錯庫

1. I'm never <u>satisfied with</u> my life.

（第 28 章：很多形容詞後面需要介係詞，對的介係詞！）

2. Hey, I like chain store<u>s</u>!

（第 5 章：表達一般性的看法或意見時，可數名詞要用複數。）

3. It's kind of embarrass<u>ing</u>.

（第 17 章：無聊有兩種：你很 boring 還是很 bored，你真的不能不管！）

4. Previous<u>ly</u>, Hong Kong <u>was</u> not a rich country.

（本章；第 3 章：描述過去發生的事，動詞要用過去式。）

5. 正確無誤！

6. In my neighborhood <u>there is</u> a park, but some people don't like to go <s>to</s> there.

（第 9 章：here 與 there 並不會「有」東西！；第 10 章：here 和 there 前面通常不會放介係詞）

7. You need a <u>strict</u> law.（本章）

8. You can visit <s>to</s> them.

（第 14 章：這個動詞後面不需要加介係詞！）

住在大城市非常方便

詞性搞錯了（二）：形容詞 vs. 名詞

✗ I'm very curiosity.

> 形容詞真麻煩。
> 　上一章我們說了形容詞與副詞的問題。這一章，形容詞還是我們的焦點，
> 我們要討論的是，形容詞和名詞搞混的情況。

　常常，大家說名詞的時候，實際上應該是要說形容詞。上面開場的句子就是個例子。在 I'm very 的後面，我們需要形容詞，以下才是正確的：

✔ I'm very <u>curious</u>.

　現在我列出學生常搞錯的字。

錯誤用了名詞	其實應該用形容詞	
America	American	（美國的）
beauty	beautiful	（美麗的）
China	Chinese	（中國的）
convenience	convenient	（方便的）
curiousity	curious	（好奇的）
difficulty	difficult	（難的）
economy	economic	（經濟的）
England	English	（英國的）
Europe	European	（歐洲的）
fashion	fashionable	（時髦的）
health	healthy	（健康的）

loyalty	loyal	（忠貞的）
nature	natural	（自然的）
nutrition	nutritious	（營養的）
obesity	obese	（肥胖的）

Taiwan	Taiwanese	（台灣的）
expense	expensive	（貴的）
peace	peaceful	（和平的）
poison	poisonous	（有毒的）
religion	religious	（宗教的）

respect	respectful	（佩服的）
Russia	Russian	（俄國的）
safety	safe	（安全的）
Thailand	Thai	（泰國的）
trouble	troublesome	（麻煩的）

| unemployment | unemployed | （失業的） |
| Vietnam | Vietnamese | （越南的） |

我們先看一些例子：

✗ Scott, you should eat more fruit. They're very nutrition.
✔ Scott, you should eat more fruit. They're very <u>nutritious</u>.

✗ It's more safety to stay home at night.
✔ It's <u>safer</u> to stay home at night.

現在，我想強調一些特別常見的錯誤類型。

一個是說國家的事情。在前面的清單裡，你應該注意到了有很多國家的名詞和形容詞，它們的拼法都有一點不一樣。如果要當形容詞，不可以直接拿國家的名稱來用喔！例如：

✗　I saw a beautiful Russia girl.

girl 是名詞，前面要用一個形容詞，你應該說：

✔　I saw a beautiful <u>Russian</u> girl.

說自己是台灣人，卻說 Taiwan people！十年來我一直聽，聽到快要抓狂的地步，這個說法是「台灣人」的「懶惰呆板醜翻譯」！好，聽我說，說人是哪一國的，可以有一點彈性。下面除了第一個，其它的都可以：

✗　I am a Taiwan person.
✔　I am a <u>Taiwanese</u> person.
✔　I am <u>Taiwanese</u>.
✔　I am a <u>Taiwanese</u>.

上面這三個正確的句子，後面兩個比較常用。注意，國家的形容詞也可以當作名詞。以第二句來說，Taiwanese 是形容詞，而第三句，Taiwanese 是名詞，兩個都是正確的。所以，無論如何都不會說 Taiwan！要說 Taiwanese 才行。

再舉個例子，原則一模一樣：

✗　On our vacation we met some Japan people.
✔　On our vacation we met some <u>Japanese people</u>.
✔　On our vacation we met some <u>Japanese</u>.

以下還有一些：

✘ Taiwan food is so good.

✔ <u>Taiwanese</u> food is so good.

✘ China people work hard.

✔ <u>Chinese</u> people work hard.

✘ I'm interested in Europe culture.

✔ I'm interested in <u>European</u> culture.

我還有一點要強調，就是 convenience 這個字。

convenience 這個字特別容易搞錯。我覺得是因為有 convenience store（便利商店）這個說法。說實在的， convenience 是一個名詞，通常，在形容名詞或代名詞的時候，我們只能說 convenient。convenience store 是一種特殊的說法。

✘ Living in a big city is very convenience.

✔ Living is a big city is very <u>convenient</u>.

✘ That's a very convenience backpack.

✔ That's a very <u>convenient</u> backpack.

還有一個特別的字。我偶爾會在街頭上聽到兩個美女講話，講中文，但話裡會夾帶一個英文字， 然後這樣說：

你的髮型好 fashion 喔!

中文裡，fashion 好像可以當形容詞，但是，請注意，在英文裡它是個名詞，它的形容詞是 fashionable。上面這句中文千萬不能用英文說：

✘ Your hairstyle is so fashion!

這樣才對：

✔ Your hairstyle is so <u>fashionable</u>!

再來：

✘ Everything that shop sells is so fashion.

✔ Everything that shop sells is so <u>fashionable</u>.

那，我建議你下次用中文聊時髦，你就應該這樣說：

喔，寶貝，你的包包好 fashionable！

我覺得連說中文的時候都用正確的英文詞性實在太帥了！（或者太咬文嚼字，我不清楚。）

 再細說一組字彙：luxury 與 luxurious

這兩個字都是「豪華」的意思，不過，luxury 是個名詞，luxurious 是個形容詞。以下是很典型的錯誤：

✘ His lifestyle is so luxury.

✔ His lifestyle is so <u>luxurious</u>.

不過，我的一些學生會堅持說：「我真的有看過 fashion 當形容詞這個用法。你看，我的流行雜誌裡就有……。」果然，流行雜誌裡有一個廣告在推 luxury watches。沒錯，在這兒，luxury 固然是個形容詞，但是，luxury 與 luxurious 不通用，不能隨便交換。

怎麼判斷哪個用法是對的呢？就是這樣：luxury 當形容詞，是說商品的一個正式種類，就是「奢華類商品」、「精品」。luxurious 只是一個形容，只是一般「豪華」的意思。

比方說，你去手錶店。裡面有很多種：運動手錶、兒童手錶，還有奢華手錶。

這裡，你可以說：

✔ Today I want to buy a <u>luxury watch</u>. I really want LV!

因為你是說手錶的哪一種。

但是，如果豪華的東西不是一個商品種類，就只能說 luxurious。比方，你聽說有個人，早上在巴黎吃飯，下午搭他的私人飛機飛到倫敦逛街，晚上飛到紐約看戲，你不能說：

✘ Wow, that's so luxury.

因為我們不是說商品的某一類，我們是說這個人的行為，所以，只能說：

✔ Wow, that's so <u>luxurious</u>!

還有一個生活原則可以幫我們判斷應該用哪一個。就是，luxury 當形容詞，99% 的時候，是用在說商品名字的前面：

luxury goods

luxury car

luxury hotel

luxury hotel room

luxury watch

luxury cruise（豪華遊輪）

luxury spa　（精品 spa）

luxury sauna（精品三溫暖）

這裡，luxury 是說哪一種 goods、哪一種 car、哪一種 hotel、哪一種 watch、哪一種 hotel room。而且，這八個字（goods、car、hotel、hotel room、watch、cruise、spa、sauna）就是 luxury 主要會搭配的名詞。

因此，如果不是說買的東西，而是說生活方式，我們通常會說 luxurious。簡

單地說，如果你用 lifestyle 這個英文字，他 99%會跟 luxurious，而不是luxury 搭配。就是這節開頭的例子：His lifestyle is so luxurious.

下面這兩個句子，想一下：

✔ My friend is staying in a luxury hotel.
✔ My friend is staying in a luxurious hotel.

「欸，為什麼這兩句都有『正確』的標誌呢？其中一個一定是錯的！」

不一定喔！這兩個句子都是正確的，但是意思不一樣。你能夠根據上面的討論去歸納它們的不同嗎？

就是，第一句是說你朋友的 hotel 是哪一種，是歸類用的，你要強調不是 budget hotel（平價旅館），也不是 business hotel（商務旅館），也不是 youth hostel（青年旅社）等等，而是說 hotel 是奢華類的，所謂精品旅館。第二句不是歸類用的，只是形容這個 hotel 是什麼樣的 hotel，就是很豪華的！所以，選 luxury 還是 luxurious，看你要說什麼！我們可以整理出這個：

名　　詞：只能說 luxury
形容詞：說 luxury 來歸類
　　　　　說 luxurious 來形容

應該用名詞，卻誤用了形容詞

現在，我們來看一下相反的情況，就是說，你用了形容詞，但其實應該用名詞。一樣，我列出最常用錯的字：

用錯了形容詞	其實應該用名詞	
dangerous	danger	（危險）
economic	economy	（經濟）
free	freedom	（自由）
German	Germany	（德國）
healthy	health	（健康）

interesting	interest	（興趣、嗜好）
Japanese	Japan	（日本）
meaningful	meaning	（意思）
ugly	ugliness	（醜）
political	politics	（政治）
spicy	spice	（香料）

注意，很多情況就是上面的詞性剛好相反。特別常見的錯誤是 interesting 這個字：

✗ Swimming is an interesting of mine.

✔ Swimming is an <u>interest</u> of mine.

✗ Jogging is my interesting.

✔ Jogging is my <u>interest</u>.（請看以下說明。）

說到 interest，我得多做一些說明。通常做自我介紹時，interest 有兩個我們最習慣的說法：

（1）X <u>is an interest of mine</u>.（一個興趣）

（2）X <u>is one of my interests</u>.（一個興趣）

（3）X, Y, <u>and</u> Z <u>are among my interests</u>.（超過一個興趣）

（4）<u>My interests include</u> X, Y, <u>and</u> Z.（超過一個興趣）

上面的例子，Jogging is my interest. 雖然不是錯的，可是我們比較不會這樣說。

好，再來一些各種各樣的對錯比較：

✗ I really want to go to Japanese.

✔ I really want to go to <u>Japan</u>.

✗ If you go there, try to avoid dangerous.

✔ If you go there, try to avoid <u>danger</u>.

✘ I've been interested in political since college.

✔ I've been interested in <u>politics</u> since college.

　之前我列出了前三名「通緝犯」：（1）lack、（2）news、（3）really vs. real，現在我們來認識第四個！就是 economy 與 economic。economy 是名詞，economic 是形容詞。典型的例子如下：

✘　Our economic is getting worse and worse.

✔　Our <u>economy</u> is getting worse and worse.

✘　I need to read more about economy issues.（issues = 主題、問題）

✔　I need to read more about <u>economic</u> issues.

　用法已經是一個問題，此外，它們的發音也常出問題。economy（名詞）的重音在第二個音節，economic 的重音在第三個音節。為了讓你們清楚一點，也為了紓緩我心裡的痛苦，我整理了下面這張圖表：

名詞	形容詞
e-**CON**-o-my	e-co-**NOM**-ic

　除了練習之外，我不知道有什麼辦法。我建議你左邊、右邊各朗誦幾次，然後出外和人說話時刻意說正確的，這樣持續一陣子，你就會習慣了。

　下面的造句練習，建議你也用 economy、economic 來試試看。

 史考特的句子

　我會從第一個和第二個清單各挑些字來造句：

1. The older I get, the less I care about being <u>fashionable</u>.

2. Some <u>Thai</u> food is too sour and spicy for me.

3. I understand the <u>meaning</u> of my philosophy book.
   （philosophy = 哲學）

4. Many Americans love <u>freedom</u> more than anything else.

5. America's <u>economy</u> didn't recover for a long time after the stock market crash.

 你的句子

我希望你也從第一個和第二個清單各挑兩個字來造句。你應該選對你比較有挑戰性的字，這樣才會有進步。

1. _____

2. _____

 超簡單改錯

1. （年輕人）Their hair is too fashion!

2. They're just curiosity about it.

3.（某個城市）It's a place in Japanese.

4. My interesting is singing and dancing.

1.（一般的想法）People is easy to notice celebrities.

2.（某一部電影）It talks about relationships.

3. We celebrated the country's free.

4. Most of my friends don't wear very fashionable clothes.

5. Personal, I am on her side.

6. I like listen to music.

7. China people just throw away their trash anywhere.

8. I speak very few Japanese.（這裡，Japanese是日文的意思）

解答

超簡單改錯

1. Their hair is too <u>fashionable</u>!

2. They're just <u>curious</u> about it.

3. It's a place in <u>Japan</u>.

4. My <u>interests include</u> singing and dancing.

錯庫

1. People notice celebrities <u>easily</u>. （或）<u>It's easy</u> for people <u>to</u> notice celebrities.

　（第 23 章：說「容易」不一定很容易！）

2. It's <u>about</u> relationships.

　（第 8 章：電影不會說話！）

3. We celebrated the country's <u>freedom</u>.（本章）

4. 正確無誤！

5. <u>Personally,</u> I am on her side.

　（第 30 章：詞性搞錯了（一）：形容詞 vs. 副詞）

6. I like <u>listening</u> to music.（或） I like <u>to listen</u> to music.

　（第 12 章：like、don't like、love、hate後面要小心放什麼字！）

7. <u>Chinese</u> people just throw away their trash anywhere.（本章）

8. I speak very <u>little</u> Japanese.

　（第 19 章：名詞是可數的還是不可數的？）

第 31 章

哇，什麼樣的服務呢?!

詞性搞錯了（三）：名詞 vs. 動詞

✘　I can't communication with foreigners very well.

　　這是探討「搞錯詞性」的最後一章。這一章我們要看的是名詞和動詞搞混的問題。我們先來看「用了名詞，其實應該用動詞」的這種情況。

　　你大概已經知道上面的句子裡錯誤在哪裡。communication 是名詞，但是在 can't 後面應該放動詞。communication 的動詞是什麼呢？就是 communicate：

✔　I can't <u>communicate</u> with foreigners very well.

我們應該再列出一些常用錯的字。來了：

用錯的名詞	應該用的動詞	
argument	argue	（爭論、辯論）
behavior	behave	（行為）
communication	communicate	（溝通）
conversation	converse	（聊）
injection	inject	（打針、注射）
memory	remember	（memory = 記憶力, remember = 記得）
performance	perform	（表演）
pollution	pollute	（污染）
prediction	predict	（預言、預估）
product	produce	（product = 產品, produce = 產生、製作）
rehearsal	rehearse	（排演）
service	serve	（服務）
success	succeed	（成功）
survival	survive	（殘存、存活）

上面清單有兩個字我需要特別說明。第一個是 conversation。它是名詞，所以不可以說：

✘ I want to conversation with him.

你可以把 conversation 改成動詞 converse，像這樣:

✔ I want to <u>converse</u> with him.

但是，實際上我們比較會這樣說：

✔ （更好）I want to <u>have a conversation</u> with him.

這就是我們的習慣。

還有一個特別危險的字，就是 service。通常，service 是個名詞。例如：

✔ That restaurant has good service.

service 可以當動詞，但是指兩個人之間的關係，service 的意思就是「跟某人作愛」，而且通常指的是「專業」提供這項服務的工作。所以，如果你要說：

我們要好好地服務我們的客人。

那，你千萬不可以說：

✘ We have to service our customers well.

哇，這樣會變成「我們要好好地跟我們的客人作愛」的意思！

你應該說：

✔ We have to <u>serve</u> our customers well.

要確保安全的話，請背下這個原則：

名詞說 service，動詞說 serve 就對了。你那麼正經的人，不應該會有機會說 service 這個動詞，對不對？！

那麼，我們再來看一兩個比較正經的對錯比較：

✘ I always argument with my dad.
✔ I always <u>argue</u> with my dad.

✘ The dancers performance really beautifully.
✔ The dancers <u>perform</u> really beautifully.

現在，我們來看相反的情況。就是說，你說了動詞，但其實應該要說名詞。根據我的經驗，這個問題比較少見，但是還是會有。一樣，先列一個常錯的清單：

用錯了動詞	其實應該用名詞	
argue	argument	（爭論、辯論）
choose	choice	（選擇）
cook	cooking	（主菜）
mean	meaning	（意思）
memorize	memorization	（背〈書〉）
pronounce	pronunciation	（發音）

以下這些對錯比較，你們應該會覺得很簡單吧：

✘ Scott's Chinese pronounce is a little weird.
✔ Scott's Chinese <u>pronunciation</u> is a little weird.

✘ I had an argue with my boss.
✔ I had an <u>argument</u> with my boss.

 史考特的句子

我們從上面兩個清單各選需要多練習的字來造句，好不好？

1. I'm happy that I can **communicate** with my students so

well.

2. I hope that this book **succeeds**, and I make a lot of money!

3. **Pronunciation** is an important part of learning a foreign language.

4. I hope the students understand the **meaning** of what I say in class.

5. The flight attendants on China Airlines **serve** their customers really well. (flight attendant = 空姐)

 你的句子

1. _____

2. _____

3. _____

4. _____

超簡單改錯

1.（原住民）They have the skill to performance very well.

2. I learned how to communication with stars.

3. I had an argue with my son about whether we should visit Hitler's house or not.（Hitler = 希特勒）

4.（跟誰結婚）That's my choose!

錯庫！蒐集自台灣人真正犯過的英文錯誤，一起來除錯！

1. I like to listen music.

2. Europe cars are more expensive.

3. I like there very much.

4. He must argument with his friend.

5. Talk to him very interesting.

6. I always argue with my girlfriend about one of our

problems.

7. There have a gorge. （gorge = 峽谷）

8. My pronounce is not very correct.

解答

超簡單改錯

1. They have the skill to <u>perform</u> very well.

2. I learned how to <u>communicate</u> with stars.

3. I had an <u>argument</u> with my son about whether we should visit Hitler's house or not.

4. That's my <u>choice</u>!

錯庫

1. I like to <u>listen</u> <u>to</u> music.

（第 24 章：這個動詞後面要放介係詞！）

2. <u>European</u> cars are more expensive.

（第 30 章：詞性搞錯了（二）：形容詞 vs.名詞）

3. I like <u>it</u> there very much.

（第 11 章：here 與 there 不可以當成受詞和主詞）

4. He must <u>argue</u> with his friend.

（本章）

5. Talk<u>ing</u> to him <u>is</u> very interesting.

（第 18 章：動詞開頭的句子，要用加 ing 的動名詞；第 26 章：嘿，你忘了動詞！）

6. 正確無誤！

7. There <u>is</u> a gorge <u>there</u>.

（第 9 章：here 與 there 並不會「有」東西！）

8. My <u>pronunciation</u> is not very correct.

（本章）

我看過那部電影

現在完成式形成得不正確

✘　Oh, I seen that movie.

看過那部電影，還不錯。但如果你看不出錯誤在哪裡，這一章的內容也值得你好好看一看。

> 這一章，就像這本書一開始的前幾章，都是你應該早就已經「知道」的東西。不過，我真的還是得幫你們複習一下。

現在完成式的形成其實很簡單，就是用 have 這個動詞加上過去分詞。正確的是：

✔　Oh, I've seen that movie.

注意，口語的英文裡，have 通常會縮成 've。seen 就是 see 的過去分詞。

會產生錯誤，常見的原因就是根本忘記了用 have 這個動詞。例如：

✘　I been to Thailand.（Thailand = 泰國）
✔　I have been to Thailand.

另外一個原因，是不用過去分詞，直接就用一般的動詞，這也是錯誤的：

✘　I have visit my girlfriend's hometown.

visit 的過去分詞就是 visited。這樣說才正確：

✔　I have visited my girlfriend's hometown.

再一個。很多人用過去式的動詞當作過去分詞，這是不正確的：

✘　I have went to Australia.

✔　I <u>have gone</u> to Australia.

 過去完成式怎麼用？

還有一個問題是，用了過去完成式，但其實應該用現在完成式才對：

✘　I had read that book.

✔　I <u>have</u> read that book.

這裡請特別注意。過去完成式只會在特殊的情況下使用。什麼情況呢？同時要說過去發生的兩件事時才會使用。例如：

✔　I got my first job last year. Two months earlier I <u>had</u> graduated from college.

過去完成式是用來強調，這兩件過去的事情中，一個是前面發生的，一個是後面發生的。也就是說，過去完成式在正確使用的情況下，一定有兩件事：一個是以前發生的，另外一個是更早以前發生的。

在上面的例子裡，got my job 是以前發生的（注意它是用簡單過去式），然後，had graduated 是更早以前發生的，它才會用過去完成式。

簡而言之，現在完成式是現在之前發生的，過去完成式是在某一個過去的事之前發生的。

而，通常要說「我做過那件事」的時候，現在完成式就足夠表達了。

這樣清楚了嗎？

再來看一些對錯的比較：

✘　I eaten a lot of Korean food.

✔　I <u>have</u> eaten a lot of Korean food.

✘   I have go to Disney World in Florida.

✔   I have <u>gone</u> to Disney world in Florida.

✘   I had tried several English schools.

✔   I <u>have</u> tried several English schools.

再注意：I have...常常縮寫成I've...。

 史考特的句子

1. <u>I've been</u> to Canada.

2. <u>I've eaten</u> most of Taiwan's foods.

 你的句子

1. _____

2. _____

 超簡單改錯

1. （某一國）I've never go there.

2. Sure, I seen that movie.

錯庫！蒐集自台灣人真正犯過的英文錯誤，一起來除錯！

1. （某種食物）It have much calories.

2. （悲觀的學生）I will never success.

3. One of my friends has seen Niagara Falls.
   （Niagara Falls = 尼加拉瀑布）

4. Have you ever ate bamboo?（bamboo = 竹子，竹筍）

5. I impressed for one hotel.

解答

超簡單改錯

1. I've never <u>gone</u> there.

2. Sure, I've seen that movie.

錯庫

1. It <u>has many</u> calories.
   （第 1 章：第三人稱現在式動詞忘記加 s / es；第 19 章：名詞是可數的還是不可數的？）

2. I will never <u>succeed</u>.
   （第 31 章：詞性搞錯了（三）：名詞 vs. 動詞）

3. 正確無誤！

4. Have you ever <u>eaten</u> bamboo?
   （本章）

5. I'm impressed <u>by/with</u> one hotel.
   （第 26 章：嘿，你忘了動詞！；第 28 章：很多形容詞後面需要介係詞，對的介係詞！）

我吃過法國菜

第33章 一般的句子不會用 ever

「我曾經去過美國。」

恭喜你喔。我也去過,住過25年,其實是在那裡出生的。但是如果你跟我說:

✘　I have ever been to America.

……我就不會讓你再回去!我有這個權利,我是美國的文法警察。

我的冷笑話你沒反應,我注意到了。好,我們延續上一章,繼續討論現在完成式。

> 你應該還記得,學校的英文課本說,現在完成式這個時態常常用來表達你的經驗,比如,你去過的地方,你做過的事,什麼的。
>
> 那是沒錯的。但是,害你不能再去美國的那個句子,為什麼是錯的?
>
> 這又是「中式英文」的問題。
>
> 很多人好像一定要把「我曾經去過美國」裡面的那個「曾經」或「過」翻譯成 ever。在英文裡是不必要的,而且是錯誤的。

一般的句子不會用 ever 這個字!
因此,上面那個錯誤的句子要改成:

✔　I have been to America.

那麼,什麼時候才會用 ever 呢?
ever 只會在特殊的幾個情況下使用。比方說,它常常運用在問題裡。例如:

✔ Have you ever eaten French food?

可是你要注意，這個問題的回答不能有 ever：

✘ Yes, I've ever eaten French food.
✔ Yes, I've eaten French food.

　　還有一個特殊的用法，就是用 ever 來形容極端的事件、經驗、人們等等，通常是要傳遞「最」的意思或含意。可能是最好、最爛、最漂亮、最醜、最長、最短什麼的。譬如說：

✔ That's the best meal I've ever had.（best meal 是「最」的東西）
✔ That's the ugliest dog I've ever seen!（ugliest 是「最」的東西）
✔ You're the kindest person I've ever met.（kindest 是「最」的東西）
✔ This book is the most boring I've ever read.
　　（most boring 是「最」的東西）

　　ever 另外一個特殊的用法，是用在 ever since 這個片語裡。ever since 是「……之後，都……」的意思。例如：

✔ Ever since I broke up with my girlfirend, I've been sad.
　　（翻譯：我跟女朋友分手之後，一直很難過。）
✔ This apartment has been noisy ever since that new guy moved in.（翻譯：那個新的家伙搬進來之後，這個公寓都很吵。）
✔ Ever since I moved abroad, my life has been more interesting.
　　（翻譯：我搬到國外之後，我的生活都比較有趣。）

　　總之，ever 有三個特殊用法：
　　（1）它用在問題裡面（但回答時不能使用！）。
　　（2）它用在極端的情況，表達「最」的意思時。

（3）它用在 ever since，「之後」這個意思的片語裡。

還有一些非常冷僻的例外，但現在先不管了。這章只要記得 ever 不會用在一般句子裡就好了！

 史考特的句子

為了好好的練習，我會寫兩個沒有 ever 的現在完成式句子，還有兩個有 ever 的特殊句子。我建議你也跟我一樣這樣造句。

1. I've been to Canada.（一般的句子，沒有 ever）

2. I have read a lot of good books in my life.
   （一般的句子，沒有ever）

3. The best meal I've ever had was in Thailand.
   （表達「最」的特殊句子，有ever）

4. Have you ever spoken English outside class?
   （用來發問的特殊句子，有 ever）

 你的句子

勸你和我一樣，寫兩個沒有 ever、兩個有 ever 的句子。

1. _____

2. _____

3. _____

4. _____

 超簡單改錯

1. I have ever seen that kind of clothing.

2. （某一種工作）I have ever had this job.

 錯庫！蒐集自台灣人真正犯過的英文錯誤，一起來除錯！

1. They were easy to get angry.

2. I don't like Taiwan movies.

3. I haven't went to cram school for a while.
   （cram school = 補習班）

4. We talking about traditional culture.

5. I have a good news for everybody to enjoy.

6. He attended to a baseball game.

7. Most of my friends like to listen to pop music after school.

8. I have ever seen a show on TV about policemen.

解答

超簡單改錯

1. I have ~~ever~~ seen that kind of clothing.

2. I have ~~ever~~ had this job.

錯庫

1. They got angry <u>easily</u>.
（第 23 章：說「容易」不一定很容易！）

2. I don't like Taiwan<u>ese</u> movies.
（第 30 章：詞性搞錯了（二）：形容詞 vs.名詞）

3. I haven't <u>gone</u> to cram school for a while.
（第 32 章：現在完成式形成得不正確）

4. We <u>are</u> talking about traditional culture.
（第 16 章：進行式如果搞錯，一切都進行不了！）

5. I have <u>some</u> good news for everybody to enjoy.
（第 19 章：名詞是可數的還是不可數的？）

6. He attended <s>to</s> a baseball game.
（第 14 章：這個動詞後面不需要加介係詞！）

7. 正確無誤！

8. I have ~~ever~~ seen a show on TV about policemen.（本章）

三年前我去過泰國

如果要表達什麼時候做或發生的，用過去式就好，不可以用現在完成式。

「三年前我去過泰國。」

恭喜你。我也去過。哈！

但是，如果你是說：

✘　Three years ago I have been to Thailand.

……我就會很沮喪。

你發現了吧？！又是現在完成式！沒錯，我們討論過了，不過還沒完呢！

這一章，我要說一個很常見的問題。我們說過，現在完成式常常用來說你的經驗、你做過的事。但是，如果你要說那件事是什麼時候發生的，你不可以用現在完成式，只能用過去式。

上面說去泰國旅遊的句子，我們只能說：

✔　Three years ago I <u>went</u> to Thailand.

為什麼呢？

現在完成式，是用來表示動作或情況發生在此刻之前，而且是在過去的非特定時間裡。關鍵字是「非特定時間」。現在完成式告訴別人現在之前你做過，但是沒有明確說是什麼時候發生的。

但是在上面的例子裡，是有說特定的時間，three years ago，這是為什麼上面你要說 Three years ago I <u>went</u> to Thailand.

因為你說是什麼時候發生的，因此你要用過去式。

注意，現在完成式除了可以用來說過去發生什麼事之外，還可以用現在完成式來表達細節。譬如說，我們可以說做了幾次：

✔ I <u>have been</u> to Taipei <u>many times</u>.

✔ I <u>have eaten</u> that kind of fish <u>five times</u>.

✔ I'<u>ve been</u> to Canada <u>once</u>.

　　動作或情況持續多久了，我們也可以用現在完成式，而因為用「現在」完成式，它通常是指持續到「現在」的動作或情況。例如：

✔ I <u>have known</u> my best friend <u>for more than seven years</u>.

✔ I'<u>ve been</u> a student <u>for more than ten years</u>.

✔ I'<u>ve lived</u> here <u>for about 6 months</u>.

　　說你做了幾次或持續了多久是一回事，但是，說什麼時候發生的，卻是另外一回事。具體什麼時候發生的，就不能用現在完成式：

✘ I have visited my mom last week.

✔ I <u>visited</u> my mom last week.（last week 具體明確的時間）

✘ I have seen it about ten years ago.

✔ I <u>saw</u> it about ten years ago.（about ten years ago 具體明確的時間）

✘ When I was a kid, I have gone to Disney World.

✔ When I was a kid, I <u>went</u> to Disney World.

　　（when I was a kid 具體明確的時間）

 史考特的句子

　　為了多元化，我會寫兩個現在完成式的句子，一個說明發生了幾次，一個表示持續多久；另外再寫兩個過去式的句子，表達事情是什麼時候發生的。建議你在下面練習時也這樣做。

如果要表達什麼時候做或發生的，用過去式就好，不可以用現在完成式。

1. I've visited Kaohsiung twice.

2. I've lived in this city for two years.

3. I went to Canada when I was in high school.

4. Last year, I tried stinky tofu at the night market.
（stinky tofu = 臭豆腐）

 你的句子

就像我說的，我勸你按照上面我的模式來造句。

1. _____

2. _____

3. _____

4. _____

 超簡單改錯

1. I have been to Britain in October.（Britain = 英國、不列顛）

2. I have seen a glacier a couple of years ago.（glacier = 冰河）

1. I love ant!

2. （能不能申請某個工作） It depends your diploma.
   （diploma = 文憑）

3. Most of time, I always guess right.（guess right = 猜對）

4. When I was young, I have lived in Taipei.

5. Even I just came back from France, I forgot what I saw.

6. Scott: Long time no see! What did you do on the weekend?

   Student: I saw the movie.

7. There have an MRT.

8. My classmates and I ever raised goldfish.

解答

超簡單改錯

1. I <u>went</u> to Britain in October.

2. I <u>saw</u> a glacier a couple of years ago.

錯庫

1. I love ant<u>s</u>!

（第 5 章：表達一般性的看法或意見時，可數名詞要用複數。）

2. It <u>depends on</u> your diploma.

（第 24 章：這個動詞後面要放介係詞！）

3. Most of <u>the</u> time, I always guess right.

（第 22 章：most 的用法：可以用一個字，也可以用三個字，就是不能用兩個字！）

4. When I was young, I ~~have~~ lived in Taipei.（本章）

5. Even <u>though</u> I just came back from France, I forgot what I saw.

（第25章：even if 和 even though，不能沒有 if 和 though。）

7. （Scott） Long time no see! What did you do on the weekend?

（Student） I saw <u>a</u> movie.

（第 20 章：搞不清楚 a / an 和 the）

8. There <u>is</u> an MRT <u>there</u>.

（第 9 章：here 與 there 並不會「有」東西！）

9. My classmates and I ~~ever~~ raised goldfish.

（第 33 章：一般的句子不會用 ever）

第35章

Scott 的朋友從沒交過女朋友

一輩子都沒做的事，通常用否定的現在完成式。

我的朋友很可憐。他都沒有交過女朋友。他跟我傾訴：

✘   Oh, Scott, I never had a girlfriend.

這個人雙重悲慘，他不但從來沒有和女孩子交往過，而且他的英文很爛！不過別擔心，他還很年輕！我們慢慢地一個一個處理問題。為了讓他的悲慘減半，這一章是特別寫給他的。

在這一章我需要介紹英文的一種現象，就是，如果你要說一輩子都沒做過的事，通常我們會用現在完成式的否定句。很多人以為要用一般的過去式，但可能會讓聽者會錯意喔。

怎麼說呢？來，看看下面這兩個句子：

I never went to the park.
I have never gone to the park.

這兩句文法都是對的，但是意思不一樣。

第一句是說，「在那段時間裡，我不去公園。」這並不是說你從來沒去過，在那段時間的以前或以後，你可能去過。它也不反應現在的情況，現在你有可能常去公園。這不表示你這一輩子都沒去過。

而第二句的意思卻是，那座公園你一生連一次都沒去過。這句話意味著，從你出生一直「到現在」，都是否定的。也就是說，「一直到現在」你都沒去過公園。

根據我的經驗，我發現當學生說 I never went... 某個地方的時候，他們的意思

常常其實是 I have never gone...。

通常，說第一句的時候，說的人會說出這是在哪一段時間裡發生的，例如：

✔ When I lived in Taipei, I never went to the park.

或者說，那段時間已經包括在語境裡。比方說，你跟一個朋友在回憶大學生活，已經講了很久。如果你的朋友說：

✔ I never went to the pub.（pub = 酒吧）

這個句子的時態暗示了時間，就是「唸大學的時代」，因此，這個句子就沒有問題。

如果上下文都沒說，或者語境都沒暗示哪一段時間，意思就是一輩子都沒做過。那麼，以下這個句子就是錯的：

✘ I never ate crab.（crab = 螃蟹）

因為，沒說是哪一段時間，意思應該是「我從來沒吃過螃蟹。」所以以下這樣才是正確的：

✔ I <u>have never eaten</u> crab.

在這本書裡，我們會假定，沒有說是在哪一段時間裡不做的，就是一輩子都沒做的。

我們不妨多看一些例子。

✘ I never saw a shark.
✔ I <u>have never seen</u> a shark.

✘ I never went to Canada.
✔ I <u>have never gone</u> to Canada.

就這麼簡單。最後我還是需要幫助我可憐的朋友。你現在應該百分之百確定他會這樣說：

✔ Oh, Scott, I've never <u>had</u> a girlfriend.

啊，我的朋友，教你說漂亮的英文，就是對你最好的安慰！

 史考特的句子

1. I've never <u>been</u> to India.

2. I've never <u>eaten</u> snake meat.

 你的句子

1. _____

2. _____

 超簡單改錯

1. I never saw that.

2. （從來沒吃過的食物）I don't eat that before.

3. I don't think about that question before.

1. （某種商品）Even they just a little bit more expensive, the quality is great.

2. When I was in junior high school, I have gone to England.

3. I hate!

4. In my whole life I never buy a knock-off.（knock-off = 仿冒品）

5. Even if most of your classmates are jealous of you, you should still study hard.

6. I watched a news about the lottery.

7. （某座山）I've heard that there are poison snakes there.

8. She ever said she doesn't like me.

超簡單改錯

1. I've never seen that.

2. I've never eaten that before.

3. I've never thought about that question before.

錯庫

1. Even though they are just a little bit more expensive, the quality is great.

（第25章：even if 和 even though，不能沒有 if 和 though。；第 26 章：嘿，你忘了動詞！）

2. When I was in junior high school, I went to England.

（第34章：如果要表達什麼時候做或發生的，用過去式就好，不可以用現在完成式。）

3. I hate it/that/them!

（第13章：有些動詞後面需要接受詞）

4. In my whole life I have never bought a knock-off.（本章）

5. 正確無誤！

6. I watched some news about the lottery.

（第 19 章：名詞是可數的還是不可數的？）

7. I've heard that there are poisonous snakes there.

（第30章：詞性搞錯了（二）：形容詞 vs.名詞）

8. She ever said she doesn't like me.

（第 33 章：一般的句子不會用 ever）

第 36 章

我吃英文的苦已經15年了

持續到現在的動作,通常用現在完成式或現在完成進行式。

我寫這本書,簡單的說,是為了減少英文對你們造成的痛苦。這可能是因為上課前、下課後,有不少學生會沮喪地走過來,跟我說:

✘ I can't believe it! I studied English for 15 years. And it's still hard!

> 我真的滿懷同情啊。我自己學中文的一個原因是要親身體會、領略學外語的真實滋味。既然你們會一再地講出像以上這種句子,恐怕史考特廚師還要再煮點苦給你們吃!
>
> 怎麼找出它的問題呢?關鍵是,在上面的情況,我的學生在我的教室裡,明明還在學習英文,她的學習是一直持續到現在的。
>
> 如果你要說一個動作持續了多久,而且它還持續到現在,你必須用現在完成進行式的動詞。

「喂!完成進行式的動詞?這本書不是很人性嗎?你為什麼要把這麼不人道的文法專有名詞丟到我們頭上呢?」很抱歉,我的「老師症」又發作了。忍耐一下!完成進行式的動詞可以拆分成三個簡單的東西:

have + been + 現在分詞(動詞+ing)

舉些例子你可能會比較明白。我在現在這所學校已經教了兩年了,我可以說:

✔ I<u>'ve been teaching</u> here for two years.

簡單吧!持續的時間長短不是問題。比如,你的朋友打電話問你,「你在幹嘛?」你在上網,已經上了一個小時了。你可以說:

✔ I<u>'ve been surfing</u> the internet for an hour.

很短也可以！比方說，你在星巴克等朋友。你只等了三分鐘她就跑進來。這個好友擔心你等了很久，所以問你，Have you been waiting long? 你應該這樣回答：

✔ No, I've only <u>been waiting</u> for three minutes!

這裡很容易出錯。有些人會直接用現在式。比方說，某個人在某所大學已經唸了三年書，他可能會說：

✘ I study here for three years.

我們不會這樣說。通常我們會用所謂的現在完成進行式：

✔ I've <u>been studying</u> here for three years.

還有些人會用過去式。例如，某個人已經持續去某家餐廳10年了，現在還會去。他可能會說：

✘ I went there for ten years.

上面這一句暗示你現在不再去了。還會去的話，應該要這樣說：

✔ I've <u>been going</u> there for ten years.

你有沒有發現這是很生活化的說法？它可以說學習啊、工作啊、去餐廳啊、等朋友啊、上網啊，超級實用。我這個美國人在日常生活裡每天都會用幾十次。這個說法非要習慣說不可。

那，你應該有注意到，上面句子的動詞都是所謂的動態動詞，就是比較活動的動詞，像 teach、surf、study、go 等。如果動詞是非動態的動詞，那麼你就只能用現在完成式，絕對不能用現在完成進行式。

例如，know 沒有什麼明顯、看得出來的動作，就是個非動態動詞。那，我們

只能這樣說：

✔ I <u>have known</u> my best friend for fifteen years.

也不能用現在完成進行式：

✘ I have been knowing my best friend for fifteen years.

　　還有一點。這一章是說動作持續多久，要用現在完成進行式。但是持續多久跟發生了幾次就不一樣。要說發生了幾次，不能用現在完成進行式，只用現在完成式。比方說，你去過加拿大三次。不能說：

✘ I have been visiting Canada three times.
✔ I <u>have visited</u> Canada three times.

　　再提出一點。對某些動詞來講，現在完成進行式與現在完成式都可以用。通常這些動詞都是表示尋常的、習慣性的，或情境的動詞。比方說，這章開頭的例子：

✔ I've <u>been studying</u> English for 15 years.

也可以說：

✔ I've <u>studied</u> English for 15 years.

　　嚴格來講兩種都可以。但是，根據我的經驗，現在完成進行式比較常用一點。上面的兩個句子中，美國人比較會用第一句。

　　這個對你來說可能是個壞消息：「哇，第二個比第一個簡單一點，我為什麼不可以用第二個？」

　　你可以用啊，但是，如果你要說比較道地的英文，我勸你用第一個。

　　這一章已經太囉嗦了，那我們把它歸納成一個原則：

　　如果要說動作/活動到現在已經持續了多久了，就用現在完成進行式。

　　不難，是不是？

史考特的句子

都是關於我真的事情喔。

1. I <u>have been teaching</u> English for ten years.

2. I'<u>ve been going</u> to my favorite restaurant for six years.

3. I'<u>ve been writing</u> this chapter for forty-five minutes.
（chapter = 章節）

你的句子

1. _____

2. _____

超簡單改錯

為了不引起困擾，以下都假設是持續到現在的事。

1.（現在的新飲食習慣）I eat this way for three months.

2. I study English for ten years, since senior high school.

3. How many years do you study in this school?

1. Most of the people here like to get a discount on their food.（discount = 打折）

2. My students are easy to copy and paste using MS Word.（copy, paste = 複製、粘貼）

3. I hate there.

4.（從以前到現在都跟丈夫吵架）I fight with my husband for a long time.

5.（蛇）Even it isn't poisonous, it can still bite you.

6. My client has a Vietnam girlfriend.（client = 客戶）

7. One of my classmate was talking to a worker.

8.（一生都沒做過）I never go to Taipei's night markets.

超簡單改錯

1. I've been eating this way for three months.

2. I've been studying English for ten years, since senior high school. （或）. I've studied English for ten years, since senior high school. （第一個比較常用）

3. How many years have you been studying in this school? （或）How many years have you studied in this school? （第一個比較常用）

錯庫

1. 正確無誤！

2. My students copy and paste using MS Word easily.

（第 23 章：說「容易」不一定很容易！）

3. I hate it there.

（第 11 章：here 與 there 不可以當成受詞和主詞）

4. I have been fighting with my husband for a long time. （本章）

5. Even if/though it isn't poisonous, it can still bite you.

（第 25 章：even if 和 even though，不能沒有 if 和 though。）

6. My client has a Vietnamese girlfriend.

（第 30 章：詞性搞錯了（二）：形容詞 vs. 名詞）

7. One of my classmates was talking to a worker.

（第 6 章：one of 後面的名詞要用複數）

8. I have never gone to Taipei's night markets.

（第 35 章：一輩子都沒做的事，通常用否定的現在完成式。）

到底這道菜是你媽媽煮的，還是你愛煮你媽媽？

這個 be 動詞是多餘的！

這道菜是我媽媽煮的。

你相信我，這句話很多人會這樣講：

✘　This dish is my mom cooked.

這句英文超級奇怪。美國人聽到，可能會有兩種解讀：

（1）完全沒有意義。

（2）因為過去分詞（這裡是 cooked）可以表示人受到（包括遭受）的事，美國人可能會解讀成，「這道菜是我媽媽，我媽媽被煮了。」

那不太對吧。

這個丟臉的例子帶我們來到這章的主題：有很多很多說中文的人，說英文的時候，會習慣把多餘的 be 動詞放進他們的英文句子裡。一般英文的句子，只要一個動詞就夠了！

造成這個問題的原因很多。主要的，就像這本書裡已經點出很多問題的根源，是你的英文受到中文的干擾。為了強調，中文有一個句型：「是……的」你可以用兩個動詞，這裡就是「是」和「煮」。英文可不行，這個煮媽媽的句型，正確的說法用一般的英文句子就好了：

✔　My mom <u>cooked</u> this dish.
✔　This dish <u>was cooked</u> by my mom.

如果真的想強調「是我媽媽煮的」，有兩個選擇：

✔ My mom <u>did cook</u> this dish!

✔ This dish <u>was cooked</u> by my mom.

第一個句子，可以用 did，但是不可以用 was 來強調。第二句跟上面一樣！你可以把 was 說大聲一些來強調。

會多一個 be 動詞，還有一個可能原因是，英文有這樣的句型：是 be 動詞加形容詞。比方說，現在進行式會用 be 動詞與現在分詞：

✔ I am reading a book right now.

這個句子其實只有一個動詞，am，reading 是現在分詞，現在分詞是一種形容詞。

這個句型可能會引起大家的誤會：「哦，這裡有 be 動詞和另外一個動詞放在一起，所以這樣是可以的。」並不是！

又有一個可能是，英文的被動句型。例如：

✔ He was killed in a car crash.

這個句子也只有一個動詞，was，killed 是過去分詞，也是一種形容詞。記住，英文的句子一般只會有一個主要動詞。

所以，說英文的時候，你要判斷清楚，什麼是動詞，什麼只不過是現在分詞或過去分詞。

但是，有些多餘的 be 動詞，我根本不知道是哪裡來的，你們就會無頭無腦的、隨便把 be/am/is/are 扔進你們的句子裡！以下都是很典型、很常見的例子。

✘ Yes, I am agree with him.

agree 是主要動詞，它一個就夠了！不需要那個 am。這樣才對：

✔ Yes, I <u>agree</u> with him.

再來看些例子吧：

✘   I was major in economics.（economics = 經濟學）

major 是「主修」的意思，在英文裡是動詞，不用別的動詞哦！

✔   I majored in economics.

✘   She was lived in Taoyuan when she was younger.（Taoyuan = 桃園）
✔   She lived in Taoyuan when she was younger.

不知道為什麼，有四個動詞特別容易搞錯：happen、die、depend 以及 belong。

很多人會說：

✘   What's happened?

happen 就是動詞，它一個就夠了。

✔   What happened？

還有：

✘   He was died last year.

die 也是動詞，不是過去分詞也不是現在分詞，was 要拿掉：

✔   He died last year.

然後：

✘   It's depend on what time the restaurant opens.
✔   It depends on what time the restaurant opens.

再來：

✘   That jacket is belong to me.

✔   That jacket <u>belongs</u> to me.

另外，還有一個問題。有些動詞是助動詞，助動詞後面要加一個動詞。

✔   I <u>should go</u> to sleep.

但是有很多人，在助動詞與後面的動詞之間竟然會加個 be 動詞，這太多餘了。像這樣：

✘   I should be go to sleep.

不用那個 be 哦！should 是一個常常弄錯的詞。另外一個常錯的助動詞是 will：

✘   He will be come later.

✔   He <u>will come</u> later.

因為這一章強調多餘的東西，不需要說的東西，我們就不會造句，因此直接來到超簡單的改錯。

 超簡單改錯

1. They are love to eat fast food.

2. Those computers is belong to this company.

3. His wife was died.

4. I should be say something different.

5. Vegetables will be benefit our health.

錯庫！蒐集自台灣人真正犯過的英文錯誤，一起來除錯！

1. I don't care anything!

2. I was so angry at my boyfriend yesterday.

3. （某個問題）There are two theories about how to respond it.（theory = 理論, respond = 反應）

4. One part of the movie is talk about vampires.
   （vampire = 吸血鬼）

5. （說老人的福利，一般的想法）Society doesn't pay enough to old person.

6. （某一所天主教學校）It's religious school.

7. （某個語言）It can replace to English.

8. （有名的脫口秀主持人）I have ever heard that she gives cars to her audience!

超簡單改錯

1. They ~~are~~ love to eat fast food.

2. Those computers ~~is~~ belong to this company.

3. His wife ~~was~~ died.

4. I should ~~be~~ say something different.

5. Vegetables will ~~be~~ benefit our health.

錯庫

1. I don't care about anything!

（第 28 章：很多形容詞後面需要介係詞，對的介係詞！）

2. 正確無誤！

3. There are two theories about how to respond to it.

（第 24 章：這個動詞後面要放介係詞！）

4. One part of the movie is ~~talk~~ about vampires.

（第 8 章：電影不會說話！）

5. Society doesn't pay enough to old people.

（第 5 章：表達一般性的看法或意見時，可數名詞要用複數。）

6. It's a religious school.

（第 21 章：一樣東西〈是可數的話〉前面需要冠詞！）

7. It can replace ~~to~~ English.

（第 14 章：這個動詞後面不需要加介係詞！）

8. I have ~~ever~~ heard that she gives cars to her audience!

（第 33 章：一般的句子不會用 ever）

老闆經常要我出差

第 38 章

let 與 make 後面該怎麼說?

「夏天的時候,我父母會讓我去游泳。」

不錯,不錯。游泳的確很健康。但是,這個英文怎麼表達呢?

✘ My parents will let me to go swimming during the summer.

啊,現在你就不准去游泳了,你整個夏天要待在家裡 K 英文。

這一章我們便要K這兩個字的用法:let(讓)和 make(使)。它們的意思很簡單,很常用,但是也很容易用錯。幸好,這個錯誤還蠻單純的,就是在 let 或 make 的受詞後面多加一個 to。我們這一章開頭的句子應該這樣說:

✔ My parents will <u>let</u> me <u>go</u> swimming during the summer.

原來有多餘的 to,拿掉就好了。

make 的問題一模一樣:

✘ My boss makes me to take a lot of business trips.
✔ My boss <u>makes</u> me <u>take</u> a lot of business trips.

注意,有時,後面的動作/行為會乾脆省略:

✔ She <u>let</u> me.
✔ He <u>made</u> me.

後面不一定要繼續講,但若要繼續的話,不可以有 to!

但是,make 與 let,到底該用哪一個?

上面我們討論了 let 與 make 的用法。但它們的意思不一樣喔!看一下:

✘ My boss is such a bad guy. He lets me so angry!

「親愛的英文，我到底哪裡錯了？看起來蠻正確的啊！」警告！大警告！英文的 let 與中文的「讓」不一樣。上面的想法你用中文可以說「他讓我很生氣！」但英文裡，let 只有「允許」或「准」的意思，沒有「使」、「害」的意思。所以，上面錯誤的句子的「意思」會變成：「我老闆是個壞人。他允許我很生氣。」這樣說超怪，更何況，文法是錯的！現在，我們可以定一個「原則」：使人有某種情緒上的反應，英文只能說 make。請看：

<u>對</u>	<u>錯</u>
Sad movies <u>make</u> me <u>cry</u>.	Sad movies let me cry.
My son <u>makes</u> me <u>lose my temper</u>. （發火）	My son lets me lose my temper.
He <u>makes</u> me <u>laugh</u>.	He lets me laugh.
She <u>makes</u> me <u>happy</u>.	She lets me happy.
Tests <u>make</u> me <u>nervous</u>.	Tests let me nervous.
That <u>makes</u> him <u>scared</u>.	That lets him scared.

後面是情緒上的反應，前面一律都是 make。

上面的對錯比較，後面三句之所以是錯的，有另外一個原因：就是，make 後面可以加形容詞，但是 let 不可以。前三句是用動詞（cry、lose、laugh），所以只是用法上的錯誤；後三句是用形容詞（happy、nervous、scared），用法、文法通通都錯了！

那，有壞老闆的人應該這樣抱怨：

✔ My boss is such a bad guy. He <u>makes</u> me so angry!

不過，讀這章 makes you happy，不是嗎？既然如此，造句 will make you even more happy。

史考特的句子

為了練習，我會造一個 let + 動詞的句子，一個 make + 動詞的句子，還有一個 make + 形容詞的句子。我建議你也這樣做。

1. When I was little, my parents <u>let</u> me do a lot of fun things.

2. My company <u>makes</u> me <u>travel</u> to two different cities.

3. When students speak a lot of Chinese in my English class, it <u>makes</u> me <u>angry</u>.

你的句子

1. _____

2. _____

3. _____

超簡單改錯

1. My mom doesn't let me to read tabloids.（tabloid = 八卦小報）

2. My parents make me to clean my room every Sunday.

3. （養孩子）You have to let them happy.

1. One of my friends graduated from high school this year.

2. （約會讓男生很失望）The girl too boring.

3. I read a news before that crime will go up.

4. What if we let the perverts to live next to you?
   （pervert = 變態）

5. I have went to an ancient trail last year.
   （ancient = 古老; trail = 小路）

6. （以前的事）My father was work there.

7. （跟父母爭執）That lets me angry!

8. （鄰居）They make loudly noises.

解答

超簡單改錯

1. My mom doesn't let me ~~to~~ read tabloids.

2. My parents make me ~~to~~ clean my room every Sunday.

3. You have to <u>make</u> them happy.

錯庫

1. 正確無誤！

2. The girl <u>was</u> too boring.

（第 26 章：嘿，你忘了動詞！）

3. I read <u>some</u> news before that crime will go up.

（第 19 章：名詞是可數的還是不可數的？）

4. What if we let the perverts ~~to~~ live next to you?（本章）

5. I <u>went</u> to an ancient trail last year.

（第 34 章：如果要表達什麼時候做或發生的，用過去式就好，不可以用現在完成式。）

6. My father <u>worked</u> there.（或）My father <u>was working</u> there.

（第 37 章：這個 be 動詞是多餘的！）

7. That <u>makes</u> me angry!（本章）

8. They make <u>loud</u> noises.

（第 29 章：詞性搞錯了（一）：形容詞 vs. 副詞）

史考特的書真的值得看

「值得」很值得學!

「史考特的書真的值得看。」

我告訴你,如果你說:

✘ Scott's book is really worth to read.

> ……那,這一章真的很值得看!
>
> 不瞞你說,英文的「五大頭號通緝犯」的第五個就是 worth 喔!到處可見錯誤!這個字非常常見,格外有用,一定要弄清楚。那我們開始慢慢搞懂它。
>
> 「值得」這個意思在中文也很常見。但是,在英文裡要表達這個意思,可沒有中文那麼簡單,有些陷阱我們得要避免。

會出錯,多半都是因為「中式英文」引起的。用中文的話,「值得」的後面可以直接放動詞,像:

那部電影,值得看。

但是英文不能放一般動詞:

✘ That movie is worth see.

不定式的也不對:

✘ That movie is worth to see.

如果你用 worth 這個英文字,後面要放加 ing 的動名詞,可不能放一般動詞,也不能放加了 to 的不定詞動詞。後面放動名詞才對:

✔ That movie is <u>worth</u> see<u>ing</u>.

現在，我們就可以來處理掉這章一開頭的句子，內容百分之百正確，但是英文用法大有問題：

✔ Scott's book is really <u>worth</u> read<u>ing</u>.

啊，內容對，文法也正確，人生多美好！
但還有一個問題。<u>worth 後面一定要接動名詞或名詞</u>，沒有的話就錯了！

✘ （某一個事件）It's worth.
✔ It's <u>worth</u> do<u>ing</u> / see<u>ing</u> / read<u>ing</u>.（這些動名詞都對）

其實，一般的名詞也可以：

✔ It's <u>worth</u> the money / the time / a look / a try.

有時，我們會簡單的把 it 當做 worth 的受詞。比方說，你想買某個東西，你可以問：

✔ Is it <u>worth</u> it?（在這裡，it 表示那個東西的價錢）

假如你花了很多時間完成某件事，你覺得成果很好，你可以說：

✔ It was <u>worth</u> it!（在這裡 it 表示你花的時間、投注的心力）

也要注意喔，<u>worth 跟後面的名詞之間沒有介係詞</u>：

✘ It's worth of it.
✔ It's worth it.

✘ It's worth for the price!
✔ It's worth the price!

接下來，我們要討論相關的問題。

worth 與 worthwhile 有什麼差別？

意思差不多，但是用法很不一樣。

worthwhile 後面不用接名詞，可以單獨使用：

✔   This activity is <u>worthwhile</u>.

這就是 worthwhile 與 worth 主要的不同。就像上面說的，worth 不可以單獨使用：

✘   This activity is worth.（上面的才對）

就我們上面討論過的，若要用 worth 的話，後面需要接一些東西：

✔   This activity is <u>worth</u> do<u>ing</u>.

還有一個重要的問題。

worth 與 worthy 有什麼差別呢？

worthy 比較表示這個東西值得尊敬，因為他/她/它有道德上的條件。

比方說，你有一位老師，他很努力，很願意幫助人，學問也豐富，這算是在德性很成功吧，我們就可以說 worthy：

✔   Our teacher is <u>worthy of</u> respect.

注意：worth 後面可以直接接名詞或動名詞，可是 worthy 要加 of 這個字。

worthy 也可以直接放在名詞的前面：

✔ Helping poor people is a <u>worthy</u> cause.

（在這裡 cause = 社會活動、運動）

根據上面的說明，你能夠猜測下面兩句的不同嗎？

✔ This book is <u>worth</u> <u>reading</u>.
✔ This is a <u>worthy</u> book.

這兩個句子很可能是說兩本不一樣的書！一般的書都可以說 worth 或 worthwhile，有道德的價值、對社會有貢獻的才能說 worthy。上面的第一句可能是指網路小說、理財書、一般的歷史書等。第二句大概是說偉大的經典，像論語、莎士比亞等。

我們這裡多探索一下 worth 和 worthy 在意義上的不同。因為 worthy 指重要貢獻、道德的意義，它有「應得的回報」的意思，而 worth 並沒有。比方說，一位科學家搞出了一些醫療研究上的大突破，你覺得他應該獲得諾貝爾獎。我們就會說：

✔ He is <u>worthy of</u> the Nobel Prize.

這裡，Nobel Prize 就是 he 應該得到的東西。很多 worthy 的句子是表示這樣的想法：

✔ This movie is <u>worthy of</u> an award. 這部電影應該得獎。
✔ Our teacher is <u>worthy of</u> respect. 尊敬是我們老師應得的回報。
✔ Overcoming obstacles is <u>worthy of</u> admiration. 克服障礙，應該獲得我們的佩服。

worthy of 後面的那個東西（award、respect、admiration）就是主詞應該得到的獎賞。也請注意到，worthy 後面有 of。至於 worth，像上面說的，後面沒有介係詞。

但是 worth 不是用來說人們應得的回報，而是說聽者應該做什麼。例如：

✔ This restaurant is <u>worth</u> try<u>ing</u>.
✔ That mountain area is <u>worth</u> visit<u>ing</u>.
✔ Your high school history book is <u>worth</u> read<u>ing</u>.

這裡，worth 後面的東西不是什麼獎賞，而是你該去做的事！

來看看兩個文法正確的句子：

✔ Scott, this movie is <u>worth</u> see<u>ing</u>.
✔ Scott, this movie is <u>worthy of</u> an award.

第一句，你是說我的事，是說我花我自己的錢、自己的時間去看這部電影也不會後悔。這句話是個建議。

第二句不是說我的事，而是說電影的事。你是說那部電影應該得到什麼樣的回報，這裡就是獎盃。這不是建議，而是你在發表想法。我什麼事都不用做。說不定你知道我已經看過那部電影，現在只是要進行對電影的評論。

有時候，translation is worth doing，看懂了上面的內容，你就知道現在有事情要做了……

 翻譯

為了加強我們對這一章的了解，我們來做些翻譯訓練。我拍拍胸脯答應你，這絕對不是「老是為了給功課的功課」。翻譯出來的句子都是很常用，每天都需要說的事情，都是「現成的生活英語」。在此，我誠摯邀請你把下面的句子翻譯成英文：

1.（東西好吃的餐廳）這家餐廳值得去。

2.（精采的武俠小說）這本書很值得讀！

3.（教授很認真）她值得那個獎！

---

4. 去那個觀光勝地，值得的。

5.（新筆）它值得試試看。

---

6. 他值得人們的尊敬!

7.（拿了諾貝爾獎的人）他該得的！

---

8. 那些維他命值得吃。

---

9. 運動很值得。

---

10. 史考特的書值得看！

史考特的句子

為了練習，我會用一個 worth，一個 worthwhile，還有一個 worthy。我建議你也這樣做。

1. The temple near my apartment is <u>worth</u> going to.

2. Creating an exercise program is <u>worthwhile</u>.

3. My father is <u>worthy of</u> respect.

你的句子

1. _____

2. _____

3. _____

超簡單改錯

1.（某一個課程）It's worth to take.

2. Do you think it's worth?

3. This action movie is worthy.（action movie = 動作片）

4. It's worth.

5. Jinmen is quite worth to travel to.（Jinmen = 金門）

錯庫！蒐集自台灣人真正犯過的英文錯誤，一起來除錯！

1. （某個人的名字）I like the pronounce.

2. It was worth to see.

3. （某個演員）Most of Taiwanese can't stand her DVD.

4. We are talk about our house.

5. It will let her to cry.

6. I have ever been robbed on Hutou Mountain.
   （Hutou 是虎頭的拼音）

7. It's worth for ten dollars.

8. （說第一次坐飛機的經驗）My first flight go to America.

9. （電影院）There have a lot of people in there.

10. （父母）Even they punished me, I still did the same thing.

翻譯

1. This restaurant is <u>worth</u> <u>going</u> to.
2. This book is <u>worthwhile</u>.
   （或） This book is <u>worth</u> <u>read</u>ing.
3. He is <u>worthy of</u> the/that prize.
4. That tourist area is <u>worthwhile</u>.
   （或）That tourist area is <u>worth</u> <u>going</u> to.
5. It's <u>worth</u> <u>try</u>ing.
6. He is <u>worthy of</u> respect.
7. He is a <u>worthy</u> winner.（或） He is <u>worthy of</u> the prize.
8. Those vitamins are <u>worth</u> <u>tak</u>ing.
9. Exercise is <u>worthwhile</u>.
   （或）Exercise is <u>worth</u> <u>do</u>ing.
10. Scott's book is <u>worth</u> <u>read</u>ing.

超簡單改錯

1. It's <u>worth</u> <u>tak</u>ing.
2. Do you think it's <u>worthwhile</u>?
   （或）Do you think it's <u>worth it</u>?
3. This action movie is <u>worthwhile</u>.
   （或）This action movie is <u>worth</u> <u>watch</u>ing.
4. It's <u>worth it</u>.（或）It's <u>worthwhile</u>.
5. Jinmen is quite <u>worth</u> <u>travel</u>ing to.

錯庫

1. I like the <u>pronounciation</u>.
   （第 31 章：詞性搞錯了（三）：名詞 vs. 動詞）
2. It was <u>worth</u> <u>see</u>ing.（本章）
3. Most ~~of the~~ Taiwanese can't stand her DVD.
   （第 22 章：most 的用法：可以用一個字，也可以用三個字，就是不能用兩個字！）
3. We <u>are</u> <u>talk</u>ing about our house.
   （第 16 章：進行式如果搞錯，一切都進行不了！）
5. It will make her ~~to~~ cry.（上一章）
6. I have ~~ever~~ been robbed on Hutou Mountain.
   （第33章：一般的句子不會用 ever）
7. It's worth ~~for~~ ten dollars.（本章）
8. My first flight <u>went</u> to America.
   （第 3 章：描述過去發生的事，動詞要用過去式。）
10. <u>There are</u> a lot of people ~~in~~ there.
   （第 9 章：here 與 there 並不會「有」東西！；第 10 章：here 和 there 前面通常不會放介係詞。）
11. Even <u>though</u> they punished me, I still did the same thing.
   （第 25 章：even if 和 even though，不能沒有 if 和 though。）

第 5 關
親愛的英文，我愈來愈了解你了

- 我建議他找不一樣的工作。
  用對 recommend，建議才有用啊！（第 42 章）

- 我兩個鐘頭後打電話給你。
  two hours later? in two hours? 選一個！（第 45 章）

- 我想做一個好老師。
  to be or to do？搞錯會讓人臉紅啊！（第 48 章）

去樓上就會發現學英文的祕訣

去某一個地方，需不需要 to？

「我很想去德國。」

我也很想去啊。我們意見一致。而且，你應該知道，這句話用英文表達就是：

✔ I want to go to Germany.

但是，如果我回答你：

✘ Oh, yeah, I also want to go to there.

你應該會覺得怪怪的。為什麼呢？因為你讀過這本書第 10 章啊！你這個英文高手明明知道 here 與 there 前面不會加 to 的，一般來講，這兩個字前面不會有任何介係詞。所以，有人跟你說他想去德國，我知道你會帥帥地、從容不迫地回答：

✔ Oh, yeah, I also want to <u>go there</u>.

我們來看另外一個句子：「如果你到樓上去，Scott 老師會告訴你學英文的一個祕訣。」這句英文怎麼說呢？提示：前面我才剛複習 here 跟 there，這是一個暗示，希望你不會掉入陷阱！

✘ If you go to upstairs, Scott will tell you a tip for learning English.

還是掉進陷阱了？！我來救你：

✔ If you <u>go upstairs</u>, Scott will tell you a tip for learning English.

現在看懂了嗎？我們先複習 here 與 there，是因為 upstairs 是 here 和 there 的弟弟。我是很正經的：英文詞彙裡面有一種類型，它們前面都不太會放介係詞。這個「家庭」裡面，here 和 there 只不過是「大哥」和「二哥」而已，還有很多「弟弟」。我們來認識這一家人：

here	（這兒）	overseas	（海外，國外）
there	（那兒）	somewhere	（某地方）
home	（家）	anwhere	（任何的地方）
upstairs	（樓上）	nowhere	（無地）
downstairs	（樓下）	inside	（裡面）
abroad	（國外）	outside	（外面）

還是先複習一下 here 跟 there。Practice makes perfect!（熟能生巧）

✘ Our city is a pretty nice place! You should come to here for a trip.

✔ Our city is a pretty nice place! You should <u>come here</u> for a trip.

沒有 to 就對了！

我們多欣賞幾個這類型的正確用法。

✘ I went to home.

✔ I <u>went home</u>.

✘ I want to go to abroad.

✔ I want to <u>go abroad</u>.

✘ I don't want to go to anywhere!

✔ I don't want to <u>go anywhere</u>!

✘ I think he went to upstairs.

✔ I think he <u>went upstairs</u>.

✘ It's cold. Let's go to inside.

✔ It's cold. Let's <u>go inside</u>.

上面這些字，一般來說，前面不需要加任何介係詞。我之所以在上面強調多餘的 to，是因為這是最常見的錯誤。不過，我們應該也要看一些其它介係詞的錯誤：

✘　He's in upstairs.
✔　He's <u>upstairs</u>.

✘　My son is studying for his Ph.D. at abroad.（Ph.D. = 博士）
✔　My son is studying for his Ph.D. <u>abroad</u>.

✘　He's at outside.
✔　He's <u>outside</u>.

有一個例外是 home。你可以說 He's at home. 這就是「他在家」的意思。

我應該提醒一下，上面「怪家庭的兄弟」都是特別的目的地，也帶有特別的用法。不過，到一般的目的地，就是大部分的地方，我們都會說 to。 像：

✔　I went <u>to the store</u>.（商店）
✔　I went <u>to the park</u>.（公園）
✔　I went <u>to the beach</u>.（海灘）
✔　I went <u>to school</u>.（學校）
✔　I went <u>to the hospital</u>.（醫院）
✔　I went <u>to France</u>.（法國）
✔　I went <u>to Taipei</u>.（台北）

假如我列出英文裡你能夠去的地方，前面不用說 to 的，可能只會占 5%，就是這章介紹的一家「怪咖」（here、there、home、upstairs、downstairs、abroad、overseas、somewhere、anwhere、nowhere、inside、outside）。

簡單的說，去一般的地方說 to，怪咖才不說 to。

即使如此，有些人說一般的地方，也會忘掉說 to！這是比較少見的問題，可是還是會有：

✘　I went school.（一般的地方啊！）

✔　I went <u>to</u> school.

✘　I went Thailand.（一般的地方啊！）

✔　I went <u>to</u> Thailand.

　　這些應該都是你「知道」的事情。但是我們學外語都知道「知道」不一定等於「會用對」。既然你已經上樓了，我就告訴你一個學英文的祕訣。就是，我叫你造句時寫真實的事，是為了：一，讓你發現有些英文說法很有用；二、我希望這些生活事你能真的開口說出來。要說出來，是因為學英文的祕訣就是：

　　說就是記。

　　比如生字說出來，會幫助你記得它。說出口就容易記下來。

　　「欸，Scott，你的邏輯不太對。我說了它表示我已經記得它。」但是，學外語真的是這樣嗎？我也是個外語學生。根據我的經驗，學習外語是個「學而忘，忘而學」的循環。讀寫聽說都很重要，都對你的英文學習有幫助。但是，以我的經驗而言，在學習生字這方面，說的效率比讀寫聽高很多，如果我說高一百倍，一點都沒有誇張。

　　譬如，我自己學中文，有些字，我查字典，已經查了幾十遍，但是下次碰到，哇，又忘了，要再查！你不要騙我說你不會，我知道在學習英文的路上你也遇到過這個情況！

　　我自己的體會是，日常生活中，在合適的情境下，我只要說對一個生字，說了五次之後，我通常就記得了。

　　那麼，請你告訴我，讀了幾十次還記不得，和說了五次就記牢，哪一個比較有效率？

　　人類可能是很自我中心的動物：我們最記得的東西往往是我們自己說的！這可能是個不值得讚揚的事實，但還是事實。如果你能接受這個事實，你的

學習效率就會暴增。

　很多學習語言的人覺得「要學好，才去用。」我跟你說不不不不不，再一個大大的「不！」

　「嘿，不記得，怎麼用？我還是懷疑你的邏輯。」就是刻意地去用。一學到，就強迫自己去用。「說」不是學好之後的享受，而是學習過程不可或缺的一部分！

　說就是記。所以，你看這本書的時候，或者造句的時候，我希望你會註記哪些說法很不錯，準備日後在真實生活裡運用，然後到時候強迫自己說！

　啊！啊！啊！是不是覺得很有啟發！那，我們就來想幾個比較沒有把握的字彙，邁向「說五次就精通」之路。

 史考特的句子

　　1. I don't want to <u>go outside</u>, because it's raining.

　　2. I <u>go downstairs</u> every day to get my mail.

　　3. I usually <u>go home</u> right after I finish teaching English.

 你的句子

　　1. _____

　　2. _____

3. _____

 超簡單改錯

1. I've never gone to abroad by airplane.

2. The train stopped in somewhere.

3. If you go to upstairs, you'll feel hot.

錯庫！蒐集自台灣人真正犯過的英文錯誤，一起來除錯！

1. Which countries do you like to travel?

2. Many elementary school students go to there.

3. There's a research about this subject.

4. It's worth to visit?

5. How long do you come to this school?

6. At that time, we didn't consider of the air pollution.

7. You can go to anywhere you want.

8. One of my friends is going to go to the movies tomorrow.

解答

超簡單單改錯

1. I've never gone ~~to~~ abroad by airplane.

2. The train stopped ~~in~~ somewhere.

3. If you go ~~to~~ upstairs, you'll feel hot.

錯庫

1. Which countries do you like to travel to?

（第 24 章：這個動詞後面要放介係詞！）

2. Many elementary school students go ~~to~~ there.

（第 10 章：here和 there前面通常不會放介係詞）

3. There's some research about this subject.

（第 19 章：名詞是可數的還是不可數的？）

4. It's worth visiting?（第39章：「值得」很值得學!）

5. How long have you been coming to this school?

（第 36 章：持續到現在的動作，通常用現在完成式或現在完成進行式。）

6. At that time, we didn't consider ~~of~~ the air pollution.

（第 14 章：這個動詞後面不需要加介係詞！）

7. You can go ~~to~~ anywhere you want.（本章）

8. 正確無誤！

第 41 章

我喜歡讀雜誌裡的名人八卦

這個名詞前面的介係詞錯了！

「Scott, 這個星期天我請你吃飯，好不好？」

謝啦！我可以選餐廳嗎？王品牛排！王品牛排！

嘿，等一下，這本書不是要說食物，是要討論怎麼在生活裡說很自然的英文。抱歉，我說食物，是很忘我的事。那，話說回來，「Scott, 這個星期天我請你吃飯，好不好」，英文怎麼說？

很可惜，我一個桃園的朋友真的跟我這樣說：

✘ I'll treat you to lunch at Sunday, OK?

我最後原諒了她，因為她真的請我吃王品！（這是真的事喔）敝人只能帶著笑容、很溫柔地、委委婉婉地提醒貴人，她可能要「考慮」另外一個說法：

✔ I'll treat you to lunch **on** Sunday, OK?

啊，你可能已經隱約感覺出，我們已經進入英文的一個很奇特的世界，就是介係詞的世界。

> 　　在第 24 章，「這個動詞後面要加介係詞」，我們學到了有些動詞後面經常會有一種介係詞片語。也就是說，這些動詞後面，有話要繼續講的時候，記得要加介係詞。
>
> 　　在這一章，我們要換一個角度，看哪一個介係詞應該搭配某個名詞。有時候，某個名詞前面需要加特定的介係詞，大家往往很容易搞錯。

就像朋友會請我吃飯的 Sunday，星期幾前面的介係詞都是用 on：

✔ I've got to <u>turn in</u> my homework **on** <u>Friday</u>.（turn in = 交給老師）

名詞前面放錯了介係詞，這類錯誤有很多種。為了比較有系統的討論，我把錯誤類型分成以下幾種。

> 　　不過，我要先給你一點鼓勵。介係詞的用法是件很細微的事。連英文高手也常會有問題。我自己覺得，精通歐洲語系的語言，要過的最後一個關就是介係詞。不要沮喪！
>
> 　　我也再給你一個建議。你記得我們在上面討論過一個字的「行為」嗎？就是，如果你真的號稱你「了解」一個字，你一定要知道它會在什麼情況出現，也需要知道它跟哪些字在一起用。

　　舉上面的 Friday 來講。前面的 on 與後面的 Friday 不需要分開學，你只要知道 on 就是 Friday 的「朋友」，它們會在一起出現。on 就是 Friday 的一種行為。然後，你乾脆把它們當成一個片語：on Friday。這樣一來，你不太用去「背」Friday 前面應該說 on。需要說的時候，你可以直接從腦海裡拿出這一組來用。

　　字的行為，跟哪些介係詞在一起，是很重要的一種喔！

　　所以，下面的介係詞/名詞，我建議你開始把它們看做一組，也練習把這一組字順順利利地說出口。記得一組，就不用過度辛苦去「背」。

　　來看看幾個常見的介係詞和名詞成為死黨的例子：

娛樂：看電視、看電影

通常，看電視的時候，我們看什麼節目 on TV。例如：

✘　I saw an interesting show in TV.

✔　I saw an interesting show **on** TV.

說電視的哪一個頻道也說 on。這包括 channel 這個統稱，和頻道的名字：

✘ I saw the program from my favorite channel.

✔ I saw the program **on** my favorite channel.

✘ I saw it at the National Geographic Channel.（National Geographic = 國家地理）

✔ I saw it **on** the National Geographic Channel.

簡單的說，任何有螢幕的東西通常都會 on，包括電腦的螢幕：

✔ I saw a funny video **on** my computer.

有一個例外。如果我們從電視節目裡面得到某個東西，像知識，我們會說 from。這是因為我們不光只是看，我們還把看的內容，弄到我們身上（應該說移植到我們的大腦裡）。這個 from 常常跟 learn 這個字搭配：

✘ I learned a lot on TV.

✔ I learned a lot **from** TV.

✘ I learned a lot on the Yahoo video.

✔ I learned a lot **from** the Yahoo video.

 上網

說上網跟說電視很像。如果我們上網看資訊或玩，我們說 on the internet。

✘ I saw an interesting picture in the internet.

✔ I saw an interesting picture **on** the internet.

✘ I was playing games at the internet.

✔ I was playing games **on** the <u>internet</u>.

✘ I was chatting with my friend in the internet.
✔ I was chatting with my friend **on** the <u>internet</u>.

✘ I watched a movie in Tudou.（Tudou 是土豆網的英文名字）
✔ I watched a movie **on** <u>Tudou</u>.

例外也跟電視一樣。如果你把網路上的東西弄到你自己身上，你就可以說 from、over、或 through，這包括知識、下載的東西、還有透過網路訂購的東西。

✘ I've learned a lot about English at the internet.
✔ I've learned a lot about English **from** the <u>internet</u>.
（注意：on、through 也可以）

✘ I ordered a book in the internet.
✔ I ordered a book **from** the <u>internet</u>.（注意：on、over、through 也可以）

 看書、看報紙

通常我們看書、看報紙的時候，介係詞是 in，我們看內容 in a book 或 in a newspaper 或 in a magazine。注意，這跟電視不一樣了，我們看什麼節目 on TV，但是看雜誌是 in a magazine。

√ 平的、螢幕性的東西說 on。要打開的讀物說 in。

例子：

✘ I read something really interesting on the newspaper.
✔ I read something really interesting **in** the <u>newspaper</u>.

✘　I read about Chinese history on my textbook. (textbook = 課本)

✔　I read about Chinese history **in** my <u>textbook</u>.

✘　I like to read celebrity gossip on magazines.

✔　I like to read celebrity gossip **in** <u>magazines</u>.
　　（celebrity = 名人; gossip = 八卦）

　　例外，跟之前是一樣的，如果你拿到或學到東西，你要改說 from。比方說，雜誌裡有很漂亮的圖片，你撕下來：

✔　I got a beautiful picture **from** the <u>magazine</u>.

　　或者，你學到了很多知識：

✔　I learned a lot about dinosaurs **from** the <u>book</u>. (dinosaur = 恐龍)

　　「電子書呢？」哈，被問這個，連偉大的史考特也愣了一下。根據我們提出的原則，你猜得出來嗎？你想：用來看電子書的平板電腦是平的東西，也是有螢幕的東西，那，就是……

✔　I'm reading a book **on** my <u>iPad</u>.

討論娛樂、讀物裡面的內容

　　上面，我們只不過是說你是用什麼樣的媒體工具來得到資訊。如果你說，I'm watching sports on TV，這只告訴我，「我在用一個平的東西。」如果你說，I'm reading an article in the newspaper，這只告訴我，「我在用一個可以摺起來的東西。」但是如果要說這部電影的內容呢？這個文章裡面的理論呢？這個電子書長篇小說的情節呢？就是：

　說內容，一律都說 in。

譬如說，你這樣說是對的：

✔ I watched a movie **on** my <u>computer</u>.

沒錯。不過，你如果要繼續說那部電影：

✘ There are some really great characters on the movie.

啊！這樣就是錯的。第一句是說你用什麼具體的載具來看電影，第二句是說電影裡面的內容，這裡我們英文是母語的人都會說 in：

✔ There are some really great characters **in** the <u>movie</u>.

上面的 characters 是虛構的，由演員演出的人物。不過，說電影裡面的演員，這些真的人，也會說 in。

✘ I saw Brad Pitt on the movie.
✔ I saw Brad Pitt **in** the <u>movie</u>.

如果要在句子開頭廣泛的指出整個演出，也會說 in。

✘ On the TV show, the bad guy is so evil!（evil = 邪惡）
✔ **In** the <u>TV show</u>, the bad guy is so evil!

書刊類型的東西比較簡單，因為說媒體工具，說裡面的內容，都是說 in。你可以僥倖的活下去，哈。

✔ There was an interesting story **in** the <u>newspaper</u>.（說媒體工具）
✔ **In** the <u>story</u>, there were some big surprises.（說內容）

不過，現代生活很複雜！電子書，上面的例外，要小心！

✘　I was reading a novel in my iPad.

✔　I was reading a novel **on** my <u>iPad</u>.（說媒體工具：平的、螢幕的！）

✔　There were some really sad parts **in** the <u>novel</u>.（說內容）

 交通工具

　在車上，英文怎麼說呢？那得看看是什麼樣的車子了。

＼／大部分的車子，我們會說 on，包括這些：motorcyle、bus、train、boat。下
面都是對的：

<table>
<tr><td>I'm on my <u>motorcyle</u>.</td><td>I got on the <u>motorcyle</u>.</td></tr>
<tr><td>I'm on the <u>bus</u>.</td><td>I got on the <u>bus</u>.</td></tr>
<tr><td>I'm on the <u>train</u>.</td><td>I got on the <u>train</u>.</td></tr>
<tr><td>I'm on a <u>boat</u>!</td><td>I got on a <u>boat</u>!</td></tr>
<tr><td>I'm on <u>the MRT</u>.</td><td>I got on <u>the MRT</u>.</td></tr>
</table>

　汽車就不一樣了。汽車我們都說 in：

　　I'm **in** the <u>car</u>.　　　　　　I **got in** the <u>car</u>.

　這包括特別的汽車，像計程車：

　　I'm **in** a <u>taxi</u>.　　　　　　I **got in** a <u>taxi</u>.

　好，我們來看一些對錯比較吧！

✘　I was in the train when my friend called me.

✔　I was **on** the <u>train</u> when my friend called me.

✘　I'm on my car on the way to work.

✔　I'm **in** my <u>car</u> on the way to work.（on the car 表示你在車頂的上面！）

✗ I get in the bus at 4:30pm every afternoon.
✔ I get on the bus at 4:30pm every afternoon.

✗ Hey, get in my motorcyle, and I'll give you a ride!
✔ Hey, get on my motorcyle, and I'll give you a ride!

 時間

說幾點都是at：

✗ Class starts on 10:30 am.
✔ Class starts at 10:30 am.

任何的一天就說 on。就像這章一開頭所說的，一星期的某一天要說 on。

✗ I'll meet you at Monday, OK?
✔ I'll meet you on Monday, OK?

一日，就是月曆方式的說年月日，也是 on：

✗ I was born at January 26th, 1975.
✔ I was born on January 26th, 1975.

✗ The meeting is at April 2nd.
✔ The meeting is on April 2nd.

weekend（週末），就算是兩天，還是可以說 on。但是，weekend 也可以說 over 或 during。絕對不可以說 at。

✗ I'll clean my apartment at the weekend.
✔ I'll clean my apartment on / over / during the weekend.

節日，如果是一天的節日，也按照我們「一天說 on」的規則，就要說 on.

✘　I'll be with my parents in Christmas Day.

✔　I'll be with my parents on Christmas Day.

✘　I'll give her a present at Valentine's Day.（Valentine's Day = 情人節）

✔　I'll give her a present on Valentine's Day.

✓ 但是如果節日超過一天，我們就要說 during 或 over。on 在這裡就是錯的。拿 Chinese New Year （過年）來說：

✘　I'll watch a lot of TV on Chinese New Year.

✔　I'll watch a lot of TV over / during Chinese New Year.

　　那麼，一天的一部分，像 morning（早上）、afternoon（下午）、night（晚上）呢？用法其實都不太一樣喔：

in the morning （早上）

in the afternoon （下午）

in the evening （晚上）

at night （夜裡）

✓ 非常晚的話，我們會說：

late at night （差不多 10pm - 2 am 左右）

in the middle of the night （差不多 1 am - 5 am 左右）

　　若要表示非常晚，很多人會說成 at midnight，這是錯的。midnight 是指 12 點整，不超過一秒鐘的那個剎那！如果不是 12 點整，就要說 late at night 或 in the middle of the night。

　　我們來看一些對錯比較：

✘ I woke up at 6 o'clock at the morning.
✔ I woke up at 6 o'clock **in** the <u>morning</u>.

✘ I'll see you on the afternoon!
✔ I'll see you **in** the <u>afternoon</u>.

✘ I always do my homework in the night.
✔ I always do my homework **at** <u>night</u>. （注意：night 前面不用 the）

✘ （晚上12點半打電話）He called me at the midnight.
✔ He called me <u>late at night</u>.

✘ （凌晨3點被吵醒了）A dog woke me up at the midnight!
✔ A dog woke me up <u>in the middle of the night</u>!

 但是，如果說是星期幾的早上、中午、晚上，我們需要說 on：

說星期幾	沒說
on <u>Wednesday morning</u>	**in** the <u>morning</u>
on <u>Friday afternoon</u>	**in** the <u>afternoon</u>
on <u>Sunday night</u>	**at** <u>night</u>

很容易記啊：說星期幾是 on，說星期幾的何時也是 on！

✘ I'll call you at Tuesday night.
✔ I'll call you **on** <u>Tuesday night</u>.

✘ I'll pick you up in Wednesday morning.
✔ I'll pick you up **on** <u>Wednesday morning</u>.

那，要說 that time（那個時候），這個很廣泛的詞呢，通常要說 at：

at that time

✘ （小時候）In that time, I was a happy little kid.

✔ **At** <u>that time</u>, I was a happy little kid.

 其他主題

我在這裡列出很多名詞，大家常常放錯它們前面的介係詞，以下名詞按照字母
順列排列，前面放正確的介係詞：

in a <u>book</u>	（書）
in the <u>car / taxi</u>	（汽車、計程車）
in the <u>chair / wheelchair</u>	（椅子、輪椅）
in <u>sixth grade</u>	（學校的六年級，每年級都這樣）
on the <u>ground</u>	（地上）
for your <u>health</u>	（身體健康）
at <u>home</u>	（在家）
on <u>the internet</u>	（網路，注意上面討論的例外）
on my <u>itinerary</u>	（旅遊計畫）
in a <u>foreign language / English / Chinese</u>	（外文、英文、中文）
on <u>Wednesday morning</u>	（週三早上，注意上面討論的例外）
in <u>the mountains</u>	（山區）
in the <u>newspaper</u>	（報紙）
at <u>night</u>	（晚上，注意上面討論的例外）
on <u>that night</u>	（那天晚上）
in <u>school</u>	（學校）

on the shelf　　　　　　　　　　　（書架、架子）

in space　　　　　　　　　　　　　（太空）

in the sun　　　　　　　　　　　　（太陽下）

on the test / the TOEFL　　　　　　（考試、託福測驗，什麼考試都是這樣）

at that time　　　　　　　　　　　（那個時候）

on the train　　　　　　　　　　　（火車）

on the weekend　　　　　　　　　　（週末）

at work　　　　　　　　　　　　　（工作）

別擔心太多了！就算很多，你也不是每一個都會弄錯。你要記得，如果你要精通英文，要過的最後一關就是介係詞。學會了這章的內容，你應該向「精通英文」邁進了一大步。

 史考特的句子

1. I usually study Chinese on Sunday.

2. In my opinion, there aren't many good shows on TV.

3. I like to read news on the internet.

4. On the bus, it's so crowded.

5. There are a lot of interesting things in Scott's book about English mistakes!

 你的句子

1. _____

2. _____

3. _____

4. _____

5. _____

 超簡單改錯

1. （吃太多）It's not good to your health.

2. Those teachers give higher scores in tests.

3. I am at sixth grade.

1. I ever studied Spanish.

2. The Hong Kong action movies on TV were boring.
（action movies＝動作片）

3. I have done a research.

4. （80年代的明星）She is popular in that time.

5. Vacation is important in our life.

6. I'm afraid at water.

7. It's worth.

8. How do you communication with your family?

解答

超簡單改錯

1. It's not good <u>for</u> your <u>health</u>.
2. Those teachers give higher scores <u>on tests</u>.
3. I am <u>in</u> sixth <u>grade</u>.

錯庫

1. I <u>have</u> ~~ever~~ studied Spanish.
   （第 33 章：一般的句子不會用 ever）
2. 正確無誤！
3. I have done ~~a~~ <u>some</u> research.
   （第 19 章：名詞是可數的還是不可數的？）

4. She ~~is~~ was popular ~~in~~ <u>at that time</u>.
   （本章；第 3 章：描述過去發生的事，動詞要用過去式。）
5. Vacation<u>s</u> ~~is~~ <u>are</u> important in our life.
   （第 5 章：表達一般性的看法或意見時，可數名詞要用複數。）
6. I'm <u>afraid</u> ~~at~~ <u>of</u> water.
   （第 28 章：很多形容詞後面需要介係詞，對的介係詞！）
7. It's worth <u>it</u>. 或 It's <u>worthwhile</u>.
   （第 39 章：「值得」很值得學!）
8. How do you <u>communicate</u> with your family?
   （第 31 章：詞性搞錯了（三）：名詞 vs. 動詞）

老師，我建議你多運動

recommend 以及 suggest 的用法很特別

在我的學校，我的學生都是很典型的台灣人：活潑、用功、健康、身材都瘦瘦的。至於英文老師呢，我們也都是蠻典型的西方人：親切、幽默、開朗、身材……喔，啊，身材怎麼交代呢？應該可以說是稍微有一點點……不瘦。

而且，你們對外籍老師們非常好，希望可以幫助我們，讓我們在國外過很愉快的生活，也希望我們健康，所以我本人聽了好幾十次的這個：

✘　I suggest you to exercise more.

喔，我舉雙手同意學生的建議100%適合我。但是，要我多運動之前，你們要先多動腦，如下：

suggest（建議）和 recommend（推薦）並不是很難懂。但是，他們的用法有一點特別，因此，是大家特別容易說錯的兩個字。

主要的問題是，很多人在 suggest 和 recommend 之後，會……

（1）用代名詞受詞的形態，然後……

（2）再接個 to。

比方說：

✘　I suggested him to study harder.

這是錯的。固然很多詞的用法是那樣，像 want：

✔　I wanted him to study harder.

suggest 與 recommend 卻不同。suggest 和 recommend 後面的代名詞應該是主詞狀態的，也不需要 to。應該要這樣說才對：

✔　I suggested <u>he</u> study harder.

suggested 後面也可以接個 that：

✔　I suggested <u>that he</u> study harder.

suggest / suggest that 後面有一點像一個句子，對不對？主詞，然後動詞……

不過！

這是一個相當大的「不過」。你應該要特別注意，在上面的句子裡，he 後面的動詞不是 studies，而是 study。

> 這是很特別的用法。只要你記得 recommend 與 suggest 後面沒有 to，沒有加 s / es 或 ed 的原形動詞，就對了。
>
> 假如你受得了一點文法專有名詞，我們可以這樣說明：這兩個字代表的是所謂的「假設語氣」。假設語氣有幾個用途，其中一個就是給他人建議。「假設語氣」的用法跟一般「語氣」有些不一樣。

簡單的說，建議就是你 should 做的事情，不是嗎？果然，recommend 跟 suggest 沒有第三人稱的 s /es，就是因為它們後面有個省略的 should。上面的例句，放回省略的詞，就是：

✔　I suggested <u>(that) he (should)</u> study harder.

should 後面是原型動詞，所以第一、二、三人稱都不改變。你看：

✘　I recommend you to apply to New York University.
✔　I recommend <u>you apply</u> to New York University.
✔　（放回省略的）I recommend <u>(that) you (should)</u> apply to New York University.

✗   I recommend her to look for a different job.

✔   I recommend <u>she look</u> for a different job.

✔   （放回省略的）I recommend <u>(that) she (should) look</u> for a different job.

✗   I recommend him to be nicer to his coworkers.

✔   I recommend <u>he be</u> nicer to his coworkers.

✔   （放回省略的）I recommend <u>(that) he (should) be</u> nicer to his coworkers.

那，現在建議你的老師多運動，就易如反掌了：

✔   I suggest <u>you exercise</u> more.

✔   （放回省略的）I suggest <u>(that) you (should) exercise</u> more.

可以說 suggest 跟 recommend 後面有 should 的句子，只是省略了 should！

 suggest 和 recommend 也可以簡單用

我上面一直說 suggest 與 recommend 後面的句子，是因為這是你們常常說錯的句型。但其實，我也應該提醒你們，這兩個字後面不一定要說句子，一般的名詞或名字也行。比方說，我跟朋友找東西吃，然後我知道附近有一家攤子賣還蠻好吃的三明治。我可以簡單的：

✔   I suggest sandwiches.

這是比較不會說錯的。recommend 稍微難一點，因為說推薦的時候習慣會有一個對象。

✗   I recommend you that clinic.（clinic = 診所）

我到底哪裡錯？recommend 後面的東西只能說你推薦什麼，不能說是給誰的

推薦。給誰推薦的是在 to 的介係詞片語裡：

✔ I <u>recommend</u> that clinic **to** you.

而且，如果只有一個受詞，只能說推薦的東西，不可以說給誰推薦的。譬如，你已經跟我說服很久說我們應該去吃漢堡王，你不可以說：

✘ Trust me. I recommend you.

recommend後面只有一個東西的話，就是推薦的東西：

✔ Trust me. I recommend Burger King.
好，現在 I recommend we make some sentences!

 史考特的句子

1. I recommend you practice English outside of class.

2. I suggest you visit the beach in California.

3. I don't recommend Mos Burger to you. The burgers are too small!（Mos Burger = 摩斯漢堡）

4.（說應該去哪裡剪頭髮）I suggest a little family barbershop.
（family barbershop = 家庭理髮）

 你的句子

1. _____

2. _____

超簡單改錯

1. I suggested her to try the new teacher's class.

2. I recommended my friend to go to New Zealand, because of the scenery.（scenery = 風景）

3.（陪好友買鞋子的時候）I recommend you Nike's shoes. They're the best.

錯庫！蒐集自台灣人真正犯過的英文錯誤，一起來除錯！

1. I have ever travelled Indonesia.（Indonesia = 印尼）

2. Don't confused.

3. I recommend you to visit the temples in China or Taiwan.

4.（某國）In 1955, they have earthquake.

5.（某些女生）They learn how to put on make-up to let

themselves beautiful.

6. Lots of Taiwanese people like to littering. (litter = 亂丟垃圾)

7. I suggest that you read more books that you enjoy.

8. They felt safe in the night.

解答

超簡單改錯

1. I suggested <u>she try</u> the new teacher's class.

2. I recommended <u>my friend go</u> to New Zealand, because of the scenery.

3. I recommend <u>Nike's shoes to you</u>. They're the best. (注意：to you 可以省略)

錯庫

1. I have travelled <u>to</u> Indonesia.
   (第 33 章：一般的句子不會用 ever；第 40 章：去某一個地方，需不需要 to？)

2. Don't <u>be/get</u> confused.
   (第 27 章：說了助動詞，卻忘了主要動詞！)

3. I recommend <u>you visit</u> the temples in China or Taiwan. (本章)

4. In 1955, they <u>had an</u> earthquake.
   (第 3 章：描述過去發生的事，動詞要用過去式。；第 21 章：一個東西（是可數的話）前面需要冠詞！)

5. They learn how to put on make-up to <u>make</u> themselves beautiful.
   (第 38 章：let 與 make 後面該怎麼說？)

6. Lots of Taiwanese people like <u>to litter</u>. (或) Lots of Taiwanese people like <u>littering</u>.
   (第 12 章：like、don't like、love、hate 後面要小心放什麼字！)

7. 正確無誤！

8. They felt safe <u>at night</u>. (第 41 章：這個名詞前面的介係詞錯了！)

第 43 章

我阻止了一個小孩跑到馬路上去

如何表達阻止、預防、防止、制止這些意思

小孩跑到馬路中間，你當然會跑過去救他回來。那怎麼報告你的英勇行為呢？

✘ I stopped a little kid to run into the road.

當時你的英姿超讚，但你的「英譯」超爛。

表示「阻止」的意思的英文字很多，像 prevent 與 stop。它們的用法其實很簡單，但是大家仍然常常犯錯。

問題就在後面的介係詞。很多人會用 to、at、for。像上面的 to。但是，事實上，有「阻止」的意思的動詞，後面的介係詞都是 from：

✔ I <u>stopped</u> a little kid **from** runn**ing** into the road.

注意，from 是介係詞，所以後面要加動詞時需要有 ing 的動名詞。上面是用 stop 這個例子，如果用 prevent，用法一模一樣：

✘ The police prevented him to commit suicide.（commit suicide = 畏罪自殺）
✔ The police <u>prevented</u> him **from** commit**ting** suicide.

ban（禁止）的用法也一樣：

✘ We should ban people to play loud music at night!
✔ We should <u>ban</u> people **from** play**ing** loud music at night!

有些人，他們雖然動名詞用對了，但是介係詞還是錯的。at 也是不對的：

✘ I stopped my friend at taking the wrong book.

from 才對：

✔ I <u>stopped</u> my friend **from** taking the wrong book.

有人則是根本漏掉 from。請千萬不要忘記！

✘　The teacher prevented us making mistakes on the test.

✔　The teacher <u>prevented</u> us <mark>from</mark> making mistakes on the test.

但是，這不是說 prevent、stop、ban 後面一定要接 from。這樣的動詞，你也可以後面直接接一般的名詞，然後結束句子：

✔　My friend wanted to steal something, but I stopped her.

✔　This medicine prevents disease.（disease = 病）

✔　We should ban smoking!

也可以直接用動名詞：

✔　I stopped talking.

在這裡，stop 比較偏向停止的意思。

好，就是這樣。我們造句吧。我有沒有說，造句時，我們應該說真人真事，為了準備一些在日常生活裡用得到的句子？有？那，我不再囉唆。

 史考特的句子

1. My students try to <u>prevent</u> me <mark>from</mark> eat<u>ing</u> unhealthy foods.

2. You have to try to <u>stop</u> naughty students <mark>from</mark> talk<u>ing</u> too much in class.

3. I <u>stop</u> reading when it gets too late.

4. If a criminal tries to rob my apartment, I'll <u>stop</u> him.

5. Somebody <u>blocked</u> me <mark>from</mark> get<mark>ting</mark> on the train.

（block = 擋住）

你的句子

1. _____

2. _____

超簡單改錯

1. （某國王不喜歡移民）The king tried to stop people to come in.

2. I can't stop you to chat with other people.

錯庫！蒐集自台灣人真正犯過的英文錯誤，一起來除錯！

1. If you want to drive on the mountain areas, you have to be careful.

2. （某種食物）It has to delicious and expensive.

3.（某一個地方的政府）They blocked the store to open in this area.

4. One of my friends prevented me from making a big mistake.

5. We had to performance in Japan.

6. Most of men are effeminate nowadays.
   （effeminate = 女性化、娘娘腔）

7. I have been to the cram school when I was in high school.

8. I just read on the newspaper.

超簡單改錯

1. The king tried to <u>stop</u> people ~~to~~ <u>from</u> coming in.

2. I can't <u>stop</u> you ~~to~~ <u>from</u> chatting with other people.

錯庫

1. If you want to drive ~~on~~ <u>in</u> the mountain areas, you have to be careful.

（第 41 章：這個名詞前面的介係詞錯了）

2. It has to <u>be</u> delicious and expensive.

（第 26 章：嘿，你忘了動詞！）

3. They blocked the store <u>from</u> <u>opening</u> in this area.（本章）

4. 正確無誤！

5. We had to ~~performance~~ perform in Japan.

（第 31 章：詞性搞錯了（三）：名詞 vs. 動詞）

6. Most ~~of~~ men are effeminate nowadays.

（第 22 章：most 的用法：可以用一個字，也可以用三個字，就是不能用兩個字！）

7. I ~~have been~~ <u>went</u> to the cram school when I was in high school.

（第 34 章：如果要表達什麼時候做或發生的，用過去式就好，不可以用現在完成式。）

8. I just read <u>it</u> ~~on~~ <u>in</u> the newspaper.

（第 13 章：有些動詞後面需要接受詞；第 41 章：這個名詞前面的介係詞錯了）

我的老闆已經讓我抓狂幾百次了

要說做了多少次，前面不可以說 for！

啊，中文！好美的語言！有很多事情，英文要考慮好幾個差別極小的用法，但中文卻只有一個說法。

例如，講中文，如果你要說做了多久，或者要說做了幾次，這兩種沒有什麼差別，都可以直接說：

我做了五個小時。

我做了五次。

啊，看起來很簡單、很正經、很乖的兩個句子，卻藏著英文的陷阱。遇到這兩個情況，英文怎麼說呢？

✔ I did it for five hours.

✘ I did it for five times.

有沒有掉進去？大家都知道，用英文說做了多久，前面要說 for。以下這些都是對的：

✔ I played computer games **for** two hours.

✔ I went to Japan **for** ten days.

✔ I lived in Los Angeles **for** three years.

因此，很多人以為要說做了幾次，也可以說 for：

✘ I've been to Thailand for two times.

說實在的，說幾次前面不會用 for：

✔ I've been to Thailand two times.

所以，這章開頭的「陷阱」，自然正確的英文應該是：

✔ I did it five <u>times</u>.

直接說幾次就好了，真的不用說 for。但是，相信我，這是非常、非常常見的錯誤。

✘ I studied this English word for many times, but I forgot it!
✔ I studied this English word many <u>times</u>, but I forgot it!

✘ I reminded him for three times.（remind = 提醒）
✔ I reminded him three <u>times</u>.

✘ My boss has made me angry for a million times!
✔ My boss has made me angry a million <u>times</u>!

once 跟 twice 也不例外，它們也是說次數的詞：

✘ I've only been there for once.
✔ I've only been there <u>once</u>.

✘ It rained for twice today!
✔ It rained <u>twice</u> today!

就這麼簡單。

 史考特的句子

1. I went to the buffet <u>once</u> today.（buffet = 自助餐廳）

2. I've been to my favorite bookstore so many <u>times</u>.

你的句子

說說你自己，應該要用到 once、twice、還有 times。

1. _____

2. _____

3. _____

超簡單改錯

1. I've been to Japan for five times.

2. I've already done it for seven or eight times.

錯庫！蒐集自台灣人真正犯過的英文錯誤，一起來除錯！

1. （父母還在種蔬菜）My parents grow vegetables for about one year.

2. My dad lets me go to one of the best and most expensive restaurants in town.

3.（旅遊時）I don't care the hotels.

4. Order some clothes make me feel better.

5.（借了一件衣服）I borrowed from my friend.

6.（寵物）Keep it inside to prevent it to get too much sunshine.

7.（某個工廠）It pollution the sea.

8. You forgot for three times.

解答

超簡單改錯

1. I've been to Japan ~~for~~ five times.

2. I've already done it ~~for~~ seven or eight times.

錯庫

1. My parents ~~grow~~ have been growing vegetables for about one year.
　（第 36 章：持續到現在的動作，通常用現在完成式或現在完成進行式。）

2. 正確無誤！

3. I don't care about the hotels.
　（第 24 章：這個動詞後面要放介係詞！）

4. Ordering some clothes makes me feel better.
　（第 1 章：第三人稱現在式動詞忘記加 s / es；第 18 章：動詞開頭的句子，要用加 ing 的動名詞。）

5. I borrowed it from my friend.（第 13 章：有些動詞後面需要接受詞）

6. Keep it inside to prevent it ~~to~~ from getting too much sunshine.
　（第 43 章：如何表達阻止、預防、防止、制止這些意思）

7. It ~~pollution~~ pollutes the sea.
　（第 31 章：詞性搞錯了（三）：名詞 vs. 動詞）

8. You forgot ~~for~~ three times.（本章）

我兩個鐘頭後必須離開

第 45 章

✓ 要表達現在之後某一個時間點，要用 in，不用 later。

正確表達時間很重要，不是嗎？中文很簡單，比方說，跟朋友說，過兩個星期你會打電話給她，你可以說：

兩個星期之後我會打電話給你。

可能因為中文的句型是這樣，很多人用英文說這個想法的時候，會這樣說：

✗ I'll call you two weeks later.

說實在的，如果要說**現在之後的某一時刻**，你不可以在句子的後面加 later！在時間前面加 in 才對：

✔ I'll call you **in** two weeks.

「咦？」我聽到你的質疑了。「later 的意思不就是之後嗎？它也行吧！」

不行。讓我來告訴你，你不可以把「之後」硬幫幫地翻譯成 later。later 要用在正確的地方。什麼地方？就是<u>同時有兩件事要說</u>，<u>而且這兩件事都必須是發生在過去的。</u>

舉個例子。這是真實發生在我自己身上的事。之前申請簽證，這是過去的事，過了兩個星期，我去領我新的簽證，這也是過去的事。在這裡，就可以用 later：

✔ I applied for my visa. Two weeks <u>later</u> I picked it up.

我們可以用一個小圖表來分辨 later 跟 in 的用法：

in：現在以後的一個時間點

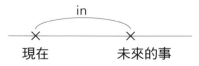

later：兩件事都發生在過去，第二件事在第一件之後。

過去的事1　　　過去的事2　　　現在

再舉幾個例子來加強我們的了解。假設都是現在說的：

✘　The teacher told us to write a paper. We have to finish it two weeks later.

✔　The teacher told us to write a paper. We have to finish it **in** two weeks.

✘　I have to go! I've got to meet my friend 15 minutes later!

✔　I have to go! I've got to meet my friend **in** 15 minutes!

✘　Well, I just started high school. I'll graduate three years later.

✔　Well, I just started high school. I'll graduate **in** three years.

「救命啊！可是我已經先把時間說出來了！」

這是很常見的問題。因為中文的說法是多少時間「……之後」，說英文的時候，很容易會先把時間說出來，就來不及說前面的 in 了。例如：

I have to leave two hours...

看到了嗎？two hours 已經說出口，來不及說 in 了！

這個其實有辦法！表達「現在之後的時刻」，還有有另外一個說法，就是，在時間之後加 from now。像下面這個例子：

✔　I have to leave two hours **from now**.

🖊 一般的美國人，在日常生活裡，真正會說的還是：

　要表達現在之後某一個時間點，要用 in，不用 later。

✔ I have to leave **in** two hours.

不過，I have to leave two hours from now. 還是百分之百正確的。

我們可以整理原則如下：

說從此之後的時間，時間前面要用 in；如果不小心先說出了時間，時間後面可以加 from now。但是，絕絕對對不可以說 later！

再來一個例子：

✘ I have to go to dinner a few hours later.

✔ I have to go to dinner **in** a few hours.

✔ I have to go to dinner a few hours **from now**.

之前對錯比較的例子也都可以用 from now 的句型。

好，表現的時候到了！

 史考特的句子

都是以我此時的角度來說的：

1. I'm going to go to Taichung **in** a few days.（Taichung = 台中）

2. I'll go to the buffet **in** about forty-five minutes.
   （buffet = 自助餐廳）

3. Three days **from now**, I have to substitute a class.
   （substitute = 代課）

你的句子

1. _____

2. _____

3. _____

超簡單改錯

1. The museum will close a few years later.

2.（等10天就要開始準備出國）Ten days later, I have to prepare for my trip.

錯庫！蒐集自台灣人真正犯過的英文錯誤，一起來除錯！

1. It's worth to do it.

2. Most of Taiwanese are civilized.（civilized = 文明）

3. One of my friends went to the supermarket several times this week.

✓ 4. I have never go on a road trip.

✓ 5. （以前旅行過的地方）I think there is a wonderful place.

6. I drive my car on highway.

7. （說喜不喜歡某一所學校的制服）I like!

8. You have to do it for several times.

9. We must consider about our children and grandchildren.

10. I believe the gas will run out fifty years later.（gas＝油）

解答

超簡單改錯

1. The museum will close in a few years later.（或） The museum will close a few years later from now.

2. In ten days later, I have to prepare for my trip.（或）Ten days later from now, I have to prepare for my trip.

錯庫

1. It's worth to doing it.
　（第 39 章：「值得」很值得學！）

2. Most of Taiwanese are civilized.
　（第 22 章：most 的用法：可以用一個字，也可以用三個字，就是不能用兩個字！）

3. 正確無誤！

4. I have never gone on a road trip.
　（第32章：現在完成式形成得不正確）

5. I think it there is a wonderful place.
　（第 11 章：here 與 there 不可以當成受詞和主詞）

6. I drive my car on the highway.
　（第 21 章：一樣東西〈是可數的話〉前面需要冠詞！）

7. I like it/them!（或）I do!（第 13 章：有些動詞後面需要接受詞）

8. You have to do it for several times.
　（第 44 章：要說做了多少次，前面不可以說 for！）

9. We must consider about our children and grandchildren.
　（第 14 章：這個動詞後面不需要加介係詞！）

10. I believe the gas will run out in fifty years later.（本章）

　要表達現在之後某一個時間點，要用 in，不用 later。

我一定要贏得這場比賽

這個 to 是多餘的!

　　我知道你很好強、很好勝,要不然,你怎麼可以撐到這本書的第 46 章呢?因此,我知道,如果叫你參加英文比賽的話,你非贏不可。我聽到我很多學生強烈的回應我:

✘　I must to win this contest!

　　其實,我真的當過英文比賽的裁判。說這句話的人我給他打零分!祝他明年運氣好一點吧,或者更好,希望他好好讀這一章!

　　我覺得這是一般人「知道」的事,你在紙上看到上面那個句子,一定知道多說了 to。只是一不小心,錯誤就溜出了口,覆水難收。正確的當然是:

✔　I must win this contest!

　　很多人會在助動詞和動詞中間多餘的加了一個 to。should 也一樣:

✘　I should to study harder.
✔　I should study harder.

　　錯誤產生的原因可能是,有一些助動詞後面的動詞是 to 開始的不定詞。像以下這兩個例子:

✔　I <u>want to go</u> to the store.
✔　I <u>have to do</u> more exercise.

　　習慣說這些 to,就在不應該說的地方也不小心的說了。其實,大部分的助動詞後面是不需要加 to 的。以下,我們列出這些助動詞:

can、could、might、must、should、will、would

「史考特，為什麼有些說 to，但是有些卻沒有說呢？」啊，我的好朋友，我有一個壞消息：沒有人知道。我自己說有 to 的 have to，同時說沒有 to 的 must，是因為我爸爸是這樣說的。他是這樣說的因為他的爸爸是這樣說的。他的爸爸為什麼是這樣說的？沒有人記得。

我有點半開玩笑啦，你了解吧？！嚴格說來，針對這個問題，語言學家有追溯到古英文時期，但是古英文是人們八百年前就不再說的語言！現代的人可能只需要知道，有些有 to，有些沒有 to，是因為它們的來源及演變的過程不一樣。

喔，我忘記了你們很好勝！如果你真的要一個原則，我們可以這樣說，根據語言學家的看法：

很多助動詞是用來表示對後面內容的態度或看法。

例如：

I should exercise more.

這比較偏向我對運動的態度/看法，但是我可能不用做什麼，只是個看法而已。

但是很久以前，to 真的是「到」的意思，就是說一個人會「到」某一個地方辦某一件事。所以，我說：

I have to exercise more.

比較意味著我要做什麼。那個 to 稍微暗示我真的要動身。

沒有 to 的比較偏向看法，有 to 的比較偏向需要辦的事。

但是，現代的英文裡，我覺得你只要記得後面有沒有 to。這就是助動詞很重要的「行為」之一。

比方說，現代的英文裡，have to 與 must 真的很像。你就是要記得，have 有

to，must 卻沒有。但是，說到 have to 與 must，我需要現在跟你講：日常生活的英文，have to 比 must 常見多了。我猜測，華人說「得」、「要」、「一定要」、「需要」等的情況中，我們美國人有99%的情況都會說 have to。must 的語氣非常強烈，我們會保留，好在很激烈的情況下才用。以美國人的標準來說，你們說太多 must，我覺得不太自然。這是相當重要的一點。為了強調，我弄了這個表：

字	美國人真的說出口的比率	表示需要的程度/迫切性
have to	99%	從習慣的事到很迫切的事
must	1%	非常迫切，屬於緊急情況

還可以補一點：have to（需要的意思）裡面的 v 其實發 /f/ 的發音，have（一個字，「有」的意思）裡面的 v 發 /v/ 的發音。

好了，說明太多了。我們回去看生活裡用得到的句子。

例句：

✘　I can to get a better job soon.
✔　I <u>can get</u> a better job soon.

✘　You should to prepare for the typhoon.（typhoon = 颱風）
✔　You <u>should prepare</u> for the typhoon.

✘　You had better to be nice to the teacher.
✔　You <u>had better be</u> nice to the teacher.

就這麼簡單。

副詞後面也不用 to。

多餘的 to，還會發生在一個情況，就是副詞跟動詞之間。例如：

✘ I seldom to travel abroad.

✔ I <u>seldom travel</u> abroad.

　seldom（偶爾、不常的意思）是副詞，travel 是動詞，根本不需要 to！不知道為什麼，seldom 是最常見的慣犯。它就是我們頭號通緝犯的第 6 名，蠻氣人的字！我們來大聲宣傳一下：

seldom 後面<u>不需要</u> to！

多餘的 to，第二常見的副詞是 always：

✘ My sister always to takes my clothes!

✔ My sister <u>always takes</u> my clothes!

　好啦，你應該迫不及待想要造句！You must make sentences to improve your English!

 史考特的句子

我從容易錯的助動詞和副詞選字來造句：

　　1. I should practice my Taiwanese more!（這裡 Taiwanese ＝ 台語）

　　2. I seldom go swimming.

 你的句子

　　1. ＿＿＿＿＿＿＿＿＿＿＿＿＿＿＿＿＿＿＿＿＿＿＿＿＿

　　2. ＿＿＿＿＿＿＿＿＿＿＿＿＿＿＿＿＿＿＿＿＿＿＿＿＿

超簡單改錯

1.（解釋運動有什麼好處）You can to interact with people.
（interact = 互動）

2. I seldom to give my opinion in class.

錯庫！蒐集自台灣人真正犯過的英文錯誤，一起來除錯！

1.（說某個公司要慢慢地改變）They must be evolve. 〔ɪ`vɑlv〕 演進/進化

2. I will suggest them to do this one.

3.（玩電動的青少年）They think they will hero.

4.（以前看電影）Two people were sleep in the theater.
（theater = 電影院）

5.（某些人）They discriminate the black people.
〔dɪ`skrɪmə͵net〕   discriminate against

6. One of my friends hates dogs.

7.（某一個政治人物）He has good image.（這裡，image = 形象）

8. （有毒的廢物）It pollution the water.

∨ 9. （某種新食物一輩子都沒吃）I never eat!

10. People should to learn English.

解答

超簡單改錯

1. You can ~~to~~ interact with people.

2. I seldom ~~to~~ give my opinion in class.

錯庫

1. They must ~~be~~ evolve.

（第 37 章：這個 be 動詞是多餘的！）

2. I will suggest (that) ~~them~~ they to do this one.（第 42 章：recommend 以及 suggest 的用法很特別）

3. They think they will ~~be~~ hero<u>es</u>.

（第 27 章：你説了助動詞，卻忘記了主要動詞！；第 2 章：複數名詞忘了加 s／es）

4. Two people were sleep<u>ing</u> in the theater.（第 16 章：進行式如果搞錯，一切都進行不了！）

5. They <u>discriminate</u> <u>against</u> the black people.（第 24 章：這個動詞後面要放介係詞！）

6. 正確無誤！

7. He has <u>a</u> good image.

（第 21 章：一樣東西〈是可數的話〉前面需要冠詞！）

8. It ~~pollution~~ <u>pollutes</u> the water.

（第 31 章：詞性搞錯了（三）：名詞 vs. 動詞）

9. I <u>have</u> never eat<u>en</u> <u>it</u>!

（第 35 章：一輩子都沒做的事，通常用否定的現在完成式；第 13 章：有些動詞後面需要接受詞）

10. People should ~~to~~ learn English.

（本章）

第 47 章

我不吃辣

形容詞不可以當主詞或受詞

我不吃辣！

假如不會講中文的外國朋友請你吃辣辣的咖哩，然後你是不吃辣的，你會怎麼跟他交代呢？很多台灣人真的是這樣跟我交代的：

✗　I don't eat spicy!

啊，你現在還有另外一件事要交代！

這純粹是「中式英文」。你是不是已經發現很多英文的錯誤受中文的影響？

在中文裡，形容詞可以當主詞和受詞。但是，英文可不行。

在英文裡，spicy 是個形容詞，但是 eat 後面需要受詞，受詞就是名詞。你應該這樣講：

✔　I don't eat <u>spicy food</u>!

說實在的，你有很多選擇，只要 spicy 後面有任何的名詞就好了：

✔　I don't eat <u>spicy dishes</u>!
✔　I don't like <u>spicy stuff</u>!
✔　I can't eat <u>spicy things</u>!
✔　I can't stand <u>spicy curry</u>!

以上等等都對。

天氣也常常產生這種問題。例如：

✗　I don't like hot!
✔　I don't like <u>hot weather</u>!（或任何合適代替 weather 的名詞都可以）

前面討論的都是受詞。主詞也常常出問題。比方說，建議怎麼跟人相處，中文

可以說：

親切比較好。

但是，這樣的說法不可以：

✗   Friendly is better.

應該說：

✔   <u>Being friendly</u> is better.

在此，being 是動名詞（gerund），也是一種名詞。
我們可以歸納出一個原則：
<u>形容詞當主詞，可以在前面放 being。</u>

✗   Arrogant is not polite!（arrogant = 高傲、傲慢）[ˈærəɡənt]
✔   <u>Being arrogant</u> is not polite!

有時，你不用說 being，也可以把那個形容詞改成它名詞的形式：

✗   Happy is the most important thing in life.

✔   (1) <u>Being happy</u> is the most important thing in life.
✔   (2) <u>Happiness</u> is the most important thing in life.

簡單地說，有時大家「知道」需要用名詞，但好像就是會忘記。比方說，去逛
街，東西要買最大的：

✗   The big is the best!
✔   The <u>big one</u> is the best!

這兒，問題可能是，中文加了「的」，就是一個名詞，以上面的案子來說，中
文可以說：

大的最好！

英文不行，說英文，你還得說大的什麼。

史考特的句子

1. I don't like <u>sour food</u>.

2. <u>Being confident</u> is the key to success at work.

你的句子

1. _____

2. _____

超簡單改錯

1. （某個餐廳的食物）Special is sausage with eggs.（sausage ＝ 臘腸）

2. （美國）One interesting is, traffic regulations are different there.（traffic regulations ＝ 交通規則）

錯庫！蒐集自台灣人真正犯過的英文錯誤，一起來除錯！

1. （唸碩士的學生）They'll spend one or two years on abroad.

2. I haven't been to Canada for 20 years.

3. （對對象的條件）Considerate is most important.
   （considerate = 周到、貼心）

4. （以前的出差）I must go to Hualian.

5. Most of people didn't want to leave their houses during the holiday.

6. Lots of Taiwanese people like to chewing betel nuts.
   （chew betel nuts = 嚼檳榔）

7. I didn't understand what the movie was talking about.

8. I was doing very good at the beginning.

9. （某些壞人）They are lack of education.

10. （某一個補習班的學生）You seldom to take exams.

解答

超簡單改錯

1. A special <u>thing</u> is sausage with eggs.（合理的名詞、冠詞就行，有很多選擇）

2. One interesting <u>thing</u> is, traffic regulations are different there.（任何合適的名詞也可以代替 thing）

錯庫

1. They'll spend one or two years ~~on~~ abroad.（第 40 章：去某一個地方，需不需要 to？）

2. 正確無誤！

3. <u>Being considerate</u> is most important.（本章）

4. I ~~must~~ <u>had to</u> go to Hualian.（第 3 章：描述過去發生的事，動詞要用過去式。）

5. <u>Most</u> ~~of~~ people didn't want to leave their houses during the holiday.

或 <u>Most of the</u> people didn't want to leave their houses during the holiday.

（第 22 章：most 的用法：可以用一個字，也可以用三個字，就是不能用兩個字！）

6. Lots of Taiwanese people like <u>to chew</u> betel nuts. 或Lots of Taiwanese people <u>like chewing</u> betel nuts.

（第 12 章：like、don't like、love、hate 等動詞，要小心後面放什麼字！）

7. I didn't understand what the movie was ~~talking~~ about.

（第 8 章：電影不會說話！）

8. I was doing very ~~good~~ <u>well</u> at the beginning.（第 29 章：詞性搞錯了（一）：形容詞 vs. 副詞）

9. They <u>lack</u> education.

或 They <u>are lacking in</u> education.

或 They <u>have a lack of</u> education.

（第 15 章：細說一個字：lack）

10. You seldom ~~to~~ take exams.（第 46 章：這個 to 是多餘的！）

你要做什麼你？！

do 和 be 搞混了！

啊，做老師還不錯。學生會送你東西吃，也會當導遊陪你出去玩。公立學校的老師暑假很長，我們補習班老師下午才上課。人生多美好啊！因此，很多年輕人想做老師。有一天，上課時，一個可愛的少女舉手，居然說了這句話：

✘ Scott, I want to do a teacher just like you.

然後，我的臉紅了，我結結巴巴地說不出話來，開始考慮衝出教室的門。

你知道為什麼嗎？

> 因為在英文裡，說 do，然後說一個人，意思是，跟那個人做愛！上面句子的意思是：
>
> 「史考特，我希望我可以跟一個像你這樣的老師做愛。」
>
> 哇！再一個哇！我真的掙扎著保持鎮定，然後假裝沒事教下去。
>
> 當時，我不會中文。現在我了解這個單純的少女是很正經的表達「老師，我希望可以做像你這樣的老師。」有些事情中文說「做」它們，英文只會說 be。

上面的英文，這樣才正經：

✔ Scott, I want to <u>be</u> a teacher just like you.

這些我現在都了解。但是當時……哇！再一個哇。

這就帶我們來到這一章的重點：do 和 be 要搞清楚！

do 和 be 動詞很常見，可能就是因為他們那麼常用，就被濫用，也被爛用！

主要有兩種錯誤。

問題 A：你說了 be 動詞，但其實應該說 do

最常見的錯誤是否定的句子。

我們來複習一下國小的英文文法課！你應該知道吧，否定的句子是這樣形成的：

do not / don't + 動詞

就這麼簡單！但是很多人偏偏會說或寫成這樣：

✘ I'm not care about him!

care 是動詞啊，我們不會說 I am 什麼動詞。應該是這樣：

✔ I <u>don't</u> care about him!

再來一個例子：

✘ Young people is not listen to their parents!
✔ Young people <u>do</u> not listen to their parents!

問句也會造成問題。一般動詞的問句，第一個字是 do / does.

✘ Are you suggest I exercise more?

suggest（建議的意思）是動詞啊！

✔ <u>Do</u> you suggest I exercise more?

前面有「疑問代名詞 」（where、when、why、how、who等）的問句也常常會出錯：

✘ What are you do on weekends?
✔ What <u>do</u> you do on weekends?

否定的句子和問句是最容易出錯的，一般肯定的句子比較少。

你只要記得，如果這個否定句/問句是用一般動詞，前面要說 do。

313

這裡，我要囉唆一下。學英文有一個重要的事，就是要培養「詞性感」，這個字屬於什麼詞性，字的前前後後要怎麼使用，疑問句及否定句要怎麼改，這要透過練習來熟悉，真的會了的時候，憑直覺就可以判斷詞性，也就不容易出錯。

現在，我們來看相反的情況：

問題 B：你說了 do，但其實應該說 be 動詞

這就是我說的「詞性感」，請看看下面這一句：

✘　I don't really interested in Korean TV shows.

在這兒，interested 是形容詞，你感覺到了嗎？句子的動詞應該是 be 動詞：

✔　<u>I'm not</u> really interested in Korean TV shows.

否定的句子也會產生一樣的錯誤。

例如，過去的事，你要說，發生某一件事，你們並不感到丟臉，有人會這樣說：

✘　We didn't be embarrassed.

這個錯誤很糟糕啊。有那個 be 動詞，表示說者的文法概念差不多是對的，但是那個 didn't 是多餘的。embarrassed 是形容詞，be 動詞就可以了：

✔　We <u>weren't</u> embarrassed.

所以，你看，就是詞性的問題啊！

注意，上面的兩個例子，關鍵字是 interested 和 embarrassed。這兩個字都是所謂的過去分詞。你應該還記得國中老師怎麼說過去分詞的？它是動詞三個時

態裡的第三個：

原型動詞： interest
過去式： interested
過去分詞： interested

你要小心哦！前兩個是動詞，第三個其實是形容詞！美國人都感覺得出來。就算他們的拼法一模一樣，他們的詞性卻是不一樣的！

再一次強調這個原則：

過去分詞是形容詞！

因為拼法一樣，你就要對語境很敏感，然後感覺出這個東西是動詞形態還是形容詞形態。例子：

✘ I don't excited by Hollywood movies.
✔ <u>I'm not</u> excited by Hollywood movies.

現在分詞一樣！它也是形容詞啊！

✘ He don't boring. He's a funny teacher.

這裡 boring 是現在分詞，就是形容詞啊，需要 be 動詞：

✔ He <u>isn't</u> boring. He's a funny teacher.

不過，一般的形容詞也會產生這個問題。不知道為什麼，形容詞 sure（確定、肯定的意思）出現在很多這樣的錯誤裡：

✘ I don't sure what time the movie starts.
✔ I'<u>m not</u> sure what time the movie starts.

✘ She doesn't sure about the answer.
✔ She <u>isn't</u> sure about the answer.

做？用 do 還是 be 動詞？

現在，回到這章開頭的「鬧劇」。就是，很多中文說「做」或「當」的情況，英文其實不會說 do，而是說 be 動詞。

說人的例子真的很危險！比方說，你要跟妳的孩子表示「當你媽媽是很幸福的事。」英文要說：

✔ I'm so happy to <u>be</u> your mother.

它錯誤的版本我根本不敢寫出來。

不過，說東西也會有這個問題。比方說，下雨，只能用報紙「當作」雨傘：

✘ I'm OK. This can do my umbrella!
✔ I'm OK. This can <u>be</u> my umbrella!

總而言之：小心！

 超簡單改錯

1. I don't really interested in detective novels.
   （detective novels = 偵探小說）

2. He's not respect people.

錯庫！蒐集自台灣人真正犯過的英文錯誤，一起來除錯！

 1. I'm very interesting to this subject.

2. This movie talks about three warriors.（warrior = 戰士、鬥士）

['wɔrɪɚ]

3. （說喜歡跟不喜歡的食物）I don't like sweet.

4. （幾年前去泰國）It's happy experience!

5. They felt bored in the night.

6. （現在住台灣的人）I lived in Taiwan for forty years.

7. （說個不想幫助別人的人）Even he is a man and really strong, he doesn't help others.

8. Comic books are not very interesting.

9. （美國的政治家）They think that they are easy to control any other country.

10. What are you do in your free time?

超簡單改錯

1. ~~I don't~~ I'm not really interested in detective novels

2. He doesn't respect people.

錯庫

1. I'm very ~~interesting to~~ interested in this subject. (第 17 章：無聊有兩種：你很boring 還是很 bored，你真的不能不管！；第 28 章：很多形容詞後面需要介係詞，對的介係詞！)

2. This movie is about three warriors. (第 8 章：電影不會說話！)

3. I don't like sweet food. (第 47 章：形容詞不可以當主詞或受詞。注意：任何適合的名子都可以代替 food)

4. ~~It's~~ It was a happy experience! (第 3 章：描述過去發生的事，動詞要用過去式。；第 21 章：一樣東西〈是可數的話〉前面需要冠詞！)

5. They felt bored ~~in the~~ at night. (第 41 章：這個名詞前面的介係詞錯了！)

6. I have lived in Taiwan for forty years. (或) I have been living in Taiwan for forty years. (第 36 章：持續到現在的動作，通常用現在完成式或現在完成進行式)

7. Even though he is a man and really strong, he doesn't help others. (第 25 章：even if 和 even though，不能沒有 if 和 though。)

8. 正確無誤！

9. They think that they ~~are easy to~~ control any other country easily. (第 23 章：說「容易」不一定很容易！)

10. What ~~are~~ do you do in your free time? (本章)

我很好奇你的英文有多好？

間接問句怎麼問？

恭喜你！活到第 49 章了。都已經到了這個階段，你應該知道怎麼問問題。比方說，你要知道對方年紀多大，「你幾歲？」英文當然是：

✔ How old are you?

這是直接的問。但是，有些人委婉一點，會說：「我不知道你幾歲。」目的也是想問，但不是那麼直接。這句中文要說成英文的時候，很多人就直接在上面那個英文句子前面加上「我不知道」，就變成：

✘ I don't know how old are you.

這很明顯落入「中式英文」的陷阱了，用中文的語法說英文。

說到這裡，再看看上面那句錯誤的英文，你可能隱約地回想起國中曾上過的文法。沒錯，這就是所謂的「間接問句」。

現在，我要請你忍耐一下，讓我發表一下對台灣英文教育的看法。

我個人認為，台灣英文課本的內容，70%在現實生活中幫不上你的忙，只有剩下的30%是日常用得到的。這一章我們討論的「間接問句」，是你唸國中的時候就學了，可能課本的內容很枯燥、很乏味，呆板、正經八百，你背過、考過，但是用不到，因此你早忘記了。

其實，這個間接問句就是屬於那珍貴、有用的30%！這是日常生活裡嘗試要溝通的時候很常用到的句法，而很多台灣學生就因為用錯了，讓人家覺得他們的英文很破，而心生挫折，更害怕講英文了。沒事的！我們現在就來對症下藥，改正這個錯誤。

你可能依稀記得，間接問句，要改變問句的詞序。

詞序是什麼？就是句子組成的秩序。一般的句子，就是：主詞+動詞+受

詞／介係詞片語；而問句，主詞和動詞要顛倒。間接問句，雖然是問句，但
這個問句是包在前面這個句子裡面的，屬性會變成一般的句子，原本顛倒的
主詞和動詞就要變成「正」的。

所以，前面那句錯誤的句子，要改成以下這樣才對：

✔ I don't know how old <u>you are</u>.

任何問句，只要前面加了字，都會變成間接問句。這些都蠻常見：

I want to know...	Tell me...
I don't know...	Can you tell me...
I wonder...	I'm really curious about...
I'd like to know...	Tell me more about...
I forgot...	I need to find out...

I found out...
My friend told me...
I learned...
I can't remember...

　用中文的邏輯，來看英文，當然很不習慣，但是沒辦法，學英文，就是學英文
說寫的方式。不過，以這個間接問句來說，我覺得很多台灣學生會說錯的原因
是，他們不習慣句子最後面是用動詞結尾，他們覺得怪怪的。

　我告訴你，一點也不奇怪！一般的美國人，一天裡，可能會說出幾百個句尾是
動詞的句子，這對我們而言是家常便飯！

　為了讓你深深地習慣句子的最後一個字是動詞，習慣後才有可能精通，以下的
句子請你熟讀朗誦背起來！這些句子100% 自然、100% 正確。為了讓你可以參

考比較，前面會附上直接問句，下面間接問句的動詞底下會劃線，特別強調出來。

（What's her name?）
✔ I'd like to know what her name is.

（How good is the movie?）
✔ I want to know how good the movie is.

（Where are they?）
✔ I totally forgot where they are.

（How good is your English?）
✔ Scott is curious about how good your English is.

這些句子真的沒問題，相信我！

還有一點要說。就是，很多問句的開頭是 do / does / did。在間接問句裡，do / does / did 要拿掉。比方說，原來的句子是 Where does he like to eat? 然後，你要在前面放 I want to find out，那要怎麼做呢？

✘ I want to find out where does he like to eat.
✔ I want to find out where he likes to eat.

注意：原來的句子（Where does he like to eat?）裡，第三人稱現在式的動詞由 does 來代表，但是在間接問句裡，like 要加 s，反應第三人稱現在式的時態。

如果是過去式，那麼就要小心 did。比方說，原來的直接問句是 Where did you go yesterday? 前面要加上 I forgot，那會是怎麼樣呢？

✘ I forgot where did you go yesterday.
✔ I forgot where you went yesterday.

注意：原來的句子（Where did you go yesterday?）裡，是直接問句，主詞動詞的詞序顛倒，動詞是由 did 這個助動詞來表示，而且是過去式的時態，後面的 go 就維持原型。但是在間接問句裡，詞序變「正」，不需要助動詞 did 了，go 要用過去式，所以是 went。

我們再看一個例子：

✘ Can you tell me when did she get back from the airport?

✔ Can you tell me when <u>she got</u> back from the airport?

yes / no 疑問句的間接問句

問句還沒完喔！還有一種問句。還記得嗎？你的國中老師教過的？

沒關係，我提醒你，就是 yes / no 問句。顧名思義，這種問句的答案不是 yes 就是 no。比方說：

Are you an American?

那，間接的問句可要小心了！是以下這樣嗎？

✘ I'd like to know are you an American.

只要是 yes / no 問句，前面加了字，變成間接問句，就要加一個字：if 或 whether。

✔ I'd like to know <u>if you are</u> an American.

你應該還記得吧，句子的最後面你也可以加 or not：

✔ I'd like to know <u>if you are</u> an American <u>or not</u>.

但是，在一般會話的時候，通常不會直接跟對方說 or not，因為感覺像是你在

審問、質問對方，要逼迫他回答。不過，如果是在說一個不在場的第三方，是比較沒有問題的。此外，在會話裡，if 比 whether 常見，whether 比較會在正式的寫作裡出現。請看：

✗　I can't tell did my students finish their homework.
✔　I can't tell <u>if</u> my students <u>finished</u> their homework <u>or not</u>.

　　注意，正確的句子裡，finished 是過去式的。後面的 or not 是可放可不放的。

　　哇，這一章落落長！終於到了可以說真心話的時候了，不說不快，趕快來說，不然會後悔啊！

 **史考特的句子**

1.（後天放假，會跟朋友吃飯）I'm not sure where my friend wants to go for lunch.（原來的短問題：Where does my friend want to go for lunch?）

2. I can't remember when the bookstore closes.（原：When does the bookstore close?）

3.（喜歡的女生）I don't know if she wants to go on a date with me or not.（原：Does she want to go on a date with me?）

4.（跟一個補習班同事說的）Hi, I'd like to know if you can substitute my class.（原：Hi, can you substitute my class?）（substitute = 代課）

 你的句子

希望你嘗試用兩個有疑問詞的（what、when、where、why、how、who）

以及兩個 yes / no 問句的。

1. _____

2. _____

3. _____

4. _____

超簡單改錯

1. I don't know what's that.

2. （某些地圖）They show where is the bus.

錯庫！蒐集自台灣人真正犯過的英文錯誤，一起來除錯！

1. I recommend Mia to see this movie.

2. （比較現在的台灣人與上一代）Lifestyle of older generation is better than our generation's.

3. I want to do an accountant.（accountant = 會計師）

4.（以前去加拿大旅行）I have been to Canada two months ago.

5.（說孩子喜歡玩什麼）They'll play the toy guns.

6.（說家的狗）When he want to sleep, my mother have to hold.

7.（最近去逛街）I wondered what should I buy.

8.（說老人申請社會福利的條件）You have to more than 65 years old.

9.（比較台北跟桃園一般開車的人）Driver in Taipei is kinder than in Taoyuan.

10.（小狗）He let me to touch him.

超簡單改錯

1. I don't know ~~what's that~~ <u>what that is</u>.

2. They show where ~~is the bus~~ <u>the bus is</u>.

錯庫

1. I recommend <u>(that)</u> Mia ~~to~~ see this movie.（第 42 章：recommend 以及 suggest 的用法很特別。注意：that可用可不用）

2. <u>The</u> lifestyle of <u>the</u> older generation is better than our generation's.
（第 21 章：一樣東西〈是可數的話〉前面需要冠詞！）

3. I want to ~~do~~ <u>be</u> an accountant.（第 48 章：do 和 be 搞混了！）

4. I ~~have been~~ <u>went</u> to Canada two months ago.（第 34 章：如果要表達什麼時候做或發生的，用過去式就

好，不可以用現在完成式。）

5. They'll <u>play with</u> the toy guns.
（第 24 章：這個動詞後面要放介係詞！）

6. When he want<u>s</u> to sleep, my mother ~~have~~ <u>has</u> to hold <u>him</u>.（第 1 章：第三人稱現在式動詞忘記加 s / es；第 13 章：有些動詞後面需要接受詞）

7. I wondered what ~~should I~~ <u>I should</u> buy.（本章）

8. You have to <u>be</u> more than 65 years old.（第 27 章：你說了助動詞，卻忘記了主要動詞！）

9. Drivers in Taipei ~~is~~ <u>are</u> kinder than in Taoyuan.（第 5 章：表達一般性的看法或意見時，可數名詞要用複數。）

10. He let me ~~to~~ touch him.（第 38 章：let 與 make 後面該怎麼說？）

第 50 章

你快要說對了，還是快要說錯了？

啊……我們快要結束了。

你的英文經過這段時間的鍛鍊，已經變得好厲害了。看完這一章的內容，最後的錯庫發瘋，應該可以一瞬間就處理掉吧！然後，你大概就會衝出門，跑進公司、跑到學校，大聲吶喊，有沒有和英文有關的事，找我！找我！跟以前一見英文就躲，你現在簡直判若兩人！我說的對不對啊？

情願、自願、主動爭取要做事，這很好，不過，我們還是得提醒一下。比方說，你上我的英文課，我問你們問題，你蹦蹦跳跳馬上舉手說，「我先說！」危險的是，用英文的話，你可能馬上就說錯：

✗　Ooh, ooh, ooh, I go first!

這是錯的喔。就算這是相當口語的話，英文還是會謹守時態的。你還沒做，對吧，這是未來的事！怎麼說呢？就算你一兩秒鐘內就要回答了，這個動作還是在未來！以下這樣說才對：

✔　Ooh, ooh, ooh, I'<u>ll</u> go first!

注意：說快要做的事，我們都會說縮寫的 I'll，不太會說兩個字 I will。I'll、you'll、he'll、she'll 都會這樣。這只是一個習慣問題，但是，大家都有共同的習慣，就可以說是原則了。

那，我們可以來寫個簡單的原則，就是：

你答應快要做某事的時候，就算過幾秒鐘就開始做，你說的時候，事情還在未來！不遠的未來還是未來。

這個原則超級常用，因為說出來可以幫助他人、團體等，碰到這種情況，這個語境就會出現。比方說，我常常叫我的學生用生字來造句，所以幾乎每天都會遇到這個情況：

✘ Scott: Who wants to make a sentence?
Student: I do it!

雖然快要做，但是說的時候還沒做，就是在未來！

✔ Scott: Who wants to make a sentence?
Student: I'll do it!

在職場上，有新的老闆，當然要讓他留下深刻的印象。因此，老闆一提出新的案子，當然要主動積極地說「我要做」。但是，我就曾經目睹，我在外商公司工作的台灣朋友，鬧了個笑話：

✘ Boss: Who wants to handle the new case?
Taiwanese employee: I do it!

啊！你的第一句英文，可能會讓你的外國老闆對你的印象大打折扣。簡單地說，do 表示你經常辦這個案子，這樣的回答會先讓老闆感到困惑，因為他提的是 new case。然後，他會想一下，馬上就知道這是因為你的英文不好，可能會覺得有點煩，導致他對你的第一印象不佳。應該這樣說才對：

✔ Boss: Who wants to handle the new case?
Taiwanese employee: I'll do it!

日常生活裡常會出現以下這樣的情況。電話響了，然後：

✘ Don't worry, I get it!
✔ Don't worry, I'll get it!

注意：說快要做的事，我們都會說縮寫的 I'll，不太會說兩個字 I will，這只是一個習慣問題。但是，大家共同都有的習慣，就可以說是原則了。

不過，還是有例外！你以為英文會有這麼簡單喔？！算你倒霉。

這些情況有個例外，就是，想要的話，上面講的所有情況，你都可以說：

I got it.

意思就是「我自己來」。

這是非常口語的說法，然後文法有點不正常，got 可以解讀成現在式的 I've got（我有），然後省略 've，或者過去式 I got（我得到了），感覺是「這件事我已經有把握」一樣，也就是「有把握、有信心可以辦好」的意思。

任何有那種未來馬上要做、快要做的情況都可以說 I got it。但是不能改，都是 I got it 這三個字，算是一個片語吧。主詞 I、動詞 got 或受詞 it。需要有任何改變的話，就要用這一章介紹的 I'll 這樣的句型。

第二個例外。你以為只有一個例外？哈哈！

有時，can 可以代替 'll。我問學生誰要造句，這兩個都行：

✔ I'll do it!
✔ I can do it!

還有一點。我不敢說是第三個例外。

就是，「我先！」有個超口語說法：

Me first!

這也帶著迫不及待的語氣。因為是那麼口語，可能不會跟老師或老闆說，但跟朋友真的很常用。比方說，你要在 KTV 先唱，就可以說：

✔ Ooh, me first!

在任何比較生活化的的情況下都可以說。這也算是個片語，文法不太正常也不用管！

你現在應該很有信心了吧！我敢保證，老闆或老師聽了你的第一句英文，對你應該會留下美好的印象。

史考特的句子

1. （補習班櫃台小姐問老師們誰能代課）OK, OK, I'll do it.

2. （學生有些剩下的餅乾，問有沒有人要把它們吃掉）Oh, I'll eat them if nobody else wants them.

你的句子

1. _____

2. _____

超簡單改錯

1. （體育課的教練問學生誰要做第一個短跑）Hey, I do it!

2. （史考特剛才有問相當難的問題）Well, I answer, but I'm not sure if it's right.

史考特的錯誤資料庫有好多寶貝！快來挖！

1. I ever had a crush on a pop singer.（crush = 青少年的早戀/迷戀）

2. （班上討論 ballroom dancing 社交跳舞）They don't know what are the kinds of dances.

3. （曬太陽）I'm easy to get dark skin.

4. （有些台灣電影）They are lack of music.

5. （對象的條件）Healthy is most important.

6. （下課了，但現在還在學校）I'll go home fifteen minutes later.

7. （日文課的同學）They'll speak Japanese very strange.

8. （麥當勞的食物）It's high fat.

9. （狗表現出很想出門的樣子，跟太太討論誰要遛）OK, fine, I do it.

10. （學生被問《美國隊長》電影是不是值得看）I think it's worthy.

11. （班上討論旅遊）One of my friends really likes going to Japan.

12. （以前去旅遊）I wait the train for a really long time.

解答

超簡單改錯

1. Hey, I'll do it!（情願、自願的感覺）
   （或）Hey, I got it!（有把握的感覺）
   （或）Hey, me first!（迫不及待的感覺）

2. Well, I'll answer, but I'm not sure if it's right.（這裡不能說 I got it，因為 I got it 表示有把握、有信心的樣子。而且，前面的 well 表示有一點猶豫、不想說話的樣子，所以這裡也不能說迫不及待的 Me first!）

錯庫

1. I ~~ever~~（have）had a crush on a pop singer.（have 可放可不放。 第 33 章：一般的句子不用 ever）

2. They don't know what ~~are~~ the kinds of dances are.（第 49 章：間接問句怎麼問？）

3. ~~I'm easy to~~ get dark skin easily.（或）My skin gets dark easily.（第 23 章：說「容易」不一定很容易！）

4. They lack music.（或）They are lacking in music.（或）They have a lack of music.（第 15 章：細說一個字：lack）

5. Being healthy is most important.（第 47 章：形容詞不可以當主詞或受詞）

6. I'll go home in fifteen minutes ~~later~~.（第 45 章：要表達現在之後的某一個時間點，通常用 in，不用 later。）

7. They'll speak Japanese very strangely.（第 29 章：詞性搞錯了（一）：形容詞 vs. 副詞）

8. It's high in fat.（第 28 章：很多形容詞後面需要介係詞，對的介係詞！）

9. OK, fine, I'll do it.（本章）

10. I think it's ~~worthy~~ worthwhile.（或）I think it's worth seeing.（第 39 章：「值得」很值得學。）

11. 正確無誤！

12. I waited for the train for a really long time.（第 3 章：描述過去發生的事，動詞要用過去式；第 24 章：這個動詞後面要放介係詞！）

壓軸上場　錯庫發瘋

Part 2

大家好。如果你真的學會了前面的內容，我認為你已經改掉大部分的英文錯誤了。但是，這有待證明喔！

好吧！那我們就來看一下你的厲害！

這是本書的最後一章，也是你的最後一戰。你準備好了嗎？那，開槍囉！

超大型錯誤資料庫

（注意：有些句子是正確的，有些句子的錯誤不只一個！）

1. They'll study on abroad.

2. I have ever been to Disney in Japan.

3. （說漫畫書, comic book）The story is talking about a girl who turns into a vampire.（vampire = 吸血鬼）

4. I just surfed for five times.（surf = 衝浪）

5. （以前當兵）When I in the army, I just wear one uniform.

6. （孩子要做重要的決定）I will let them to decide.

7. （舞蹈家說排演的狀況）I have to rehearsal outside.

8. （很久沒看到朋友，然後他報告近況）I found the new coffee shop that you've never heard of before!

9. I seldom to drink alcohol.

10. I have seen an interesting report on the newspaper.

11. They are lack of information.

12. （討論某個報告）I'm not sure the information is right or not.

13. I like listen music.

14. We should ban people to smoke in public.

15. It's quite tired.

16. （某一種奇怪的食物）Have you ever eat?

17. I don't want to talk this.

18. When I was elementary school student, I have been to the water park.（water park = 水上樂園）

19. The Russia people like to have parties.

20. （史考特剛問了好友最近的旅遊怎麼樣）Here, I show you some

pictures!

21. I will suggest them to do this one.

22. There have a foreign restaurant.

23. （在上課的時候說的）Twenty minutes later, the class will be over!

24. （某件事）I not worried that.

25. One of my colleague had a baby.（colleague＝同事）

26. （說新老師）Even he has be the teacher for a short time, I think he's had some good ideas.

27. （剛才看到的某一個昆蟲）It is not spider!

28. （某個東西）I just like!

29. （上史考特的課）I come to here because I want to improve my English.

30. A: Should I see the movie? B: It's not worth.

31. （上課時剛被史考特問，「你們現在聊著什麼話題?」）We talk about question number six in the book.

32. I will happy.

33. One of my friends likes to study foreign languages.

34. I don't really interested in romance novels.

35.（健身房）You can use many equipments.

36.（關於婚姻的文章）It also mentioned about the future parents-in-law.（parents-in-law = 岳父/岳母）

37. General speaking, people want to be successful.

38. I don't like banana!

39. Younger like rock and roll.

40. They very like the steamed buns.（steamed buns = 包子）

41.（某家餐廳）Even it's not good, so many people go there.

42. Get surgery is dangerous.（surgery = 手術、開刀）

43. Most of teenagers don't want to get married so quickly.

44.（小國）I never heard this country!

45. Most of my friend went to the restaurant with me.

46. （說補習班從紐西蘭來的新的英文老師）He come from New Zealand.

47. She did something dangerous, so she was die.

48. （一般的建議）If your wife wear a Hello Kitty shirt, it will be embarrassing.

49. Voters are easy to forget what politicians said.（voters = 選民/投票的人，politicians = 政客）

50. （某一個國家）There is amazing!

51. Cooking is very important thing.

52. In junior high school, I hate Chinese class.

53. I like play many sport.

54. （說孝順的責任）Everybody have to good to their parents.

55. （某個服飾店）Even you wash their clothes, you can return them.

56. （某一本書）It's worth to read.

57. I'm very admire.

58. One of my neighbor is work in that school.

59. I tried to stop my little sister to go on a date with that guy.

60. （說 Taipei 101 大建築）Have shops.

61. People very want to know what the tallest building in the world is.

62. （第一次上史考特的課，做個自我介紹）Hello, I come from Kaohsiung.

63. We often to watch movies at home.

64. Even though I was really sick this morning, I still went to work.

65. I like watch sports programs.

66. I want to see America's sceneries.

67. （說怎麼保持友誼）Call him is good!

68. （說 GM foods, 基因改變的食物）It also has some dangerous.

69. （對槍的一般的想法）Gun can kill person.

70. I'm interested in Chinese cook.

71. They don't lack of food.

72. （朋友中，只有一個人出國過）Only she has go to abroad.

73. （說者以前在麵包店 bakery 工作，現在已經沒了）I have been work in a bakery.

74. （好友）When I boring, I will call him to play basketball.

75. What are you do in your free time?

76. Two years ago, I've been to there.

77. I was not carefully.

78. When I was a child, I have been told some interesting stories.

79. （沒有工作的人）I am take a long rest now.

80. I ever read an article that was about staying healthy.

81. （說某一個商店）Most of time, it closes at 5 or 6 pm.

82. （說一輩子都很健康）I never broken a bone.

83. （以前的旅行）My boyfriend and I drive to mountain.

84. （Scott 剛問了全班一個問題，一個人舉手說這個）I go first!

85. （寵物鳥）It cannot back to nature.

86. What was the movie talking about?

87. （說跟別人坐計程車的經驗）I kept silent on taxi.

88. One of my classmate is very skinny.

89. I've been there for one time.

90. （現在是12月中）Two weeks later, I'll go to a Christmas party with my classmates.

91. （台灣的特色菜）Only Taiwan have.

92. I afraid of the cold so much!

93. My friend is my most precious!（precious = 珍貴）

94. （期末考剛考完了，跟另外一個考過的同學討論）I just finished a test. I thought it was hard. Did you?

95.（新生說為什麼要上史考特的課）They recommended me take your class.

96. I'm very interesting to economic news.

97.（孩子）Let them to do what they want.

98. Nobody knows when is the holiday.

99. I agree that.

100. We are discuss about New Zealand.

101.（學生要說他上這個補習班已經多久了）I come here only for one year.

102.（一個天氣不好的地方）I hate there!

103. Even you go to the pharmacy, you might not get the medicine.（pharmacy = 藥局）

104. I easy to become cold.

105.（另外一個人懷疑她說的話是假的）It's really!

好，朋友們，我們就到這兒。錯誤都被槍殺了。六大頭號通緝犯都被逮捕了。丟的臉已經拿回來了。

我真的很高興可以分享我教英文十年的一點心得。我希望你們不但開始用自然正確的英文，也希望你們了解為什麼會錯，這樣才可以根除頑固的壞習慣。

還是要再強調，你要記得外語的終點線不是懂而是用，終點線還在前方等著你喔。

1. They'll study ~~on~~ abroad.

   （第 40 章：去某一個地方，需不需要 to ？）

2. I have ~~ever~~ been to Disney in Japan.

   （第 33 章：一般的句子不會用 ever）

3. The story is ~~talking~~ about a girl who turns into a vampire.

   （第 8 章：電影不會說話！）

4. I just surfed ~~for~~ five times.

   （第 44 章：要說做了多少次，前面不可以說 for！）

5. When I <u>was</u> in the army, I just <u>wore</u> one uniform.

   （第 26 章：嘿，你忘了動詞了！；第 3 章：描述過去發生的事，動詞要用過去式。）

6. I will let them ~~to~~ decide.

   （第 38 章：let 和 make 後面該怎麼說？）

7. I have to ~~rehearsal~~ <u>rehearse</u> outside.

   （第 31 章：詞性搞錯了（三）：名詞 vs. 動詞）

8. I found ~~the~~ <u>a</u> new coffee shop that you've never heard of before!

   （第 20 章： 搞不清楚 a / an 和 the 這裡，因為跟朋友很久沒有見面，而且因為他沒有聽過這家咖啡店，因此就要用 a。）

9. I seldom ~~to~~ drink alcohol.

   （第 46 章：這個 to 是多餘的！）

10. I have seen an interesting report ~~on~~ <u>in</u> the newspaper.

    （第 41 章：這個名詞前面的介係詞錯了！）

11. 這裡有三個選擇：① They <u>lack</u> information. ② They <u>are lacking in</u> information. ③ They <u>have a lack of</u> information.

    （第 15 章：細說一個字：lack）

12. I'm not sure <u>if</u> the information is right or not.

    （第 49 章：間接問句怎麼問？）

13. I like listen<u>ing</u> <u>to</u> music.（或）I like <u>to listen</u> to music.

    （第 12 章：like、don't like、love、hate 後面要小心放什麼字！第 24 章：這個動詞後面要放介係詞！）

14. We should ban people ~~to smoke~~ <u>from smoking</u> in public.

    （第 43 章：如何表達阻止、預防、防止、制止這些意思）

15. It's quite ~~tired~~ tir<u>ing</u>.

    （第 17 章：無聊有兩種：你很 boring 還是很 bored，你真的不能不管！）

16. Have you ever eat<u>en</u> it?

    （第 32 章：現在完成式形成得不正確；第 13 章：有些動詞後面需要接

受詞。任何合適的名詞都可以代替 it.）

17. I don't want to ~~talk about~~ this.

（第 24 章：這個動詞後面要放介係詞！）

18. When I was an elementary school student, I ~~have been~~ went to the water park.

（第 21 章：一個東西〈是可數的話〉前面需要冠詞！；第 34 章：如果要表達什麼時候做或發生的，用過去式就好，不可以用現在完成式。）

19. The Russian people like to have parties.（第 30 章：詞性搞錯了（二）：形容詞 vs.名詞）

20. Here, I'll show you some pictures!

（第 50 章：你快要說對了，還是快要說錯了？）

21. I will suggest ~~them to~~ (that) they do this one.（第 42 章：recommend 以及 suggest 的用法很特別。that 可用可不用）

22. There ~~have~~ is a foreign restaurant (there).

（第 9 章：here 與 there 並不會「有」東西！。後面的 there 可用可不用）

23. 有兩個選擇：① In twenty minutes, the class will be over! ② Twenty minutes from now, the class will be over!

（第 45 章：要表達現在之後某一個時間點，要用 in，不用 later。）

24. I'm not worried about that.

（第 26 章：嘿，你忘了動詞了！；第 28 章：很多形容詞後面需要介係詞，對的介係詞！）

25. One of my colleagues had a baby.

（第 6 章：one of 後面的名詞要用複數）

26. Even though he has been the teacher for a short time, I think he's had some good ideas.

（第 25 章：even if 和 even though，不能沒有 if 和 though。；第 36 章：持續到現在的動作，通常用現在完成式或現在完成進行式。）

27. It is not a spider!

（第 21 章：一樣東西〈是可數的話〉前面需要冠詞！）

28. I just like it!

（第 13 章：有些動詞後面需要接受詞。任何合適的名詞都行）

29. I come ~~to~~ here because I want to improve my English.

（第 10 章：here 和 there 前面通常

不會放介係詞）

30. 有幾個選擇：① It's not worth it. ② It's not worthwhile. ③ It's not worth seeing.

（第 39 章：「值得」很值得學！）

31. We are talking about question number six in the book.

（第 16 章：進行式如果搞錯，一切都進行不了！）

32. I will be happy.

（第 27 章：你說了助動詞，卻忘記了主要動詞！）

33. 正確無誤！

34. I don't I'm not really interested in romance novels.

（第 48 章：do 和 be 搞混了！）

35. You can use many equipments a lot of equipment.

（第 19 章：名詞是可數的還是不可數的？）

36. It also mentioned about the future parents-in-law.

（第 14 章：這個動詞後面不需要加介係詞！）

37. Generally speaking, people want to be successful.

（第 29 章：詞性搞錯了（一）：形容詞 vs. 副詞）

38. I don't like bananas！

（第 5 章：表達一般性的看法或意見時，可數名詞要用複數。）

39. Younger people like rock and roll.

（第 47 章：形容詞不可以當主詞或受詞。任何合適的名詞都可以代替 people）

40. They very really like the steamed buns.

（第 7 章：動詞前面不可加 very）

41. Even though it's not good, so many people go there.

（第 25 章：even if 和 even though，不能沒有 if 和 though。）

42. Getting surgery is dangerous.

（第 18 章：動詞開頭的句子，要用加 ing 的動名詞。）

43. 看情況：如果是一般的 teenagers，你會說 Most teenagers don't want to get married so quickly. 如果是特定的一群 teenagers，你會說 Most of the teenagers don't want to get married so quickly.

（第 22 章：most 的用法：可以用一個字，也可以用三個字，就是不能用兩個字！）

44. I have never heard of this country!

（第 35 章：一輩子都沒做的事，通常用否定的現在完成式；第 24 章：這個動詞後面要放介係詞！）

45. Most of my friend<u>s</u> went to the restaurant with me.

（第 2 章：複數名詞忘了加 s／es）

46. He ~~come~~ <u>is</u> from New Zealand.

（第 4 章：你來自哪裡？用 from 還是 come from？）

47. She did something dangerous, so she ~~was~~ die<u>d</u>.

（第 37 章：這個 be 動詞是多餘的！）

48. If your wife wear<u>s</u> a Hello Kitty shirt, it will be embarrassing.

（第 1 章：第三人稱現在式動詞忘記加 s／es）

49. Voters ~~are easy to~~ <u>easily</u> forget what politicians said.

（第 23 章：説「容易」不一定很容易！）

50. <u>It's</u> amazing <u>there</u>.

（第 11 章：here 與 there 不可以當成受詞和主詞）

51. Cooking is <u>a</u> very important thing.

（第 21 章：一樣東西〈是可數的話〉前面需要冠詞！）

52. In junior high school, I hate<u>d</u> Chinese class.

（第 3 章：描述過去發生的事，動詞要用過去式。）

53. ① I like <u>to play</u> many sports. ② I like <u>playing</u> many sports.

（第 12 章：like、don't like、love、hate 後面要小心放什麼字！；第 2 章：複數名詞忘了加 s／es）

54. Everybody ~~have~~ <u>has</u> to <u>be</u> good to their parents.

（第 1 章：第三人稱現在式動詞忘記加 s／es；第 27 章：你説了助動詞，卻忘記了主要動詞！）

55. Even <u>if</u> you wash their clothes, you can return them.

（第25章：even if 和 even though，不能沒有 if 和 though。這裡比較偏向假設的情況，後面的 can 表示這個，所以在這裡 if 比 though 好一點。）

56. It's <u>worth</u> ~~to read~~ <u>reading</u>.

（第 39 章：「值得」很值得學!）

57. I'm ~~very~~ <u>really</u> admire <u>him/her/it</u>.

（第 37 章：這個 be 動詞是多餘的！；第 7 章：動詞前面不可加 very；第 13 章：有些動詞後面需要接受詞）

58. <u>One of</u> my neighbor<u>s</u> ~~is~~ work<u>s</u> in that school.

（第 6 章：one of 後面的名詞要用複數；第 37 章：這個 be 動詞是多餘的！）

59. I tried to stop my little sister ~~to go~~ <u>from</u> going on a date with that guy.

（第 43 章：如何表達阻止、預防、防

止、制止這些意思）

60. ~~Have~~ There are shops.

（第 9 章：here 與 there 並不會「有」東西！）

61. People ~~very~~ really want to know what the tallest building in the world is.

（第 7 章：動詞前面不可加 very）

62. Hello, ~~I come~~ I'm from Kaohsiung.

（第 4 章：你來自哪裡？用 from 還是 come from？）

63. We often ~~to~~ watch movies at home.

（第 46 章：這個 to 是多餘的！）

64. 正確無誤！

65. I like to watch sports programs.（或）I like watching sports programs.

（第 12 章：like、don't like、love、hate 後面要小心放什麼字！）

66. I want to see America's ~~sceneries~~ scenery.

（第 19 章：名詞是可數的還是不可數的？）

67. Calling him is good!

（第 18 章：動詞開頭的句子，要用加 ing 的動名詞。）

68. It also has some ~~dangerous~~ danger/dangers.

（第 30 章：詞性搞錯了（二）：形容

詞 vs.名詞。danger 的用法有一點特別。如果是一般的危險〈danger〉，就是不可數的，是單數的用法；如果是幾種不一樣的危險，則是可數的而且是複數的，要加 s。）

69. Guns can kill ~~person~~ people.

（第 5 章：表達一般性的看法或意見時，可數名詞要用複數。）

70. I'm interested in Chinese cooking.

（第 31 章：詞性搞錯了（三）：名詞 vs. 動詞）

71. 三個都行：① They don't lack food. ② They aren't lacking in food. ③ They don't have a lack of food.

（第 15 章：細説一個字：lack）

72. Only she has gone ~~to~~ abroad.

（第 32 章：現在完成式形成得不正確；第 40 章：去某一個地方，需不需要 to？）

73. I have ~~been~~ worked in a bakery.

（第 32 章：現在完成式形成得不正確。如果現在還在麵包店工作，就會説 I have been working in a bakery. 或 I am working in a bakery.）

74. When I am ~~boring~~ bored, I will call him to play basketball.

（第 26 章：嘿，你忘了動詞了！；第 17 章：無聊有兩種：你很boring還是很bored，你真的不能不管！）

75. What ~~are~~ <u>do</u> you do in your free time?

（第 48 章：do 和 be 搞混了！）

76. Two years ago, ~~I've been~~ <u>I went</u> to there.

（第 34 章：如果要表達什麼時候做或發生的，用過去式就好，不可以用現在完成式；第 10 章：here 和 there前面通常不會放介係詞）

77. I was not ~~carefully~~ <u>careful</u>.

（第 29 章：詞性搞錯了（一）：形容詞 vs. 副詞）

78. When I was a child, I ~~have been~~ <u>was</u> told some interesting stories.

（第 34 章：如果要表達什麼時候做或發生的，用過去式就好，不可以用現在完成式。）

79. （沒有工作的學生） I am ~~take~~ <u>taking</u> a long rest now.

（第 16 章：進行式如果搞錯，一切都進行不了！）

80. I ~~ever~~ read an article that was about staying healthy.

（第 33 章：一般的句子不會用 ever。動詞 read 跟 have read 都可以。）

81. Most of <u>the</u> time, it closes at 5 or 6 pm.

（第 22 章：most 的用法：可以用一個字，也可以用三個字，就是不能用兩個字！）

82. I <u>have</u> never broken a bone.

（第 35 章：一輩子都沒做的事，通常用否定的現在完成式。）

83. My boyfriend and I ~~drive~~ <u>drove</u> to <u>a/the</u> mountain.

（第 3 章：描述過去發生的事，動詞要用過去式。；第 21 章：一樣東西〈是可數的話〉前面需要冠詞！）

84. I'll go first!（第 50 章：你快要說對了，還是快要說錯了？）

85. It cannot <u>go</u> back to nature.

（第 27 章：你說了助動詞，卻忘記了主要動詞！任何合適的動詞，像 fly 什麼的，都可以代替 go）

86. What was the movie ~~talking~~ about?

（第 8 章：電影不會說話！）

87. I kept silent ~~on~~ <u>in the</u> taxi.

（第 41 章：這個名詞前面的介係詞錯了；第 21 章：一樣東西〈是可數的話〉前面需要冠詞！）

88. <u>One of</u> my classmates is very skinny.

（第 6 章：one of 後面的名詞要用複數）

89. I've been there ~~for~~ one time.

（第 44 章：要說做了多少次，前面不可以說 for！once 可以代替 one

time，它們的意思一模一樣。）

90. In two weeks, I'll go to a Christmas party with my classmates.

（第 45 章：要表達現在之後某一個時間點，要用 in，不用 later。）

91. Only Taiwan ~~have~~ has it.

（第 1 章：第三人稱現在式動詞忘記加 s / es；第 13 章：有些動詞後面需要接受詞。任何合適的詞都可以代替 it，像 that、this food 等等）

92. I am afraid of the cold so much!

（第 26 章：嘿，你忘了動詞了！）

93. My friend is my most precious thing/person!

（第 47 章：形容詞不可以當主詞或受詞）

94. I just finished ~~a~~ the test. I thought it was hard. Did you?

（第 20 章：搞不清楚 a / an 和 the。因為這兩個人才剛考完同樣的試，說者跟聽者都知道是特定的那一個考試，所以這裡應該說 the。）

95. They recommended ~~me~~ (that) I take your class.

（第 42 章：recommend 以及 suggest 的用法很特別）

96. I'm very ~~interesting to~~ interested in economic news.

（第 17 章：無聊有兩種：你很

boring 還是很 bored，你真的不能不管！；第 28 章：很多形容詞後面需要介係詞，對的介係詞！）

97. Let them ~~to~~ do what they want.

（第 38 章：let 與 make 後面該怎麼說？）

98. Nobody knows when the holiday is.（第 49 章：間接問句怎麼問？）

99. I agree with that.

（第 24 章：這個動詞後面要放介係詞！）

100. We are discussing ~~about~~ New Zealand.

（第 16 章：進行式如果搞錯，一切都進行不了！第 14 章：這個動詞後面不需要加介係詞！）

101. I've only been coming here for one year.

（第 36 章：持續到現在的動作，通常用現在完成式或現在完成進行式。）

102. I hate it there!

（第 11 章：here 與 there 不可以當成受詞和主詞）

103. Even if you go to the pharmacy, you might not get the medicine.

（第 25 章：even if 和 even though，不能沒有 if 和 though。後面的 might 暗示這是假設的情況，所以 if 比 though 好）

104. I ~~easy to~~ <u>easily</u> become cold.

（第 23 章：說「容易」不一定很容
易！）

105. It's ~~really~~ <u>true</u>!

（第 29 章：詞性搞錯了（一）：形容
詞 vs. 副詞）

親愛的英文，我到底哪裡錯了？

搞定 50 個你一定會犯的英文錯誤，聽說讀寫有如神助

作　　者　史考特・科斯博（Scott Cuthbert）
責　　編　高莎莎、王愛蒂
發 行 人　麥成輝
社　　長　喻小敏
總 編 輯　林毓瑜
編 輯 部　王曉瑩
行 銷 部　李明瑾
業 務 部　郭其彬、王綬晨
出 版 社　本事文化股份有限公司
　　　　　台北市中正區羅斯福路四段68號7樓之9
　　　　　電話：(02) 2363-9799　傳真：(02) 2363-9939
　　　　　E-mail：motif@motifpress.com.tw
營運統籌　大雁文化事業股份有限公司
　　　　　地址：台北市松山區復興北路333號11樓之4
　　　　　電話：(02)2718-2001
　　　　　傳真：(02)2718-1258
香港發行所　大雁(香港)出版基地・里人文化
　　　　　地址：香港荃灣橫龍街78號正好工業大廈22樓A室
　　　　　電話：852-2419-2288 傳真：852-2419-1887
　　　　　網址：anyone@biznetvigator.com
封面設計　徐小碧
內頁排版　浩瀚電腦排版股份有限公司
印　　刷　上晴彩色印刷製版有限公司
●2014（民103）5月初版
●2014（民103）8月22日初版2刷
定價350元

Copyright © 2014 by 史考特・科斯博（Scott Cuthbert）
Published by Motif Press Co., Ltd
All Rights Reserved

本書經由史考特・科斯博授權本事文化股份有限公司（Motif Press Co., Ltd）
在台灣地區印行和出版繁體中文版。

Printed in Taiwan　著作權所有，翻印必究
ISBN 978-986-6118-71-5

國家圖書館出版品預行編目資料

親愛的英文，我到底哪裡錯了？──搞定50個你一定會
犯的英文錯誤，聽說讀寫有如神助/史考特・科斯博 著；
---.初版.一 臺北市；本事文化出版 ：
本事文化發行，　2014〔民103.05〕
面 ；　公分.-
ISBN 978-986-6118-71-5(平裝)
1.英語 2.語法
805.16　　　　　　　　103004124